TED TAYLER

STRANGE BEGINNINGS

BOOKS

By Ted Tayler

The Freeman Files

Red Herring Season

Gathering Clouds

Still Standing

Vinci Books

vinci-books.com

Published by Vinci Books Ltd in 2025

1

Chapter One

Monday, 20 August 2018

"THIS MUST BE the first time we've all been here by a quarter to nine," said Neil. "Except the guv, of course. Thanks for a splendid night, Friday, by the way. Melody enjoyed meeting up with everyone."

"Did you all have a relaxing weekend?" asked Luke.

"Hardly," said Alex. "Gus and I didn't get back from Malaga until late on Saturday. Although, I suppose half a weekend is better than none."

"Or it would have been," said Lydia. "I heard from my mother on Saturday lunchtime. My father and his partner flew into Edinburgh later that afternoon. We could not get up there and back before this morning to be with them, especially as Alex slept until noon on Sunday."

"Eleanor decided to allow Chidozie to contact her then?" asked Blessing.

Neil heard the lift descend to the ground floor. Gus Freeman was on his way.

"We need to catch up on your news later," he said. "I don't know about Luke, but I've got no juicy gossip to offer. Instead, Melody and I spent two quiet days with our feet up in the garden."

"I drove to Englishcombe village for Sunday lunch with my parents," sighed Blessing.

"That sounds as if it went well," said Luke. "We want to hear your story later."

Blessing gave a more profound sigh.

Gus entered the office at one minute to nine and was pleasantly surprised to see a full house. He wondered why the conversation had faltered.

"Has Alex filled you in on the finer details of Saturday's events yet?" he asked.

"Not yet, guv," said Alex. "We were just asking one another what we'd been up to since Friday night at the Waggon & Horses."

"Well, I need the loose ends on the Hogan case tied in a neat bow as soon as possible. I want the files ready to deliver to Kenneth Truelove. I'll get my report on Saturday's events into the Freeman Files and then call London Road for a meeting with the big man."

"Have they finally confirmed him as Chief Constable, guv?" asked Neil.

"I called Geoff Mercer yesterday evening, and he updated me on a couple of matters," said Gus. "Yes, the appointment will be effective from the first of next month."

"Is that a permanent appointment, guv?" asked Luke. "You know what I mean. Will he be in post until his scheduled retirement, or will this be until they find another candidate from around the country?"

"Good question, Luke," said Gus. "No doubt, they have

a bright, young thing destined for stardom. Someone who ticks the politically correct boxes."

"They tried that with Sandra Plunkett, guv," said Neil. "Wouldn't it be better to stick with a copper's copper rather than try to appease the minority groups with somebody who isn't up to the task?"

"You'd better not let the top brass at London Road hear you say that, DS Davis," said Gus. "Your career will come to an abrupt halt. I imagine we'll get a new face in eighteen months to two years. Kenneth's wife agreed to postpone her cruises, not cancel them altogether. Eighteen months is a decent time for this team to build on its successful start. My position was always temporary. Once I've knocked you into shape and can let you get on with things without me holding your hand, I'll step aside."

"We'll miss you, guv," said Lydia.

Truth be told, Gus would miss the banter and the thrill of the chase.

Gus sat at his desk reviewing the details of Saturday's journey to the sun-kissed shores of the Mediterranean. He and Alex hadn't seen the sea except as they arrived at the airport. The Playa Malagueta was a mere name on a road sign he'd spotted as they headed towards the police station.

When they left Bristol International, Gus believed they would arrest Gerry Hogan's killer. Carl Wallace was firmly in the frame. It shows you can't judge a book by its cover. Even though violence wasn't his stock-in-trade, there were enough black marks against Carl Wallace's name to suggest they had the right man.

Yet, as soon as Carl had spotted them, their prime suspect was eager to co-operate.

Gus had a hunch that a confession was the last thing on Carl's mind, so it proved. However, when they interviewed him, Carl confirmed many of the elements of his conversation on the doorstep of Hogan's home on Trowle Common.

Carl Wallace had learned from his father, Lawrence, that Rachel Cummins had left her mother's home in Haslemere, Surrey, in 2006. Katherine Cummins had a vague recollection that Rachel moved to the West Country. It hadn't taken Carl long to trace the personal trainer. Wallace was serving a custodial sentence at HMP Leyhill in Gloucestershire, so he had time on his hands.

Carl soon found Rachel advertised extensively both online and in the local press.

Lawrence had told him Katherine reckoned Rachel lived with a wealthy, older man. Neither he nor Kate knew the man's name, but Carl uncovered it. Rachel's business address was the same as that of local business owner Gerald Hogan, a widower with two young sons.

A heated conversation in a bar between Lawrence Wallace and Rachel's father, Jim Cummins, had exposed potential leverage for blackmail. Jim Cummins had got engaged to his girlfriend, Kate, before she flew to Australia to visit relatives. She wanted to see the country before returning for their wedding in April. When she arrived on the second of January, Rachel was a honeymoon baby as far as everyone was concerned, but Jeff Cummins became suspicious.

The marriage ended after eighteen months. During their heated discussion, Lawrence Wallace bragged to Jeff about getting together with Kate, just as he had hoped when they were teenagers. They had been an item in the days before Jeff Cummins arrived in town and stole his girl. In the end, Kate and Lawrence's relationship also foundered. Perhaps she finally realised he was as a big a sleaze as Rachel had always maintained.

Gus did not know what Kate Cummins was doing these days. But Lawrence had held onto the knowledge he'd gained of what her ex-husband had said in their argument. Kate, or Kat as friends often called her, had shared one drunken night of passion with a guy she only knew as Batman because of his t-shirt. Kate discovered Batman's true identity only hours before flying home to the UK from Darwin. The man she slept with was Gerry Hogan.

Lawrence Wallace had convinced himself Gerry had to be Rachel's father. The timing was right. Kate's insistence that she and Jim have sex almost as soon as she'd got home from Heathrow sealed the deal. Jim believed Kate was desperate to cover her tracks.

Lawrence thought Carl was better placed to act on that information. His son had moved to Bristol to live after leaving HMP Leyhill and was familiar with operating on the wrong side of the law.

Carl Wallace had told Gus and Alex that buying the Beretta Tomcat in the city was a piece of cake. He'd taken the train from Temple Meads to Bradford-on-Avon. Hopped on a bus to Trowle Common and walked to Hogan's front door on May the sixth, 2012.

Gus had thought he'd known the sequence of events from there. As Carl Wallace gave them his version, Gus understood why so many people they talked to insisted Gerry Hogan was a decent man. A man who went out of his way to avoid trouble. Someone for whom even the hint of scandal would be avoided at all costs.

As Gerry had stood on his doorstep, listening to Carl Wallace tell him Rachel could be his daughter, his world collapsed around him. The girl with the cat on her t-shirt. It was just so plausible.

Gerry had grabbed the gun Carl pointed at him and

turned it on himself. Suicide was preferable to an accusation of an incestuous relationship.

Everything Carl Wallace told them about what followed the fatal shot made sense of the weapon and the missing white gloves. Carl confirmed he'd dropped the Beretta down a drain and the gloves into a waste bin at the railway station. After a night on a park bench in Bath, Carl had flown to Malaga.

He'd worked hard in local bars for six years and never got into trouble. On Saturday night, Carl had flown back to Bristol under escort, and someone else would get asked this week to prepare a case against him for the CPS. Gus was glad he wasn't involved. Only two people knew whether Carl was lying, and one of them was dead. The CPS would probably cut its losses. No jury would find Carl Wallace guilty of murder, but Carl had taken a gun with him that night, whether or not he intended to use it. Why load one bullet if you didn't plan to fire the weapon? No, there was enough to put Carl Wallace away for five years. Wiltshire's new Chief Constable would have to be satisfied with that.

Alex Hardy interrupted his reverie.

"I've had a return message from Bronwen, guv," he said. "It arrived here not long after we left on Friday afternoon."

"Don't keep us hanging, Alex," said Gus. "Spit it out."

"The girl Bronwen met on the plane was always Cat to her because of her t-shirt. Her name was Katie or Katherine, and she came from Surrey, but Bronwen couldn't remember the town's name. Hazel, something."

"What now, guv?" asked Alex.

"I called Geoff Mercer yesterday, as I said. Under escort, Carl Wallace returned to the UK, and Jeff Cummins has agreed to a DNA paternity test. We'll know the results on Thursday or Friday."

"You were inclined to believe Carl Wallace, weren't you, guv?" said Alex.

"Everything we knew about Gerry Hogan points that way, Alex. He was an honest man who avoided scandal. When Carl Wallace told him Rachel's mother, Kate, was the girl he slept with that night, everything he had worked so hard to protect was running through his fingers like sand. He could see only one way out."

"What a mess," said Lydia.

"I feel sorry for the boys," said Blessing. "They lost their mother in a tragic accident. Now they have to live with the thought their father didn't get murdered in a random attack, but he shot himself. If that wasn't bad enough, both Sean and Byron seemed to like Rachel. How will this affect their relationship now? They could be her half-brothers. Lydia's right. It couldn't be much more of a mess."

"The metadata on those Facebook photographs is academic now, Blessing," said Gus. "I don't suppose Divya has got back to you with news yet, has she?"

"She's only just started work, guv. I'll call her," said Blessing. "If Divya can attach location labels to those images, it will strengthen Carl Wallace's assertion that he stayed in Bristol after leaving Leyhill. The labels will neaten the bow on the files you hand in at London Road."

"That sounds sensible," said Gus. "I'll call Vera Butler in a few minutes to see if our leader will grant me an audience. If I have to leave before you receive the data, perhaps Divya can meet me in the foyer at London Road and hand me the necessary information?"

"I'll tell Divya to keep an eye out for your Ford Focus, guv," said Blessing.

Gus gave Blessing the thumbs-up. However, he still had at least an hour of work before making that trip.

"Those of you whose files are already complete," he said, "can you clear the decks ready for our next case, please?"

Gus heard a groan from somewhere on his left but ignored it. He needed to set up his meeting. He called Vera.

"Good morning, Ms Butler. How are you this fine Monday morning?"

"Not as chipper as you, Mr Freeman. Do you want to know when the Chief Constable is free?"

"If it's not too much trouble," said Gus.

"Noon," said Vera. "He says it will have to be a working lunch."

That made a change, thought Gus. They'd never had lunch before. Before his elevation, a cup of coffee and a sticky bun was the extent of catering to Kenneth Truelove's office. Gus foresaw problems for Geoff Mercer's waistline.

"Are you and Kassie Trotter preparing executive lunches these days?" asked Gus. "Or will it be inedible finger food large corporations have served for decades?"

"Grace Packenham is responsible for the changes, Gus," said Vera.

"I imagine that means vegan food is eaten while attempting a painful-looking position on a yoga mat," said Gus. "I'd prefer a Zoom meeting; if I knew what it was. Lydia understands that stuff. The Packenham woman has got to go. She's disrupting the status quo."

"We'll expect you at noon then?" asked Vera.

"I'll have a completed case file in one hand and the other hand extended to receive our next cold case. If this Packenham regime continues, I might need to join an athletics club to learn the art of baton changing. I could be in and out in seconds."

"There won't be any cold sausages or cheese and

pineapple chunks on cocktail sticks," said Vera. "The food comes from a company that runs a fleet of refrigerated vans to deliver their goods. Their sandwiches, bloomer sandwiches, sub rolls, tortilla wraps, bacon and sausage baps, panini, pasta salads and salads are hand-prepared daily. They use local suppliers to source the best produce whenever possible."

"I hope the public never learns that this outrageous expense is coming out of their wage packets," said Gus. "You mentioned a bacon bap. Please put me down for one. Reduce Geoff Mercer's order from two to one. I'll see you at noon, Vera."

With that, Gus ended the call.

It was time to tie those loose ends together. As Gus stepped through his files, he reflected on the interrupted weekend that had just passed. The trip to Malaga meant there was little time for him and Suzie to do anything on Saturday except eat and sleep.

Suzie told him she had driven to Worton for her final hack around the local tracks and lanes on her favourite horse. Then in the afternoon, she'd called Vicky Bennison for a brief chat. Gus was happy to hear Suzie hadn't let the grass grow under her feet. Vicky wouldn't rush back to work with the people she believed failed her in her hour of need, but Suzie making a move within twenty-four hours of him and Vicky's first meeting showed a commitment to mend fences.

Not that Gus had needed reminding, but soon after Alex dropped him off at the bungalow, Suzie told him she had called the surgery and asked them to arrange her twelve-week scan for the second week in September.

After two plane journeys sandwiching a hot, sticky day, Gus was tired and fell asleep as soon as his head hit the pillow. When he awoke just before seven in the morning, he'd tried to work out when the baby might arrive. His best guess was the second week in February. Gus wondered about the central heating. Would the little mite cope with another Beast from the East like the one that arrived this year?

Gus was still making a mental list of the things he needed to check were in order when Suzie had stirred beside him.

"Are you ready for an early breakfast?" he asked.

"Did you sleep well?" asked Suzie.

"I'm as hale and hearty as any sixty-one-year-old can expect," he'd replied.

"In that case, my vote is for brunch," said Suzie.

Later, after they had got up, showered, dressed, and feasted on waffles, they moved from the kitchen into the lounge. Gus retrieved the file folder from the end of the album rack, and he and Suzie spent an hour with coffee and a notepad, making adjustments to Gus's existing will.

"I need to make *my* will as soon as possible," said Suzie. "Seeing what you had to put together will help me make my way through the jargon. It's not something you consider when you're young. It seems so final."

"In your job, it's a good idea to get something in place," said Gus. "Criminals carry weapons far more often than when I started in uniform. It only takes one idiot with a knife, or worse, to lash out when you're responding to a shout. If there's nothing on paper, it can cause grieving relatives extra headaches they could do without. Anyway, that's enough of the morbid stuff for today. Let's get outside and enjoy the sunshine."

"Not that we're relatives, but I take your point. An afternoon on the allotment it is," said Suzie. "Shall we eat at the Lamb tonight?"

"That sounds like a plan. I have plenty of catching up to do on the allotment. We'll aim to get into the pub by six or half-past and then get back here for an early night."

"Easy, tiger," said Suzie.

"It will be a busy day tomorrow," said Gus. "I need to get a good night's sleep."

"You raise a girl's hopes, then crush them, Gus Freeman."

"I try my best," said Gus.

They left the bungalow just before three o'clock and walked along the lane.

"Do you ever read your horoscope, Gus," asked Suzie as they passed the Lamb.

"Not likely," he'd replied. "Why take any notice of a comment that's so general it's bound to strike a chord with somebody, somewhere. Why do you ask?"

"Our baby will be born under the sign of Aquarius. Bob Marley was an Aquarian."

"Marley? An interesting character. Perhaps we should call the little one Marley? It sounds gender-fluid. That's all the rage, so they tell me."

"Never in a million years," said Suzie. "Anyway, Marley is a girl's name. It comes from Old English and means 'pleasant seaside meadow'. I read it in a magazine at the doctor's when I was there six weeks ago."

"One additional fact every day is the high road to success," said Gus. "Are names another thing I need to add to my mental list?"

"What list?" asked Suzie as they walked through the gates to the allotments.

"Things to do to the bungalow before the baby arrives," said Gus. "I might need a bank loan."

"This is a novel experience for both of us, Gus," said Suzie, grabbing his hand. "We'll sort it out, don't fret."

"Love will find a way," laughed Gus.

"I see you two are in good humour,"

The disembodied voice belonged to Clemency Bentham, who emerged from her potting shed with a trowel and a battered floral sunhat perched on her head.

"Have you taken the day off, Reverend?" said Gus.

"Matins ended over two hours ago, Gus," said Clemency. "Which you would know if you were a regular churchgoer. I celebrated Holy Communion earlier this morning when you were still in bed. So the rest of the day is mine."

Suzie blushed, and Gus spotted it and grinned. Clemency caught the glance that passed between them.

"I tell Bert and Irene they're in danger of becoming Darby and Joan these days," said Clemency. "A couple who are content to spend their lives in quiet devotion. You two aren't far behind."

"I must protest, Reverend," said Gus. "We're not Darby and Joan. We're Ancient and Modern. You must have heard the phrase in your line of work?"

"Here and there, Gus," replied Clemency. "Bert Penman dropped by an hour ago, by the way. You missed him. He took one look at your patch of ground and shook his head. I had better let you and Suzie get stuck into knocking it back into shape."

"You're right, of course," sighed Gus. "I can't go galli-vanting around mainland Europe on a Saturday and expect my allotment to tend itself. The next three hours will be a start. We plan on eating in the Lamb later. Will you and Brett be around this evening?"

"We will," said Clemency, "although Bert and Irene have already cried off. There's a series on TV that Irene's keen on watching. Brett plans to record it, so we can watch it when we have time. He's not that bothered about the content, but it gives him something to discuss with his grandfather."

"Provided Bert doesn't fall asleep in the middle of the programme after several pints of cider in the Lamb," said Suzie.

"That's a good point," laughed Clemency. "You know we had to help him home the other night. After that short spell in the hospital, Bert won't admit it, but he was worried for Irene."

The Reverend returned to her potting shed, and Gus retrieved tools from his shed so he and Suzie could start work.

"We'll see you next door later," said Clemency, her gardening done for the day. She scooted towards the gateway, clambered aboard her trusty steed, and guided the old bicycle along the lane.

Gus selected a bunch of carrots to harvest and tried to recall when he last watched a TV series. Something always got in the way of committing an hour or two at the same time every week. As for recording things to watch at a later date, Tess had coped with that. If he missed it, he missed it since Tess died. Just like in the old days when his parents first bought a television.

Anyway, life was too short to binge-watch a considerable number of episodes while the sun was shining.

"A penny for them, Gus," said Suzie.

"I thought of another thing to add to my growing list,"

said Gus. "It's time to upgrade our television. I might not have much chance to take advantage of any added benefits in the short term, but it could come in handy for you next year."

"If you think I'll have time to sit watching TV, you've got plenty to learn," scoffed Suzie. "What do you want me to do to help?"

"I can harvest many vegetables in August," said Gus. "I've got my carrots in that box by the shed. If you check through my runner beans, beetroots, and courgettes to see what's ready to pick, I'll tackle my second early potatoes before sorting out my onions."

"What about the other rows of potatoes next door?" asked Suzie.

"That's my main crop. After that, I'll look at what's underneath the foliage in the first week in September."

"How do you know when to do everything?" asked Suzie.

"I thought you'd know, being a farmer's daughter," said Gus. "I didn't have a clue when I came to Urchfont with Tess. Bert Penman dispensed his wisdom, and I scribbled it in an unused police notebook at home. If I lost that book, I'd be in trouble. It's in a safe place in the shed."

"My older brothers were the ones who learned the basics of animal husbandry and the like at their father's knee," said Suzie. "Dad always wanted me to stick with the Pony Club and perhaps ride point-to-point the same as he and Mum did when I grew older. He didn't want me driving tractors and combine harvesters. He was happiest when we could ride out together, even if it were to exercise the horses in my teens and early twenties."

"You weren't into the competitive side of things like John and Jackie, then?"

"I had a crack at it for a few years, but once I joined the police, I didn't have the time. So I've kept up my weekly hack around the countryside in all wind and weather. I'll be back in the saddle as soon as possible after next February. That's what's important to me, not trophies and rosettes."

The conversation and gardening continued throughout the afternoon. Time flies when you're having fun; or when you're working alongside someone you love. It came as a surprise to both of them when the church clock struck six o'clock.

"Right," said Gus. "Straight home. Take a shower and ease those aching joints. A change of clothes and we can be back in the Lamb before the church clock has chimed the half-hour."

"You get no argument from me," said Suzie.

While she popped into the pub to book a table, Gus collected the tools and returned them to the shed. He took a long appreciative look at the improvements they'd made and the wooden box full of produce he had to carry back to the bungalow.

"Divya says she'll meet you in the foyer of the main building, guv."

Gus returned to the here and now at the sound of Blessing Umeh's voice.

"Thanks, Blessing," he said. The clock on the wall opposite read eleven twenty-two—time to go.

"Do we have everything ready for the Chief Constable?" Gus asked.

The chorus of voices suggested they had been waiting for him to stop daydreaming for a while.

Gus collected their files together and headed for the lift.

What delights lay in store for him at London Road, he wondered.

Chapter Two

GUS EASED the Focus into the late-morning traffic on the High Street and trundled out of town. As long as there wasn't a glut of farm vehicles between here and Caen Hill, he should make London Road with a few minutes to spare. That gave him long enough to grab the metadata on those photos from Divya and slip it into his folder.

WHILE GUS WAS en route to London Road, the rest of the team was either clearing the decks in anticipation of their next cold case or catching up on the weekend's gossip.

"Come on, Blessing," urged Lydia. "I can tell something happened that's concerning you. What's the matter?"

"My mother reminded me on Wednesday evening that my father was keen for me to get to Englishcombe in the morning. He wanted me to go with them to church. I persuaded her that Mrs Ferris needed my help first and that my washing and ironing needed doing. So I couldn't leave the farm until one o'clock at the earliest."

"Did you get lost?" asked Lydia.

"No, Dave Smith's directions were perfect. He sent me on less busy roads. I went through places with charming names, such as Farleigh Hungerford and Hinton Charterhouse."

"They sound like 1930s matinee idols," said Lydia. "Is Englishcombe as pretty a village as the name suggests?"

"If you can imagine a village at the end of a narrow, winding lane, hidden in the fold of the hills," said Blessing. "It's pretty, there is no doubt, but they don't have a shop, a school, or a pub. They're all long gone. It's easy to imagine nothing has ever happened there throughout its history. Yet, Mrs Ferris told me to check out the ruins. A Norman castle got demolished after the authorities implicated its owner in the murder of Edward the Second."

"It hasn't always been the quiet, idyllic group of houses where your parents live today, then," said Lydia. "How long did it take you to drive there?"

"Fifty minutes," said Blessing. "I arrived at a few minutes to two, just in time for Sunday dinner. My father came out of the house as soon as I parked the car. He asked if I had a pleasant journey. I told him that since my car had returned from the garage, I hadn't had any trouble. My father said he was glad I arrived safely. He hoped I didn't break the speed limit. He's so funny. My driving instructor kept asking me why, when the limit was thirty miles per hour, I preferred to travel at twenty. I told him I wanted to be on the safe side."

"Your father cares for you, Blessing," said Lydia.

"A little too much," said Blessing. "He asked whether my car was safe in John Ferris's wooden sheds. Then, he offered to buy me a wheel clamp to stop anyone from stealing it."

"Well, there have been thefts of equipment and vehicles

from rural farms," said Lydia. "Maybe that's not such a daft idea."

"My mother saved me from further interrogation by dishing up dinner," said Blessing, "but my reprieve was only temporary. I was ready to sink into a comfortable chair and relax after we'd eaten, but my parents had other ideas. They wanted to show me around the village. My father told me the fresh air would do me good. He said I spent far too long in a stuffy office."

"How did that go?" asked Lydia.

"As soon as he said that I was a dutiful daughter and he and my mother had tried to raise me correctly, my heart sank. We left the house and walked to the church they were so keen I should visit. St Peter's is another place in the village built by the Norman nobleman who came to these shores with William the Conqueror. We walked to a tithe barn constructed in the fourteenth century. Do you remember when I visited Mere with Gus? Several parts of the village and the surrounding area belonged to the Duchy of Cornwall. My mother told me yesterday afternoon that the tithe barn is privately owned and belongs to the Duchy."

"That means Charles, the Prince of Wales, owns it, Blessing," said Lydia. "Your parents are rubbing shoulders with royalty."

"I doubt he's ever been anywhere near it," said Blessing. "My father was quiet while my mother spoke with me about the village's history. I couldn't help thinking he had something on his mind."

"What do you mean?" asked Lydia.

"My parents moved to this country many years ago, but their Nigerian culture remains traditional and conservative," said Blessing. "I know my mother only wants what's best for me, but, at best, my father has tolerated my life in the police. He sees it as a passing fancy. I am twenty-one years old, Lydia, and I might already have been married for several years in Nigeria. My father believes in a marriage where men are the head of the household. Because of this, a good marriage will be my crowning glory in his world. I want a career and to wait for the right person to come along. I want to marry for love."

"Of course you do, Blessing. I know when Dave Smith broke up with you, you were hurt. You had hopes of a lasting relationship with him, didn't you?"

"I wasn't sure Dave was the one," said Blessing, "but he was the right one for right now if that makes sense. As we passed Manor Farm, another building carrying the Duchy of Cornwall crest, my father announced he had spoken to a senior member of an Igbo family in Owerri, the capital of Imo State."

"Your father wants to arrange a marriage for you?" asked Lydia. "That's shocking. Is it even possible?"

"It's not unusual, Lydia, especially in Nigeria. Often, the young bride doesn't meet her husband until the wedding day."

"I'm half-Nigerian," said Lydia, "and even I find it barbaric. What did you say?"

"I told him I didn't want to go against his wishes, but I wanted to choose my husband," said Blessing. "He reminded me I should be a dutiful daughter and realise he had my best interests at heart. Then he blamed my mother for putting fanciful ideas in my head. I left earlier than planned and drove home to Worton. Jackie Ferris let me cry on her shoulder. It was a dreadful end to the weekend."

"Poor you," said Lydia. "What happens now? Will your

father continue to plan your marriage despite your objections?"

"I can only hope my mother will work on my father over the coming days," said Blessing. "That's her way. Like water on stone, a constant drip erodes the strongest rock in time. If she can wear my father down, I shall avoid cutting myself off from the family I love. For once, I'm looking forward to my mother's phone call on Wednesday evening."

"I feel guilty sharing the news we received at the weekend now," said Lydia.

"Don't be silly," said Blessing. "Your mother and father meeting after so many years was the opportunity for a joyous occasion. Was it a success?"

"Alex thought it might be awkward for Eleanor when we heard both Chidozie and Rosa flew from Rotterdam," said Lydia. "I knew it would have been harder if Chidozie had travelled alone. Twenty-six years is a long time. They're different people now."

"I expect you will visit with your mother soon?" said Blessing.

"Alex and I plan to get away next weekend," said Lydia. "I want to hear about the time they spent together. So far, I know that Rosa de Vries and Eleanor got on like a house on fire. Chidozie took them to The Table, one of the best restaurants in the city, on Saturday evening. Eleanor told me Chidozie invited her to Dubai in the autumn. Perhaps, we can visit at the same time. That would be great."

"It certainly sounds as if there were no awkward moments," said Blessing.

"I'm sure my birth parents will follow a similar process to the one I did with Eleanor when I first made contact," said Lydia. "Small steps to give the relationship a chance to develop at its own pace. Eleanor and I will stay as friends.

We'll never be too close to one another. No doubt that's what lies ahead for Chidozie and Eleanor. No regrets. No recriminations."

"That's all that any of us can hope for," sighed Blessing.

GUS SWUNG the Ford Focus into the remaining parking space in front of the main building. He looked towards the ACC's window and corrected himself. Of course, Kenneth Truelove now had a change of scenery. Since her demise, Sandra Plunkett's former abode on the first floor had stood empty. Until the Chief Constable appointment became official, Kenneth had resisted the temptation to move in.

Change is continuous, thought Gus, but not always easy to accept.

Somehow, Gus didn't think he'd ever get used to not seeing Kenneth staring at him from above. There would now be an empty office on the right-hand side of the administration floor. It would make sense for Geoff Mercer to transfer from the dark recesses of the corridor at the back of the building. Geoff would be more likely to wave than frown when Gus arrived to sully the visitor's car park with his old banger.

Gus collected his file folder from the passenger seat and trotted up the steps to the front door. He spotted a familiar face as soon as he stepped inside the foyer.

"Divya, good to see you again."

"Blessing told me you needed these for your meeting, Gus. We found nothing untoward in the images Carl Wallace posted online. They came from within the Bristol area, with the majority focussing on Filton. The regular posts and photos across his social media accounts don't suggest he spent a long period anywhere other than Bristol or Bath."

"Thanks, Divya. That was what I expected to hear. Taken in isolation, it seems a waste of effort, but it supports everything Carl Wallace told us in an interview. Of course, not everything the Hub handles is a game-changer, but your contribution has added value to the work we mere foot-soldiers had to do in this case."

"We're a facility ready for you to use whenever the need arises, Gus," said Divya.

"Don't worry," said Gus. "The Chief Constable will make sure I don't forget that fact. The Hub is his baby. At first, I thought he needed justification for the expensive set-up costs, but there have been odd occasions when your people have provided us with the golden key to solve a mystery. I'd better let you get back to your computers."

Divya smiled and walked out of the main building towards the Hub.

Gus took the stairs two at a time up to the first floor just because he could.

Nobody saw him, which was a minor disappointment.

He couldn't spot Vera Butler or Kassie Trotter. Geoff Mercer was standing by the ACC's office door.

"Are you making plans, Geoff?" he asked.

"Kenneth had his belongings transferred over the week-end," said Geoff. "He thought you might need a guide to help you find his office."

"I can't recall ever getting an invitation to visit either of the incumbents since my return to the fray," said Gus. "There have been so many; it's hard to distinguish one from another. Was the furniture upgraded on each occasion?"

"I took a peek first thing this morning," said Geoff. "I reckon they got rid of the fixtures and fittings Sandra Plunkett favoured and reinstated the stuff Leonard Pemberton-Smythe's mate used before he had to resign."

"Every expense spared then," said Gus. "Now I understand how they can afford the executive lunches. Shouldn't we be heading over to the dark side? It's almost noon."

"Kenneth was giving an interview to the press at eleven forty-five," said Geoff. "That should be over in a few minutes. Then he wants us out of his hair by two o'clock as he's got a financial management meeting with the Police and Crime Commissioner."

"What was the meeting with the press about?" asked Gus as they arrived outside the Chief Constable's door.

"A member of the public discovered firearms on a Swindon industrial estate," said Geoff. "The local rag thought the area was out of control and accused the police of treating the estate as a no-go area."

"No truth in it, surely?"

"That's what our new Chief Constable told them. We shall not rest. No stone unturned. You know Kenneth's style. He can be persuasive."

"Yes, he has a way with words," said Gus.

A red-faced Kenneth Truelove appeared at the top of the stairs.

"There's a glow surrounding his persona, isn't there?" said Gus.

"It's the shiny new insignia on his uniform. Of course, that's a brand-new white shirt, too," said Geoff.

Kenneth had now joined the pair outside his office door.

"Did the meeting go badly, sir," asked Geoff.

"It went, Mercer," grunted the Chief Constable, opening the door and walking inside.

"I told you he had a way with words," said Gus quietly

as he and Geoff followed their leader into the light, well-appointed office.

"To business, gentlemen," said Kenneth. "Give me the bottom line on the Hogan case, Freeman."

Gus placed the file folder on the desktop as neatly as possible. The desk was always cluttered in the ACC's old office and had a lived-in look, but the new oversized desk was all straight lines and dust-free.

"Carl Wallace maintains Gerry Hogan turned the gun on himself when he suspected that Rachel Cummins was his daughter."

"Good heavens," said Kenneth. "What did you make of that, Mercer?"

"I agree with Gus's assessment, sir. I don't think it was murder."

"John Kirkpatrick won't come out of this smelling of roses," said Kenneth. "How did he miss that possibility six years ago?"

"If it walks like a duck, sir," said Gus.

"I suppose so. A prominent business owner was shot in the head on his doorstep. My first thought would be, who wanted him dead? It wouldn't be; hang on, is there any chance it was suicide?"

"Nothing in the interviews with family and friends pointed us in that direction, sir," said Gus. "Except the same theme runs throughout his life. Gerald Hogan was a decent man who always tried to avoid trouble."

"We must pass it to the detective team at Polebarn Road in Trowbridge, Freeman," said Kenneth. "They can prepare a case for the Crown Prosecution Service."

"On to the next case then, sir," said Gus.

"I'm sure you want something that allows you and the team to find a killer, Freeman," said Kenneth. "This one was rather gruesome if I remember rightly. The victim was Marion Reeves, a forty-four-year-old wife and mother. She died on the eighteenth of March back in 2011. You didn't work on the case, Freeman, but it occurred in Wilton, not five miles from your police station on Bourne Hill."

"There was a station closer than that, sir," said Gus. "The Wilton Road station closed in 2014, and I believe there's a proposal for the premises to get sold at a public auction. Village stations can play a vital role in helping to keep rural communities safe. Or at least to feel safe. Of course, I'm a voice in the wilderness. Marion Reeves worked in Salisbury, didn't she?"

"Yes, Marion Reeves was a manager at a printing firm. Her husband, Theo, was a fifty-eight-year-old graphic designer with an office in Wilton. The couple had married in 1991 and moved into a family home in Wilton. Marion's son from her first marriage, Martyn Street, was three years old and lived with Theo and Marion. In 1993, Marion gave birth to a daughter, Stephanie. Both Theo and Marion had good jobs, and the couple thrived financially. In 2010, extensive renovations began on the Wilton property that would cost around eighty thousand pounds. On the fifteenth of March 2011, Marion Reeves withdrew six thousand pounds in cash from her bank. The police believed this money was for completing another phase of the building process."

"Why do some business people insist on cash?" asked Geoff Mercer.

"Not everyone is as tech-savvy as you, Geoff," said Gus. "I once tried negotiating the minefield they called the Bankers Automated Clearing Services to make a payment transfer. It was fraught with danger. One slip and I could have sent my forty pounds to the wrong account altogether.

When you hand cash to the guy who did the work for you and get a signed receipt in return, there's no problem. He won't come knocking at the door saying you haven't paid him, will he? Imagine the headaches if you wanted to pay a building firm five or six grand weekly for three or four months. I'd feel happier paying them that way, the same as Marion Reeves, and let the builder worry about the taxman."

"Time marches on, Freeman," said the Chief Constable. "Vera and Kassie will be here with lunch before we know it. Let's get on. Right, Marion Reeves withdrew the cash on the fifteenth. Three days later, on the eighteenth, Theo Reeves left for work at eight-fifteen in the morning. That was normal behaviour. As for Marion, Theo had no concerns; she was bright and cheerful that morning. The builders arrived just as Theo Reeves drove away from the house. It was customary for Marion to talk to them before they started work. She had arranged with her employers to start work thirty minutes later each day and only take thirty minutes for lunch. Theo said it was usually around eight forty-five when his wife left home."

"What about the children?" asked Geoff. "Did they witness any discord between the couple? Or see Marion arguing with the builders, perhaps?"

"The couple's daughter, Stephanie, was eighteen," said Kenneth. "She was a matter of weeks away from sitting her A-levels at South Wilts Grammar School on Bemerton Heath. The Reeves' home was on Oakley Road in Wilton. Stephanie cycled the three and a half miles to school every weekday, taking between fifteen and twenty minutes. Stephanie left home at twenty-five minutes past eight. She told the police her parents were fine when she got downstairs that morning. They rarely argued. After her father left for work, her mother chatted to the builders while Stephanie ate her breakfast."

"Did the older lad still live with his mother and step-father?" asked Gus.

"He did," said Kenneth. "Martyn Street, twenty-three, had already left for work at eight o'clock. Martyn worked with a Grounds Maintenance team at Wilton House for the Earl and Countess of Pembroke."

"An early start," said Gus.

"The family home is one and a half miles from Wilton House," said Kenneth. "Martyn couldn't afford a car, so he walked to work. Thirty minutes each way. He spent most of his working day on his feet when the estate was open to the public. The Pembroke family has been there for over four hundred years. They had one hundred and forty employees back in 2011. Martyn had plenty of witnesses to say he arrived at work at eight-thirty that morning and, in normal circumstances, wouldn't leave until five in the afternoon."

"The Grade I buildings attract film crews," said Geoff Mercer. "Not that it applies to the case. They shot scenes for 'Tomb Raider' there last year. I think the film came out in March."

"It doesn't sound like something I would watch, Geoff," said Gus.

"They based it on a video game," said Geoff. "Lara Croft. Have you ever heard of her?"

"No, the last actress I remember seeing at the cinema was Meryl Streep. Tess was keen on watching whatever she starred in. I fell asleep twenty minutes into the film."

"Lara Croft isn't an actress, Freeman. She's a character from the video game," said Kenneth. "Don't look at me like that, Mercer. My children played video games. I'll never claim to be down with the kids, but I'm not ignorant. I think now would be a good time to take a break."

Kenneth made the call, and a knock at the door heralded the arrival of Kassie Trotter and Vera Butler.

"It will take getting used to seeing you three in the West Wing," said Kassie, wheeling her trolley across the plush carpet.

Gus could always rely on Kassie to surprise him with a fresh look when he visited London Road. Since their heart-to-heart over Rhys Evans and her news of a single sighting of Rick Chalmers getting up-close-and-personal with Vera, he had seen little of his young friend.

There was no missing Kassie's hairstyle. If that wasn't too grand a name. Kassie's head was shaved on the left side, while the dark tresses cascading over her right shoulder had red and electric blue streaks.

As Gus wondered whether to risk glancing below Kassie's shoulders, Vera whispered in his left ear.

"One bacon bap, Gus, and a black coffee, no sugar."

"Thank you, Vera," said Gus. "How's Kassie coping with the changes to her routine?"

"We distribute the healthy food options Grace Packenham insists on during these shortened lunch breaks. Then, when her back's turned, mid-morning and mid-afternoon, we still conduct a busy trade on the sticky buns and cakes."

"You enjoy being part of a group, don't you, Vera?" said Gus. "When we met, you were one of the FEW, and now you're a member of the DRM. The Devizes Resistance Movement."

Vera didn't comment. There seemed to be trouble on the other side of the room.

"Come on, Mercer," said Kenneth Truelove. "We haven't got all day. What's up now?"

"I ordered a sausage bap and a tortilla wrap, sir," said Geoff. "My bap's gone missing."

Gus tried not to smile. He mouthed a thankyou at Vera as she left the room with her trolley.

"What do you reckon to my tattoo, Mr Freeman?" asked Kassie.

She bent forward to give Gus a better view of the recent addition between her left shoulder and elbow pit. Kassie's bluebirds and love hearts quivered.

"It looks fiery, Kassie," said Gus.

"Well, it is a dragon, Mr Freeman."

"No, I mean, you should keep an eye on it. I hope it hasn't got infected."

"I've got my antibacterial ointment, Mr Freeman," said Kassie. "I've got to apply it myself, of course. I'm still looking for the man of my dreams."

"When we finish here, Kassie, can I come and see you?" asked Gus. "The boss won't let me stay for afternoon tea. He's far too busy. Perhaps, I can sneak away with one of your illicit cakes later?"

"You need to be careful, Mr Freeman. The enemy has eyes everywhere. I'll get one of my cream slices to you before you leave, don't fret."

After Kassie closed the door behind her, Kenneth Truelove looked ready to carry on with the outline of the case.

"My compliments to the chef, sir," said Gus. "I had doubts when I heard from Vera that Ms Pakenham had engaged new caterers, but I was pleasantly surprised."

"So was I," said Geoff. "I think I know who to blame for my short measures."

"Where was I," asked Kenneth. "Ah yes, we'd dealt with the whereabouts of the family's younger members. The firm Theo Reeves employed for the renovations was MP Builders Limited. Stuart Milligan and Derek Preston had worked together for two decades. Both were in their late thirties, married with children. Milligan told the police Mrs Reeves was later leaving that morning. Marion Reeves said cheerio and drove away five minutes after nine."

"Did Marion Reeves pay the builders the money she withdrew from the bank the previous Friday?" asked Gus.

"Milligan and Preston claimed Mrs Reeves didn't mention money," said Kenneth.

"That's odd," said Geoff. "I would have thought if the money were for the builders, she would have handed it over on Friday evening, not first thing Monday morning."

"It's something we can follow up on, Geoff," said Gus. "If Milligan and Preston were a well- established firm, they could have got a wife to bank their cheques and cash. To save breaking off work during the day to make a special trip into Salisbury."

"Are MP Builders still trading, sir," asked Geoff.

"I believe so," said Kenneth. "Anyway, at five past nine, Marion left her builders alone at the property to start work. She set off to drive to Salisbury in her white Lexus RX350."

"Very nice," said Geoff. "Christine keeps looking at one of those."

"At nine-thirty," said Kenneth, "witnesses reported a car of the same colour and make on Wilton Road near Quidhampton."

"That's the A36," said Gus, "It only takes ten minutes to drive from that part of Wilton into Salisbury. Where did she stop for twenty minutes? Unless there were an accident or major roadworks, she should have passed Quidhampton three or four minutes from home."

"At a quarter to twelve," said Kenneth, "police received a call from an employee at the Churchfields Industrial Estate, Bemerton. He'd discovered a woman's body in the driver's seat of a white Lexus. Someone had stabbed Marion Reeves in the chest and stomach. The police surgeon suggested the wounds came from a narrow, four-inch blade. He estimated the time of death at ten o'clock."

"At ten in the morning, an Industrial Estate like that would be busy," said Gus. "Surely, somebody saw something?"

"Nobody witnessed the Lexus arrive," said Kenneth. "Marion Reeves parked on a side-street between a light-engineering firm and a gym. Nobody saw anyone near the car, inside the car with the victim, or the murder itself. So, who killed Marion Reeves, and why?"

"Who ran the investigation?" asked Gus.

"Billie Wightman was the DI in charge," said Kenneth.

"Ably supported by DS Matt Price," said Gus. "I knew Matt. He was a good lad. As for Ms Wightman, let's say we never saw eye to eye."

"I hope that won't be an issue, Freeman," said Kenneth. "Wightman checked Marion's diaries for details of anything to explain why she didn't travel directly to her place of work. There were two diaries. One was physical, which they found in her handbag in the Lexus. The other was digital, on a laptop in her office at the print firm. There was no sign of any arranged meeting nor anything to explain the need to visit that particular Industrial Estate."

"Which way did Wightman take her investigation, sir?" asked Gus.

"She asked the family, the builders, and her work

colleagues who they thought Marion Reeves could have met. Nothing useful came from that. Then Wightman pursued the notion Marion was cheating on her husband."

"I'm not surprised," said Gus. "Billie's husband was a uniformed copper at Bourne Hill. He left her for a younger woman. An affair wouldn't have been my first thought based on the history you've given us so far, sir. Marion Reeves was a happily married, successful woman."

"Wightman's idea may have had merit, looking at things from a different angle," said Kenneth. "Theo Reeves didn't marry before he met Marion, but he had several former lovers. Wightman and Price traced and interviewed the lot but found nothing to support the idea one of them killed Marion Reeves for the opportunity to reunite with Theo."

"What happened to the cash?" asked Gus.

"We know the builders didn't get it," said Geoff. "What's to say it was in her handbag that day? She could have handed it to someone else between Friday and Monday morning."

"Fair point," said Gus.

"Forensics showed the murder took place inside the Lexus," said Kenneth. "Theo Reeves confirmed nothing had been stolen from his wife's handbag. However, her cards, keys, mobile phone, and a modest sum of cash were still inside. The six thousand pounds in cash were never recovered, but it might have gone before Monday morning, as Geoff said."

"Was there anything else?" asked Gus.

"Eyewitnesses saw Marion Reeves talking to the driver of a pick-up truck on Friday after she'd withdrawn the cash from the bank."

"We need their names," said Gus. "Did Billie Wightman

ask whether anyone saw Marion hand something to the truck driver?"

Kenneth Truelove glanced through the report.

"The driver was stopped in traffic on the opposite side of the road to the bank. He was leaning out of the cab window. If Marion Reeves had wanted to hand over an envelope, she would have had to step off the pavement, walk into the street, and offer the money up to the driver's window. You can check, but the conversation might not be relevant. The driver could have asked a pedestrian for directions."

"We'll still ask the eyewitnesses whether it looked as if the two knew one another," said Gus. "Who else did Wightman and Price speak to?"

"They interviewed and eliminated everyone who worked at the Churchfields Industrial Estate or visited premises there on Monday morning."

"They covered an awful lot of people," said Geoff, "uncovering no meaningful clues."

"Did anything turn up at the autopsy?" asked Gus.

"The attacker struck from the passenger seat," said Kenneth. "With the number of knife wounds the coroner recorded, Marion's killer had to be covered in blood."

"Why didn't anyone see them after they got out of the car at ten o'clock?" asked Gus.

"Was Theo Reeves ever a suspect?" asked Geoff. "I know the marriage sounded idyllic, but based on Gus's assessment of DI Wightman, she would have looked at the husband first."

"Theo was in a meeting when the murder occurred, " Kenneth said. "Half a dozen colleagues confirmed he hadn't left the building since arriving at work. Wightman ruled out Theo Reeves early doors. One set of fingerprints recovered from inside the car briefly gave credence to the possibility of an affair. They belonged to a neighbour, Simon Turner. He was a twenty-six-year-old primary school teacher at Manor Fields. Theo confirmed Marion picked him up on his way home one evening the previous week. Simon's car wouldn't start when he left school, and he decided to walk the two-and-a-half miles home. Marion picked him up after he'd covered half the distance. He had a classroom of school kids to offer an alibi for his where-abouts on Monday morning."

"That was everything, was it?" asked Gus.

"I'm afraid that's all I've got time for, Freeman," said Kenneth, handing Gus the case file. "I suggest you read the file, but we've covered the salient points. Six weeks after Marion Reeves's murder, DI Wightman and DS Price trans-ferred to another team working on a spate of aggravated burglaries."

Gus spotted Geoff Mercer shrug his shoulders. The recently elevated Chief Constable was already out of his chair and heading for the door.

They had suffered the first casualty of the new regime. The three friends could no longer give a case the once-over as they had in the past. Gus always found those musings beneficial.

"The Crime Review Team are in at the deep end," said Geoff.

"We'll do our best as always," said Gus.

Gus collected a cream slice from Kassie in the dark corridor leading to Geoff Mercer's office. He glanced at the brown paper bag on the passenger seat as he set off for the Old Police Station office. Change was continuous, but you didn't have to like it.

Chapter Three

"WHAT WAS the Chief Constable's office like, guv," asked Neil Davis as Gus emerged from the lift forty minutes later.

"The same as when the previous Chief Constable occupied it, Neil," replied Gus. "Kenneth Truelove brought his family photographs across the mezzanine with his chair. Apart from that, every expense was spared. The fixtures and fittings aren't important. It's the change in responsibilities that will have the greatest ramifications."

"You look troubled, guv," said Luke. "Has the Chief Constable handed us a stinker of a case this time?"

"We have a cold case from seven years ago," said Gus, "where a forty-four-year-old wife and mother got stabbed near Wilton. A murder with no witnesses, despite taking place on a busy industrial estate. The detective team interviewed one hundred people and eliminated everyone from the investigation. After six weeks, they had no useful leads to follow and definitely no suspects. There could be more detail in the murder file, but I haven't read all of it yet. The boss had to dash to a meeting with the Police and Crime Commissioner."

"I don't suppose Mr Truelove will spend as much time with you as he has in the past, guv," said Blessing.

"The PCC made the right choice in promoting the ACC to the top job," said Gus. "We'll have to make the best of things. The PCC is only concerned with getting a superb administrator and a safe pair of hands. That's exactly what the county needs after the last two characters in the post. The downside is that Kenneth Truelove is a proper copper, unlike many other senior officers who climb to the top of the greasy pole. His astute analysis of the dozen cases we've handled thus far has undoubtedly helped this team to hit the ground running. DS Mercer said we'd been thrown in the deep end for the first time."

"Then it's up to us to avoid sinking, guv," said Lydia.

"Exactly," said Gus. "We'll need maps covering Salisbury and Wilton on the walls, please. The photos from the murder scene are horrific, but keep them in a prominent position on the main whiteboard. I don't want us to lose sight of why we're hunting for the killer of Marion Reeves."

"Did you have anything to do with this case, guv?" asked Alex.

Gus shook his head.

"I'd need to check what I was working on back then, Alex. The Chief Constable mentioned that aggravated burglaries were a hot potato by the beginning of May. That's when the detectives working on the Reeves murder switched their attentions elsewhere. I remember those crimes. Wiltshire is way down the list on national statistics for violent crimes, so something like that sticks in the memory."

Lydia leafed through the murder file on Gus's desk, searching for the crime scene photos.

Neil and Blessing found the relevant street maps covering Wilton and Salisbury.

"Do you have a list of all the people interviewed in the original investigation, guv?" asked Luke Sherman.

"It's in the file, Luke. To start with, I want to talk to the victim's husband, Theo Reeves. He will be sixty-five this year. He may have retired. We'll need to speak to the daughter, Stephanie, wherever she is. She was eighteen and due to sit her A-levels. After seven years, if she went on to university, Stephanie could live and work anywhere in the world. Or she could be married and living in Salisbury. Good hunting, Luke."

"Were there any other children, guv?" asked Luke.

"The victim's son from her first marriage," said Gus. "Martyn Street. He'll be thirty now. No idea if he still works at Wilton House, but that's a good place to start. The other two on my priority list are Stuart Milligan and Derek Preston. You should find them listed under MP Builders Limited. They ran the firm renovating and extending the Oakley Road property for Theo and Marion Reeves."

"Who was in charge of the case, guv?" asked Luke.

"DI Billie Wightman and DS Matt Price from Bourne Hill nick in Salisbury," said Gus.

"Close colleagues, guv?"

"Matt Price was a good copper, Luke."

"Do you want to speak to them?"

"When we have questions that only they can answer," said Gus. "Until then, we'll plough our own furrow."

"Understood, guv," said Luke. "It's not as long a list as on our other cases, is it?"

"Ah, there's the rub, Luke," said Gus. "Wightman and

Price spoke to the best part of a hundred people and got nothing. We could ask those people a fresh set of questions and get the same result. Maybe one person they spoke to told them a pack of lies. I don't want to waste time going over the same ground the original investigation covered. Instead, we'll look for people with a connection to the victim. Two things stand out if the killer sat next to Marion Reeves in her car for several minutes before repeatedly plunging a knife into her. First, the killer was someone Marion Reeves knew. Second, the motive was personal."

"If that person was someone interviewed by Wightman and Price, they missed that personal connection, guv."

"Possibly, Luke," said Gus. "Talking of personal connections, see if you can find the victim's first husband. The Chief Constable didn't mention a name nor explain why the marriage ended. Theo and Marion married in 1991. Martyn Street was only three years old. How long was Marion married to this man? How soon after the couple separated did Marion meet Theo?"

"Either way, the courtship didn't last long, guv," said Luke. "Marion had had a child in 1988, and Theo married Marion in 1991, just three years later. Perhaps it was Martyn that caused the rift?"

"An unwanted pregnancy," said Gus. "Now, there's a fresh idea for us to follow."

"And we've only had the file for a matter of minutes, guv," said Luke.

Gus left the team to get on with setting up meetings, preparing their digital files, and familiarising themselves with the contents of the murder file.

He reflected on this afternoon's meeting at London Road.

Gus knew that as Chief Constable, Kenneth must regularly explain to the public the actions of the officers and staff he commanded. In addition, Kenneth was now responsible for keeping the county's communities safe and secure. So as well as being responsible for the officers and staff under his control, he was also accountable to the public and the PCC. Although not necessarily in that order.

A Chief Constable had to answer to the courts that apply the law for how police powers get used. Kenneth answered to the PCC on delivering efficient and effective policing and how resources and spending were managed. Gus recalled his conversation with Geoff Mercer when considering whether to come out of retirement.

Geoff discussed the strategy and aims of the PCC's police and crime plan. There were budgets to consider. It all seemed a lot of hard work to Gus. Geoff had used a more derogatory term.

It was the modern way. The words and pictures the public received had to conform to a language that Gus and his mentors didn't recognise. Villains weren't villains these days. They were stakeholders.

"What about this pick-up driver, guv," asked Neil. "Is he worth a look?"

"How will you identify him, Neil?" said Gus. "There might have been CCTV coverage of the street opposite the bank back in 2011, but the records got wiped years ago. The police only hang onto ANPR records for two years. So it's a long shot, but according to the Chief Constable, Wightman and Price interviewed eyewitnesses from the scene. So, please keep your fingers crossed they recorded the names. Maybe one witness has a photographic memory and can recall a vehicle registration or the company's name written on the side of the truck."

"If we could find the driver," said Blessing Umeh, "we

could determine whether he was one of the connections you mentioned to Luke, guv."

"We should think about how we get a list of those possible connections," said Gus. "Where to start, anyone?"

"The husband, guv," said Alex.

"Theo Reeves may never have been a suspect," said Gus, "but how can we trust that he was aware of everyone Marion knew? His view of their marriage will colour his list of names. Theo believed everything in their relationship was fine. Marion died in a vicious assault, so that has to get called into question."

"The killer could have been someone Theo was unaware of, guv," said Lydia. "Someone Marion knew through her work or from her first marriage. What do we know about that period of her life?"

"Very little," said Neil. "I found a footnote in the murder file that mentioned Graham Street, Marion's first husband. He was much older than her and will be in his early seventies now. Graham Street was wealthy, sophisticated, and mixed with people at the top of the social tree. Marion's family came from a working-class background."

"Well, there's an angle we can pursue," said Gus. "Neil, you can follow up on that footnote. We need everything you can dig up on Graham Street, how he met Marion and their relationship."

"Got it, guv," said Neil.

"We've got the names of the staff at the printing firm, guv," said Luke. "DI Wightman interviewed them seven years ago. We could look closer at how they interacted with Marion Reeves outside of work. Perhaps, we can uncover connections with clients and businesses the firm used. It's unlikely the detective team interviewed people from outside the company."

"Marion could have met that pick-up driver she talked to that day, guv," said Blessing. "He could have visited her firm and made deliveries or collections regularly. Nobody suspected Marion of conducting an affair, but it wouldn't be the first time a wife kept secret assignations from a husband."

"What a delightful turn of phrase, Blessing," said Gus. "I haven't heard it described that way for years. But you're right. We believe the killer was someone Marion knew well because she was happy to let them sit in her car. However, we also know that Marion was kind-hearted enough to stop on her way home to pick up that young schoolteacher. Simon Turner wasn't someone she knew well. He was a near neighbour, a passing acquaintance. We will have to judge each connection on its merits. The killer could be someone Marion had known well for years or someone she was having a fling with that she'd only met through work recently."

"What about the staff at the company where Theo Reeves worked, guv?" asked Luke. "We should check with Theo whether the couple met with his work colleagues on social occasions. That could throw up a connection Wightman and Price overlooked."

"Indeed," said Gus. "Let's consider other characters involved in the case. The children, for instance. Stephanie and Martyn are unlikely to add many names to our list. Is there anyone we've missed?"

"Did Martyn attend the same school as Stephanie?" asked Lydia.

"No idea," said Gus. "What difference would that make?"

"Well, Marion was more likely to attend those awkward sessions with Martyn, where the teacher discussed a child's performance with a parent. Did Theo go along too? Did they both go to South Wilts Grammar for Stephanie's appraisals?"

"Martyn was working with his hands in 2011," Gus said. "I see which way you're going now. Martyn could have left school at sixteen and not been good enough for Grammar School. How did Theo Reeves get on with his stepson? Nothing was made of their relationship by Wightman and Price."

"As soon as their alibis checked out, they didn't dig deeper, guv," said Alex. "The detectives probably thought it irrelevant. What happened after Marion's death? Did Martyn continue to live under Theo's roof? That could tell us which way the wind blew."

"Another thing to add to your list of questions when you speak to Theo Reeves, guv," said Luke.

"I'm not complaining at this stage, Luke," said Gus. "It's when we don't have a single question to ask that I get stressed."

"Is there anything else you need on the walls or white-boards, guv," asked Alex.

"What were you thinking, Alex?"

"You queried the time it took Marion Reeves to cover the distance between her home in Oakley Road and where witnesses saw her Lexus on the A36 that morning. Walking the various routes involved might not be practical, but a detailed map could offer possibilities for where she may have stopped, which explained the twenty minutes that elapsed after leaving home."

"That's not a bad idea, guv," added Luke. "It could suggest how the killer arrived at the Churchfields Industrial Estate. Was it possible to get there on foot? Were they already close by because it was where they worked? Did they drive there to meet Marion? Where did they park? Marion parked on a side street without anyone spotting her. If another car parked next to her, it increased the risk of discovery."

"If there was another vehicle," said Blessing, "say, a pick-up truck, it wouldn't have stood out given the nature of the businesses operating on the estate. Plus, it helps to explain how the killer left the area despite getting covered in blood in the attack."

"Okay, I'm sold on the idea," said Gus. "To slightly amend a well-known phrase, we'll need a bigger map."

"If we take Wilton House as the centre of operations," said Blessing, "we need something that covers Oakley Road and South Street to the west, Old Shaftesbury Drove to the south, and Netherhampton Road to the east. The Church-fields Industrial Estate is approximately three miles west of the country house. Marion Reeves drove along The Avenue from her home and joined the A36. She should have turned left and driven towards Salisbury."

"How far was it to the industrial estate?" asked Lydia.

"A little over two miles," said Blessing. "A six-minute drive."

"If we can get a map to cover all those aspects, then go for it, Alex," said Gus.

"I'll contact the Hub, guv, and get one custom-made."

"Out of interest," said Gus, "how big is the Wilton House estate?"

"Fifteen thousand acres, guv," said Luke.

"No wonder they needed one hundred and forty staff back in 2011," said Gus. "Do you have any meetings arranged for me tomorrow morning, Luke?"

"Theo Reeves retired at sixty, guv," said Luke. "He's a keen fisherman and fair-weather golfer in his retirement. He still lives at the Oakley Road address. I've forwarded you the details. Theo can see you at ten o'clock."

"Tell him I'll be there," said Gus. "Lydia, I'd like you to accompany me."

"Any instructions on what to wear, guv?" she asked.

"Something modest will fit the bill," said Gus.

Gus hoped his and Lydia's modest understanding fell in the same ballpark. The time the team had spent chewing over the case this afternoon had been valuable. At least they had several options available to them now. The tricky part would be deciding who to interview next. Perhaps it might be best to wait until they speak to Theo Reeves.

"I don't think we can do much more this afternoon," said Gus. "It's almost half-past four. Get off home, and we can start afresh in the morning."

With that, he cleared his desk and headed for the lift. Blessing made it to the door just ahead of him.

"Are you in a rush, Blessing?" he asked.

"Everyone is leaving at the same time," she said. "I will feel better if I can drive away before the others get downstairs."

"Say hello to John and Jackie for me," said Gus. "Tell them we'll get to Worton in the next week or so to see them."

Blessing nodded and trotted off to her little car. Gus slid behind the wheel of the Focus and waited until Blessing had driven towards the car park exit.

The drive through Devizes and onwards to Urchfont was trouble-free that afternoon. Suzie was due to leave London Road as Gus turned into the gateway of the bungalow. He had fifteen minutes, tops, to himself. Gus checked the fridge and decided to wait until Suzie arrived home before cooking their meal. The ingredients he saw inside could get used in two or three different ways. Knowing his luck, the recipe he chose would be the last thing Suzie wanted.

Gus entered the lounge and laid his jacket on the back of the settee. He looked at the television. Where would he find details of the series The Reverend talked about on Sunday afternoon? Gus flicked through the channels without luck and studied the remote control. Why were there so many buttons? It might be best to leave it to Suzie. She knew which buttons to press.

Two minutes later, while still daydreaming, he heard the VW Golf pulling up outside.

"Honey, I'm home," cried Suzie as she burst through the front door.

"I take it you had a good day?" asked Gus as she walked into the lounge.

"I managed to avoid punching anyone," said Suzie.

"Grace Packenham?"

"That woman is a pest," said Suzie.

"The bacon bap I had at lunchtime was delicious," said Gus. "Vera Butler informed me that the new caterers were Ms Packenham's idea."

"Why are you home early?"

"I awarded myself and the team a thirty-minute bonus for last week's stellar performance," said Gus.

"Did you get a new case today?"

"We did," said Gus. "Marion Reeves, from March 2011. Does that ring a bell?"

"Not really," said Suzie, leaving Gus to walk to the kitchen.

Gus got up, collected his jacket, and followed her.

"A stabbing inside a car between Wilton and Salisbury

at ten in the morning," he said. "No witnesses. No suspects. Next stop, cold storage."

"A married woman?"

Gus nodded.

"The percentages say it was the husband or a lover," said Suzie.

"Have you ever met DI Billie Wightman?"

"On a couple of training courses, yes," said Suzie. "Possibly the most unpleasant female copper I've ever met. Bitter doesn't go far enough to describe the woman."

"She was SIO on that murder case seven years ago."

"Because she couldn't pin it on any of the men the victim knew, she lost interest," said Suzie.

"Harsh," said Gus, "Billie and her DS, Matt Price, interviewed a hundred people over four weeks. They spoke to neighbours, work colleagues of both the victim and her husband, and people from businesses trading on the industrial estate where the murder occurred. They found nothing to implicate anyone from their long list in the murder."

"They didn't dig deep enough to find the right people to interview," said Suzie. "That was because Wightman couldn't accept it wasn't a bloke that did it. She hates every man that's still breathing."

"What, even Matt Price? They stayed together as a team for several years. Why didn't she kick him into touch and get another man-hater as her sidekick? Anyway, where is she stationed these days?"

"Gablecross," said Suzie, "DCI Billie Wightman moved into Major Incident Planning a couple of years after her promotion. DI Matt Price went to Portishead with Avon and Somerset Police. I know a few officers over there, and they tell me that Matt Price has a permanent smile on his face these days."

"Glad to hear it. I always reckoned Matt was a good copper. Thanks for the heads up. If we need their insight, I know where to find them."

"It might be best to ignore one of them," said Suzie.

She opened the fridge door.

"What did you think when you looked in here earlier?"

"That we're spoilt for choice," said Gus. "How did you know I looked?"

"I'm a detective," Suzie replied. "The cheese isn't on top of the lamb steaks where I left it this morning."

"Have you decided what we're having yet?" Gus asked. "I'll crack on cooking whatever you fancy while you shower and change."

"Don't bother," said Suzie. "Order a pizza. It will arrive by the time I've finished getting ready. After we've devoured that, we'll go to the Lamb. An evening in the beer garden with a cold drink is in order, whether it's alcoholic or not."

Gus tried to think of an objection but failed.

The couple strolled along the lane arm-in-arm to the pub at half-past seven. They would have made it earlier, but Suzie explained how to decode all the symbols on the TV remote control.

"I hope this isn't going in one ear and out of the other," she said.

"So do I," said Gus. "When I finally retire, I need to be confident I can watch the few programmes I enjoy without outside assistance."

"Did you want to drop by the allotment before we go inside?" asked Suzie.

"We did enough yesterday afternoon to keep everything alive for forty-eight hours," said Gus. "If this case doesn't drag me away, I'll spend an hour on the allotment on

Wednesday evening. Anyway, I think I can hear Bert Penman's voice."

The retired butcher perched on his usual stool at the bar. A glance at the pint pot of cider beside him told Gus that one swallow would finish the job.

"Same again, Bert?" he asked.

"I'm not one to mix my drinks, Mr Freeman. You should know me well enough by now."

Gus ordered drinks for him and Suzie. The barman waited two seconds while Bert emptied his glass and poured him a fresh pint.

"Your cider is a beautiful golden colour this year," said Suzie, "and so clear."

"I've learned my lesson over the years, Miss Ferris," said Bert. "In the old days, I drank the rough cider they kept in barrels behind the bar. One evening, I studied the wooden floor under the spigot. The steady drip had eaten away the oak floorboard and left a shallow crater. I had nightmares over what those cloudy pints of almost orange liquid were doing to my insides. I can't say I approve of all the changes in this pub over the past sixty years, but today's cider is far healthier than the stuff they served back then."

"You still need to take care of how much of it you consume, Bert," said Gus. "The Reverend tells us they needed to help you home the other night."

"I had things on my mind, Mr Freeman," said Bert.

"Irene North, no doubt," said Suzie. "Why don't you two agree to live under the same roof?"

Bert Penman took a sip of his fresh pint.

"What, live over the brush like you and Mr Freeman? What would people think?"

"Who cares? We don't, so why should you? You both live alone in houses that are too big for you. You've got double the heating costs and council tax. It still makes sense, even if it's more for companionship than love. You would be there for Irene if she had another funny turn like she did last week and vice versa."

"Brett shared the house with you for several weeks while he sorted out his work situation," said Gus. "I know it would put his mind at rest if he knew you had someone close by, day and night."

"Brett asked while he stayed with me if I'd thought of going into a home," said Bert with a shiver. "I can't think of anything worse. I hope to keep working on my allotment, having a cider at the end of a busy day, and if I turn up my toes before I get a card from the Queen, so be it. Whenever that happens, I'll be in my own home."

"We're going to sit in the garden for a while, Bert," said Suzie. "Do you want to join us?"

"That's very sociable of you, Miss Ferris," said Bert, "but I promised Irene I'd drop by to visit on my way home. I'll sit here and finish this pint, and then I'll be on my way."

"I plan on working on my allotment on Wednesday evening, Bert," said Gus. "Perhaps we'll catch up with you both then."

"Fair enough," said Bert. "If you're still outside enjoying the sunshine until nine o'clock, I reckon the Reverend will pop in for a quiet drink with my grandson. They're insepa-rable these days, rather like you two."

"It's catching, Bert," laughed Suzie. "Enjoy the rest of your evening."

Gus and Suzie found a quiet corner in the beer garden and watched the sun disappear behind the trees on the far hillside.

"Do you think Bert will notice the gentle nudge we gave him?" asked Suzie.

"Gentle?" said Gus. "Brett might have hit on the best argument to persuade Bert and Irene to move in together. Irene hates the idea of going into a home just as much as Bert."

"If we see Brett and Clemency later, we can organise a two-pronged attack," said Suzie.

"I'm not sure the Reverend can actively encourage co-habitation," said Gus. "Although there have been so many radical shifts in policy from the General Synod in the last twenty years, who knows?"

Bert Penman had disappeared when Gus returned to the bar to get their second round of drinks. As he left the bar and returned to their table, Brett and Clemency were just walking into the beer garden from the car park.

"Did you drive tonight, Brett?" he asked. "Shall I fetch two soft drinks?"

"We cycled here," said Clemency. "Our bicycles are chained together against the wall."

"I can afford to risk drinking one pint and be safe to cycle home, Gus, can't I?" grinned Brett. "Don't worry. I'll get our drinks and join you in a minute."

"How long has Brett owned a bicycle?" asked Suzie.

"He bought a mountain bike at the weekend," said Clemency. "It puts my classic steed to shame, but fewer trips in the car will mean more chance of me shifting some of this excess weight. It will be fun cycling together through the nearby countryside in the summer. Brett has also offered to accompany me during winter when I visit my sick parish-ioners. He says it isn't safe to cycle alone at night."

"It's going well, isn't it?" said Suzie.

Clemency blushed.

"It's early days, but we enjoy one another's company."

Brett returned with a pint of bitter and a white-wine spritzer for the Reverend.

"Anything interesting happening at work, Brett," asked Gus.

"The usual fare, Gus," said Brett. "We had a budgie in for a beak and nail trim, a string of routine vaccinations, and a bulldog with diarrhoea—the everyday life of a country vet. I sometimes understand why owners are afraid to bring their beloved pets to the practice because they dread hearing bad news, but one poor dog I saw today might not be suffering as much as he is if we'd seen him sooner. What about you? Another murder mystery to solve?"

"A nasty stabbing from seven years ago near Salisbury," said Gus.

"On your old patch?" asked Brett.

"I was working on another case," said Gus. "We only started looking at it today, so I haven't formed an opinion yet."

"Both our jobs are a series of beginnings and endings," said Brett, taking another sip of his beer.

"The victim in our latest case had a vicious ending," said Gus. "From my initial look at the murder file, we might need to go back to the beginning to find her killer."

"Something struck you as strange in her past?" said Brett.

"A sixth sense," said Gus.

Chapter Four

"LAST NIGHT MADE A REFRESHING CHANGE," said Gus.

"Fine weather and pleasant company," said Suzie.

"Which would you prefer, fruit and yoghurt or cereal?"

"Scrambled egg on toast."

Gus made their breakfasts, and they ate in silence.

"Steak and cheese tonight," said Gus as he headed for the shower.

"I'll have the same," said Suzie, "but without the grilled cheese."

Gus stood under the shower, wondering whether their child would have odd eating habits.

Gus didn't consider himself to be a fussy eater. His parents had made sure of that. His mother cooked one meal for the three of them, and you ate that or went hungry. Gus was rarely hungry. Whatever she put in front of him, whether he loved it or hated it, hadn't done him any harm. In the long run, it made life simpler to go with the flow. There was a large enough part of your life when you could make your own choices.

"How much longer will you be in there, Gus Freeman?"

"Sorry, boss," said Gus.

Suzie took her turn in the shower while Gus dressed, ready for another working day. Gus wondered what sort of person Theo Reeves was. Before Theo had retired, he had been a graphic designer with a small company with offices in Wilton. While waiting for Suzie to finish in the bathroom, he ran through the list of questions he had settled on as he lay awake in bed earlier. The dawn chorus could be a blessing and a curse.

This morning, it allowed him to think about what Brett said last night. Beginnings and endings. A young Marion married an older, wealthy man, Graham Street, and gave birth to Martyn. Marion divorced and soon married someone only six years younger than Street. Was that normal to a man on the same rung of the social ladder, or could that be considered a strange beginning?

Suzie joined him in the bedroom.

"What's taking you so long to get ready this morning?" she said. "Are you daydreaming again?"

"I'm just organizing my affairs ahead of my first inter-view," said Gus. "It's important I ask the right questions and understand how the answers I get will influence how we handle this case in the future."

"Are you ready now?" said Suzie.

"Yes, Mum."

"Come here. Your tie isn't straight."

Suzie adjusted the offending necktie and stood back to check Gus's attire from head to toe.

"You'll do," she said.

"I didn't polish my shoes, but rubbing the uppers on the backs of my calves has served me well for forty years."

TED TAYLER

"Incorrigible. You'll need to buck up your ideas from next February."

"Usual time tonight?" asked Gus.

"Somewhere between five-fifteen and five-thirty," said Suzie.

Gus took her in his arms and kissed her.

"We'll be late if we don't get a move on," she said.

They left the bungalow and walked to the cars. Suzie's Golf made it to the gateway first, as usual. Gus's Focus needed a minute to remember what came after the turn of the key in the ignition. Gus gave his customary wave as Suzie turned into London Road. Then he joined the procession of vehicles behind a slow-moving vehicle he remembered reading about in the local newspaper last Friday.

The abnormally wide load destined for a Ministry of Defence camp in Gloucestershire threatened to cause him to start the day on the back foot. Gus turned on the radio for the first time in ages. If he were to get delayed, he could listen to music. Three tunes later, he switched off the radio. It was a sin to call them tunes. When did someone decide two-thirds of songs should feature rap artists?

Gus parked in the Crime Review Team's allotted rank of parking bays at the rear of the Old Police Station. The clock on the dashboard said five minutes past eight. Ah, he checked it so rarely he hadn't altered it at the end of March when the clocks moved forward an hour. Gus was five minutes late because of an abnormally wide load.

Gus travelled in the lift to the first floor to find his team hard at work. Lydia Logan Barre looked up from her computer monitor and gave Gus a thousand-watt smile. Lydia had dressed conservatively for the ten o'clock meeting with Theo Reeves. By her standards, at least.

Lydia's black shoes had four-inch heels, and the black

54

leather skirt almost reached her knees. The scarf that attempted to control her wild, red hair was the colour of the rainbow to match the short-sleeved top she had elected to wear.

"We'd better get going, guv," she said. "Alex reckons it will take us forty-five minutes to reach Theo Reeves's place in Oakley Road."

"Let me grab a notebook and pen, and then we'll be off," said Gus. "Has everyone got something useful to do?"

"Still collecting everything I can find on Graham Street, guv," said Neil.

"Searching social media for Martyn Street and Stephanie Reeves, guv," said Blessing.

"I could help with that, guv," said Luke. "Until you get back with ideas on who you wish to interview next, I'll be at a loose end."

"We should get back by twelve," said Lydia.

"Maybe not," said Gus. "It might help me get my bearings if we drive the route that Marion Reeves took the day she died."

Lydia and Gus made for the lift and descended to the ground floor.

"Did you hear about Blessing's weekend, guv?"

"No," said Gus, "Why, what happened?"

"Blessing visited her parents, and her father dropped a bombshell. He's started the ball rolling on an arranged marriage. Her father is strong on tradition, and Blessing is reluctant to go against his wishes. We can't afford to lose her, guv."

"I can't see Blessing agreeing to go along with that arrangement," said Gus.

"She's hoping her mother can persuade her father that

whoever Blessing marries will be her decision. Is there anything you can do?"

"It's not for me to come between father and daughter," said Gus. "An arranged marriage differs from a forced marriage. That's been illegal in this country for four years. Her father can't force Blessing to marry against her will. Let's hope common sense prevails, and Kelechi allows his daughter to marry for love whenever she finds the right partner."

Lydia stood by her Mini and waved her car keys.

"Come on, guv," she said. "You know it makes sense."

Gus lowered himself into the bucket seat, buckled up, and hung on for grim death.

Gus had been a passenger in this Mini before and knew what to expect.

A few minutes before her forecasted arrival, Lydia turned onto The Avenue and drove onto Oakley Road. The estate had a mix of three, four and five-bedroomed properties. Gus wondered what possessed planners to accept so much variety in extensions and conversions.

Back in the Sixties, Pete Seeger had sung of 'little boxes' that all turned out the same. Here Gus spotted properties that started with the same floor space, but one owner had extended the front room on the ground floor to align with the covered porch. The porch was left open next door, as it had been originally, and a two-storey side extension had sprouted instead. The entire street was a mish-mash, where no two properties were alike.

"Wouldn't it have been cheaper to move?" Gus asked.

"For Theo Reeves, do you mean, guv?" asked Lydia.

"Don't mind me," said Gus. "I'm a dinosaur."

Lydia didn't know what Gus was on about, but she had

spotted Theo Reeves's property where he'd lived with Marion and the two kids.

"Here we are, guv," she said. "Still only five to ten."

Gus guessed that the eighty thousand pounds Theo and Marion Reeves had set out to spend in 2011 concentrated on the interior. From the outside, it looked like a standard four-bedroomed detached property with a double garage. Until they got inside, he wouldn't know whether Theo Reeves had extended the property at the rear or added an en suite bathroom with gold taps to the master bedroom.

Lydia rang the bell. Gus saw the net curtains twitch on the next-door property.

A tall, smart-looking gentleman wearing a white shirt and black trousers answered the door. His black leather shoes didn't bear a hint of a mark. His silver hair was cut short, with a side parting. Gus wondered whether the word elegant was the correct one to use for a sixty-five-year-old retired graphic designer.

"Theo Reeves?" asked Lydia. "We're from Wiltshire Police. You were expecting us."

"Of course, come in," said Theo Reeves, standing back from the door and pointing to the first door off the hallway. "Please, go through to the lounge."

The furniture and decor looked in good order. Gus wondered how much this room had changed in the past seven years, if at all. Gus spotted two photographs on the mantlepiece above the faux fireplace. One was of Theo and Marion, which looked to have been taken soon after they married. Perhaps it was a honeymoon photograph. The other showed an attractive young woman with long dark hair taken more recently, who Gus assumed was Stephanie Reeves.

There was no sign of Martyn Street.

"Your colleague informed me that this meeting concerned Marion's murder," said Theo Reeves. He sat forward in a chair near the fireplace. Gus and Lydia sat opposite ends of a four-seater sofa against the interior wall.

"That's correct," said Lydia. "I'd like to introduce my boss, Mr Freeman. He's a consultant with Wiltshire Police. Our Crime Review Team has handled a series of unsolved cases this year with considerable success. The detectives on the original investigation didn't bring your wife's killer to justice, despite their best efforts. We intend to take a fresh look at the evidence and enable our colleagues at London Road, Devizes, to bring the guilty party before the courts."

"I see," said Theo Reeves. "I cannot see how you could do that since none of the evidence has changed. How would you find fresh evidence after so many years?"

"We intend to interview some of the same people DI Wightman and DS Price spoke to back in 2011," said Gus. "However, as that didn't produce a positive result, it's clear they didn't identify the right people to speak to and possibly asked the wrong questions of those they did."

Theo Reeves didn't look convinced. Gus knew how he felt. Gus was feeling his way, trying to gauge the man who sat opposite him. It could take time to learn whether he had something to hide.

"How did you and Marion meet?" asked Gus.

"The same way most couples met thirty years ago, Mr Freeman," replied Theo. "There was no online dating in our day. Instead, I was in Salisbury for a concert at the City Hall, and we visited a nearby pub for a last drink before going home."

"You went to the concert with someone?" asked Lydia.

"A group of friends and colleagues who enjoyed comedy, drama and music," said Theo. "I can't remember exactly how many of us were there that night, but it was between six and sixteen. We didn't always sit together, but it became a habit for several years to discuss what we'd seen over a pint in the Haunch of Venison."

"The oldest pub in Salisbury," said Gus.

"You know it?" asked Theo.

"I was a copper on the beat before I became a detective," said Gus. "I spent almost forty years in the city."

"Then you know they served a good pint in the old days," said Theo. "I haven't been in there in years. No doubt it's gentrified and attracts a different crowd. They're far more reliant on food nowadays, aren't they?"

"Everywhere has changed, Mr Reeves," said Gus. "Was Marion Street with one of your group that night?"

"Not at all," said Theo. "The bar was always crowded on a Saturday night. I fought to the bar to buy a drink and spotted Marion standing alone at the far end. It was hard to miss her. Marion was by far the prettiest girl in the place that night. She was out of my league, so I was fully prepared to fight my way back through the crowds with my drink to rejoin my friends. While I waited for the barmaid to pull my pint, I looked up and realised Marion was staring at me."

"Had you ever seen Marion before?" asked Lydia.

"I may have done," said Theo. "Salisbury had forty thousand residents in those days. When you're single, as I was, you often bump into the same groups of people doing the rounds of the pubs, restaurants, and shops in the centre, day or night. They were faces you recognised without ever knowing who they were. You know what I mean, I'm sure."

"What happened next?" asked Gus.

"When I got my pint, I told the people I came in with that I had seen someone on the other side of the room I wanted to see. They expected me back any minute. I took my courage in both hands and made my way over. I discovered Marion's name. She told me she was lonely and hurting after walking out on her husband. I told her I was a good listener. That was the start of it. We married ten months later."

"You weren't out of her league after all," said Gus.

"I suppose not," said Theo.

"Was Marion still married to Graham Street when you met?" asked Gus.

"They had separated," said Theo. "Street didn't want to prolong the agony any more than Marion did. So, the divorce went through quickly enough. When you are as wealthy as that, it's easier to get things moving. Money talked back in 1990. It talks even louder today."

"Why did Marion walk out on her husband?" asked Lydia.

"Marion never spoke about the marriage," said Theo. "From that first Saturday night, she insisted we didn't dwell on the past. Marion wanted to concentrate on her future; however it turned out. I wasn't keen to learn the details of their married life, so I was happy to follow in with her wishes."

"When did you learn Marion and Graham Street had a child?" asked Gus.

"Marion brought Martyn in a pushchair on our first proper date the following weekend. We met near the Cathedral and just walked and talked in the sunshine."

"Did you both work in Salisbury?" asked Gus.

"Marion didn't need to work while she was with Street. He had more than enough money for both of them. Marion returned to work as soon as we married, and apart from taking maternity leave when Stephanie was born, she carried on in full-time employment until the day she died."

"Did you know Graham Street before you met Marion?" asked Gus.

"I'd seen him around," said Theo. "We didn't move in the same circles. He was several years older than me. That alone puts distance between people, but several of the crowd Street went around with had both class and money. The rest, including Street, were tolerated because they had money. People such as that live in a different world, Mr Freeman. That's one thing that hasn't changed out of all recognition over the years."

"There was quite an age gap between you and Marion," said Lydia, "did that concern you?"

"Why should it?" asked Theo.

"Well," said Lydia, "on that Saturday evening you first met, what caused Marion to stare? You were in your late thirties, handsome, and well-dressed, based on the man I saw this morning. Perhaps, she hoped you were her next meal ticket?"

"I walked into the bar with other people, but I was buying my own drink," said Theo. "A woman who was only interested in the size of my bank balance would have discounted me straightaway. Marion might have preferred an older man, but she knew I wasn't as well off as Graham Street. Within a few weeks, we knew we wanted to be together. I'd been in love before, but not like that. I knew Marion was the one for me."

"Did you have any reservations about taking on the responsibility for both mother and son?" asked Gus.

"Not at first," said Theo. "Marion met with Street and their solicitors frequently as the divorce went through. Graham threatened to stop proceedings altogether when he learned we were keen to set a date for our wedding. Street was a swine. He persuaded Marion to accept a derisory cash settlement for not delaying things further. After the divorce, Street washed his hands of Martyn altogether."

"Graham Street wasn't interested in his only son?" asked Gus.

"He had several children with different women, Mr Freeman. I thought you would know that."

"We're digging into his background as part of this fresh investigation, Mr Reeves," said Gus. "Twenty years had passed since the divorce, and our colleagues didn't consider Graham Street had any part in your wife's death. Graham Street's alibi checked out, and they looked elsewhere for her killer."

"That's as maybe," said Theo Reeves, "but there was another reason he wanted to rid himself of Martyn. There was nothing wrong with the boy physically, but he struggled at school. He was a slow learner. I soon became an expert in what that term meant, Mr Freeman. His IQ score classed Martyn as having a borderline intellectual disability. Thirty years ago, students like Martyn did not qualify for special services, special education, or even an individual learning plan. Marion and I did our best but couldn't bridge the gap between Martyn's academic achievements and his peers. So when Stephanie started school, my focus was on my real first child. It might have seemed cruel, but that was what happened."

"How did Martyn's condition affect your relationship with Marion?" asked Lydia.

"It brought us closer together, if anything," said Theo. "Marion needed my help with Martyn. She knew Street would never have lent a hand. The trick was to convince Martyn that whatever level he achieved in a subject was an enormous success. There were never recriminations because he fell way short of what Stephanie achieved on the same task a few years later."

"Did Martyn and Stephanie get on well?" asked Lydia.

"Stephanie knew something was amiss with her older brother when she was a toddler. But, because of how we treated Martyn, Stephanie protected him when we weren't around."

"When other children picked on him," said Lydia, "and made fun of him."

"Not while Stephanie was about; they didn't," said Theo. "Stephanie came home with a few bruises where she had stepped in to tackle an older boy or girl who bullied her brother."

"Did that closeness and protective nature remain throughout their childhood and teenage years?" asked Gus.

"As far as I could tell, yes," said Theo. "Of course, things altered somewhat when Martyn left school at sixteen. We were fortunate to find him a job at Wilton House. Martyn loved working in the open air, carrying out all manner of maintenance across the estate. His boss gave Martyn something different to do every day. Martyn found a place where he could be happy."

"Stephanie attended the grammar school," said Gus. "I imagine Martyn's secondary education took place elsewhere?"

Theo Reeves nodded.

"Did you go to the school for parent's evening events?" asked Gus.

"Once or twice," said Theo. "More often than not, Marion went alone. We tried our best, but there was never any real improvement."

"Where is Stephanie now?" asked Gus, nodding towards the photograph on the mantlepiece.

"The school thought it fairer for Stephanie to defer her A-levels until later in the year. She was in no state to sit them a matter of weeks after her mother's murder. Stephanie passed her three exams with good grades, but the fight went out of her during the long wait before she could reapply for a university place. Before I knew it, the boot was on the other foot, and Martyn was looking out for his sister. He'd make sure she got home from the pub despite her falling-down drunk. The anniversary of Marion's death was a particularly challenging time."

"When did Martyn move out?" asked Gus.

"You must remember that at the time of the murder, Martyn was already twenty-three, Mr Freeman," said Theo Reeves. "Marion and I both hoped Stephanie would go on to university in the autumn. She would have been away from home for large parts of the next three years. Who knows where she would have gone after that? Martyn and Stephanie had never given us any reason to think there was anything between them, you know? Maybe it was all in my head. I was alone, grieving for Marion, and Stephanie suffered a meltdown. So when Martyn almost carried his drunk sister through the door one Sunday morning, I suspected he was taking an unhealthy interest."

"Had Martyn gone out with other girls?" asked Lydia.

"Not as far as I was aware," said Theo. "The next day, I suggested he leave home and find a place to live."

"How did he react to that?" asked Lydia.

"Not well," said Theo. "He didn't understand. I spoke to his manager at Wilton House, and he promised to help find him somewhere closer to his work. Martyn rents a room that overlooks the woods on the edge of the estate. He has a five-minute walk to work now instead of thirty."

"And Stephanie?" asked Gus.

"She drifted for about a year, then met someone in Salisbury. They live in Downton. Stephanie works at a primary school as a teaching assistant. It wasn't the career we had imagined for our daughter, but she's happy, and the chap she lives with seems decent. I don't think Stephanie's spoken to Martyn since the day he left home."

"Do you suspect something happened?" asked Lydia.

"I pray it was all in my head," said Theo. "Nothing that happened seven years ago ever made any sense. The nightmare has never ended."

"What happened here after the murder?" asked Gus.

"I'm not sure I understand the question," said Theo. "The police spent ages questioning everyone. I had a funeral to organise. Stephanie and Martyn were a mess."

"What about MP Builders?" asked Gus. "Did they stay?"

"The builders promised they would be out of our hair by September," said Theo, "but everything was up in the air after March the eighteenth. It was the following April before we saw the back of them. I was trying to hold on to my job because I couldn't afford to take early retirement. Then, Stephanie's problems blew up, and I was trying to resolve those plus resettle Martyn. Stuart Milligan and Derek Preston pottered about finishing bits and pieces on my house in between other jobs they had taken on. I'd see them one week for two hours and then nothing for a fortnight."

"Did they know about the money?" asked Gus.

"You mean the missing six thousand pounds? They said they hadn't mentioned needing a part payment to Marion. I had told them at the outset that if they wanted something to assist their cash flow, to give me a shout, and I'd get the money for them. Marion had precious little left of the settlement Graham Street gave her to spend large amounts like that."

"Marion withdrew the cash though, Mr Reeves," said Gus. "So, you still claim to have no idea who or what the money was for?"

"None whatsoever, Mr Freeman," said Theo. "In twenty years, we had had no secrets from one another. Or at least I didn't think we did. I could never understand why Marion hadn't come to me if there was a problem."

"What happened to Marion's mobile phone?" asked Gus. "The police checked her diaries for any meetings arranged for that Monday morning and found nothing. You saw her handbag after the police recovered it from the Lexus. You told the officers nothing was missing. Marion's purse, keys, and mobile phone were still inside."

"That's correct," said Theo. "The police took the handbag into evidence. I can't recall it ever getting returned to me. Why?"

"I don't remember seeing any listing of the call history of that phone in the files," said Gus.

"You think Marion did arrange to meet someone?" asked Theo.

"No idea," said Gus. "Would you know the name of every person your wife had listed on her mobile phone?"

"I would hope I could name ninety percent of the people on that list," said Theo. "There could have been a casual acquaintance I wasn't aware of or someone Marion knew before we met. I would hope that was true for most husbands. We had no secrets."

"Was your wife's phone number the same one she'd had for a long time?" asked Lydia.

"It *was* an old number," said Theo. "Marion transferred it to her new phone every time she got a new one."

"Several phones, but the same number throughout your relationship?"

"I'm certain, yes," said Theo.

"Seven years ago, the police questioned Marion's colleagues at the printing firm," said Gus. "They also spoke with people you worked with at your offices."

"They did," said Theo, "that was when I realised they were clutching at straws."

"Did you and Marion socialise with your work colleagues?" asked Gus.

"Once or twice," said Theo. "We didn't have a Christmas meal every year like some firms. It was a handful of occasions during the marriage at most."

"Is it possible Marion met someone at one of those infrequent get-togethers and formed a long-lasting relationship?"

"Absolutely not, Mr Freeman," said Theo. "I trusted my wife and knew the people I worked with. None of them had an affair with my wife, leading to her death. Your colleagues went down this path seven years ago. They found nothing then, and you won't find anything now."

"You've been alone for seven years, Mr Reeves," said Lydia. "Have you ever entertained the idea of a new relationship?"

"Certainly not," said Theo. "As you pointed out earlier, I was single until I was thirty-seven. I had twenty wonderful years with Marion. Now, I'm sixty-five and retired and not looking for someone to share my twilight years. My memories of Marion will sustain me. Is that it now? I don't think there's anything more I can add."

"We'd like to run through the events leading up to the

murder, if we may, Mr Reeves," said Gus. "My colleague and I intend to visit the murder scene after we leave here. It helps me establish the distances involved, the relationship and the possible relevance of buildings close to the side street where Marion parked her car. Her killer left that car covered in blood, yet nobody came forward to say they had seen someone."

"You don't need to remind me of what happened to my wife, Mr Freeman," said Theo Reeves. "The police spared me the trauma of seeing Marion's injuries. When I identified her body in the morgue, all I saw was her face. That's not an experience I would wish on my worst enemy."

"I apologise if you believe I was unnecessarily graphic in my description of events at the industrial estate, Mr Reeves," said Gus. "I intend to uncover the truth of what happened that morning. If I need to ruffle a few feathers, then so be it. Seven years have passed, and people's memories of the exact sequence of events have changed. There can be several reasons for that. They lied in the first instance, omitted certain steps that might implicate them, or, at the very least, put them in a poor light. Other witnesses unintentionally get the sequence of events out of order even though they recall every single one."

Gus sat back in his seat as Theo Reeves absorbed the full impact of his comments.

Chapter Five

"HOW ON EARTH do you tell fact from fiction?" asked Theo Reeves.

"We keep asking probing questions to expose the reasons behind a witness not telling us the truth, the whole truth, and nothing but the truth," said Lydia. "The relationships within a family unit can alter significantly over time. Someone could come forward with fresh evidence today because they no longer have an allegiance to protect another family member."

"Are you talking about my family unit?" asked Theo. Lydia sensed his anger was bubbling just below the surface. A younger man might have lost control, but Theo Reeves remained calm apart from a tension in his body that wasn't there earlier.

"My colleague was commenting in general terms on how we discover which of our witnesses is lying," said Gus. "But I think you would agree; it's fair to say relationships *have* changed between you and Martyn Street in the past seven years. They aren't the same between you and

Stephanie either. She was a teenage student living under your roof when Marion died. Now she's an independent adult with a job, living with another man. No matter how often you see Stephanie and how amicable those meetings are, the situation has changed forever. You alluded to the possibility that Martyn and Stephanie's relationship changed while they still lived in this house. We don't know how that changed, but now they live separate lives. If we ask them questions about where they were and what they were doing on March the eighteenth, they might give different answers to the ones they gave the police seven years ago. Do you understand how that could happen in cases that we handle?"

"Yes, I suppose there must be instances where a husband or brother lies to protect a loved one who had become a suspect. But, surely, you must see that didn't apply in this case?"

"Everything we know of this case hinges on evidence gathered by the detective team who worked on it in 2011," said Lydia. "You are the first person we've spoken to this time around. Mr Freeman checks each element of that evidence to ensure it's still valid."

"We've clarified why we need to go over the events leading up to the eighteenth of March," said Gus. "So, let's get back to the Friday before the murder. Marion withdrew six thousand pounds in cash from her bank. Did she tell you what she'd done?"

"No," said Theo. "I don't know whether she kept the cash in her handbag all weekend or hid it somewhere in the house. I never saw it."

"Did you and Marion have a joint bank account?" asked Lydia.

"We did," said Theo. "Once we married, I closed my

current and savings accounts and opened new accounts in our married names. The account Marion retained was where she held the money her ex-husband gave her. That was Marion and Martyn's money. I'd never considered it available for me to spend. Marion hoped one day Martyn could learn to drive, and she could buy his first car."

"You mentioned the balance wasn't significant," said Gus. "Did Marion ever tell you how much was there after the divorce settlement?"

"That was another hangover from the marriage to Street that wasn't a subject for discussion," said Theo.

"What happened when solicitors dealt with probate after Marion's death?" asked Gus. "How much money remained in the account, and how did the executors disburse it?"

"The six thousand pounds Marion withdrew practically cleared it out," said Theo. "Only a few hundred pounds got transferred into our joint account later that summer. Martyn was still living here, and Stephanie was revising for her exams. I could tell they were both struggling to come to terms with everything, and I used the money to pay for a weekend away at Centreparcs at Longleat. Unfortunately, I picked a miserable, wet weekend, and Martyn had a panic attack in the escape room attraction. All three of us were on the verge of a breakdown. The whole thing was a disaster. Stephanie's drinking spiralled out of control not long after that weekend."

"If we can switch back to the weekend before the murder," said Gus. "What did you do as a family? Was there anything different in your routine? Did Marion go anywhere alone?"

"The builders were here working on Saturday morning," said Theo. "Martyn went into town before lunch and

TED TAYLER

didn't return until five or six in the evening. Then he watched TV in his room until late. Stephanie didn't get out of bed until noon, which was typical behaviour for our teenage daughter. I remember her wanting to know if the builders had left yet. She didn't like going into the bathroom for a shower while they were inside the house. The lock was temperamental. A new bathroom was on the list of jobs they still had to tackle. They had completed our en-suite in the master bedroom. I told Stephanie they were tidying up outside and that she could shower in peace. Marion and I were here throughout the morning. We didn't venture out to the shops until after lunch. Stephanie cycled to a friend's house for the afternoon. After Martyn arrived home, we had a meal together, and then Marion and I watched television here in the lounge. Stephanie sat with us but was on her phone most of the time. Any conversation was at a premium."

"How did Martyn get into town?" asked Lydia.

"Martyn walked everywhere," said Theo. "Time wasn't important to Martyn. It took him twenty minutes to walk into town. He bought fish and chips at the same place every Saturday, then spent a couple of hours in the Greyhound Inn. After an hour in the park, two if he nodded off, he'd walk back home for his evening meal. Most Saturday nights after he reached eighteen, Martyn walked into town to drink with people he knew from work. That Saturday, he stayed home."

"What about Sunday," asked Gus. "Did anything out of the ordinary happen?"

"All of us spent a quiet morning at home before eating Sunday lunch together," said Theo. "Martyn went into town again but was home earlier. Stephanie studied in her room during the afternoon. Marion drove over to Wilton

House Garden Centre and returned around four o'clock. I watched football on TV."

"Was Marion buying things for the garden?" asked Lydia. "Your front garden looks full of mature plants and shrubs."

"She bought bedding plants," said Theo, "and Marion visited the café for coffee and cake."

"Marion told you that when she got home?" asked Lydia.

"She must have," said Theo. "It's hard to remember minor details after so long."

"Marion didn't mention having met anyone while she was out," said Gus. "Perhaps that was when the cash left her handbag."

"Are you suggesting someone was blackmailing Marion?" asked Theo. "That's outrageous. What possible reason could there be for that line of enquiry?"

"The builders weren't expecting the money," said Gus. "Marion didn't withdraw that much cash for no reason, and it wasn't among her possessions after the discovery of her body the following morning. So either she handed it to someone on Sunday afternoon, or the killer took it. We need to find out whether Marion shared coffee and cake with another person on Sunday afternoon."

"Was there nothing unusual that happened after four o'clock on Sunday?" asked Lydia.

"Nothing at all," said Theo, disturbed by the blackmail suggestion. "We were at home throughout the evening. There were no visitors or phone calls. Everyone was in bed by eleven."

"So, we now come to the day of the murder itself," said Gus. He continued to watch Theo Reeves, looking for signs of stress. Was he hiding something, or was he finally coming to terms with the actual reason behind his wife's death? The vital evidence to solve this case could emerge in the next few minutes.

"I left for work at my usual time of eight-fifteen," said Theo, "I drove the short distance along The Avenue into the centre and parked just off West Street. I took a two-minute walk to the company offices, stopping at a newsagent for a paper and a lunchtime snack en route. My morning was a succession of meetings. A dozen colleagues confirmed I didn't leave the premises until the police called me at around twelve-fifteen."

"Did you make or receive any phone calls after leaving home and before the police called you?" asked Lydia.

"I received two business calls from clients," said Theo. "I can't recall making any outgoing calls on my work phone. I didn't use my mobile that morning."

"You saw Marion before you left the house?" asked Gus.

"Of course," said Theo, "we ate breakfast together. As I told the police seven years ago, Marion was fine. We hadn't argued over the weekend and didn't have words that morning. It was as normal a start to the day as one could wish. As I left the house, the builders were reversing their van into the corner of the driveway. That was where they parked each day to avoid hampering anyone visiting the house or one of us getting in or out."

"You expected Marion to chat to the builders," said Lydia. "To check everything was all set to continue their work while the house was empty during the day."

"That's right," said Theo. "Marion would check what was on their schedule for the day and then make her way into Salisbury for work. Then, she would see Stephanie off to school, and maybe fifteen minutes later, she made a move."

"Stephanie cycled to school, didn't she?" asked Lydia.

"She did," said Theo. "Marion would check Stephanie donned her helmet before leaving. You can imagine how popular one of those would be for an attractive eighteen-year-old girl. We just wanted her to stay safe. Marion told me Stephanie generally left about ten minutes after me, at twenty-five past eight."

"Did Martyn walk to work at Wilton House every day, Mr Reeves?" asked Gus. "In all winds and weather? Did he never ask for a lift from you or Marion? Or a fellow worker on the estate, perhaps?"

"I told you already. Martyn walked everywhere. He enjoyed walking. Martyn would set off at eight from here on a journey that took thirty minutes. Martyn worked outside all year round, so he had clothes to suit every occasion. Martyn never complained. I don't think asking for a lift ever crossed his mind."

"That Monday morning was different to others while the builders were on-site, though, wasn't it?" said Lydia. "Marion usually left at eight forty-five, based on your timings. The builders told the police it was almost five past nine before Marion drove away that day."

"I can't comment on that," said Theo. "I was at work attending my first meeting."

"The builders maintained it wasn't them that delayed your wife," said Lydia.

"Perhaps someone rang Marion," said Gus. "Either on the landline or her mobile. It would explain why she got delayed and didn't go directly to work as normal."

"We don't need to remind you how long it takes to cover the distance between here and the Quidhampton area on the A36," said Lydia. "A matter of minutes, regardless of the time of day."

"Yet, it was nine-thirty," said Gus. "Twenty-five minutes after Marion left home, witnesses reported seeing her white Lexus RX350 on the main road into Salisbury. Where did she go in the meantime? Where was there to go? You've driven that route a thousand times, Mr Reeves."

"I don't have a clue," said Theo.

"Where were you at eleven forty-five, Mr Reeves?" asked Lydia.

"We'd just ended a meeting, and I was sitting in my office eating an early lunch. A colleague brought me a coffee at about noon."

"Marion died at around ten o'clock," said Gus, "thirty minutes after those witnesses saw her car on the A36. Why do you think your wife drove to Churchfields, Mr Reeves? Was it to a firm she often visited, somewhere connected to her printing firm?"

"I'm sure Marion would have mentioned it if she had," said Theo. "I'd never known her to go to the Churchfields Industrial Estate. There are lots of small firms operating out of there, even today. Of course, not all the same businesses were open back then, but it's been a busy site since it opened."

"Exactly," said Gus. "A busy little site, especially at ten in the morning. We know where Marion was at nine-thirty. It took her five minutes to reach the industrial estate from that point on the main road. How on earth did Marion drive onto the industrial estate without someone seeing her? She parked her car on a side street at around nine thirty-five. Was her killer waiting for her? Did the attack start as soon as they got into the car, or was there an argument first? If blackmail was behind the meeting and Marion had the money, why did she need to die? Why did nobody see or hear anything? At some point after ten, the killer got out of the Lexus, unseen, despite being covered in Marion's blood and carrying a knife. Where did they go? How did they arrive on that side street in the first place? On foot or by car? Why did it take another hour and three-quarters before an employee from a nearby business spotted Marion slumped over the steering wheel of her car?"

"Your colleagues asked these same questions seven years ago, Mr Freeman," said Theo Reeves. "I can't explain, I'm afraid."

"Our colleagues missed something during their investigation," said Gus. "We need to uncover what lay behind that clandestine meeting."

"What did you make of the incident with the pick-up driver?" asked Lydia.

"I'm sorry, you've lost me," said Theo.

"The police heard from eyewitnesses who saw Marion talking to the driver of a pick-up truck on Friday after she withdrew the cash from her bank. Didn't the police ask if you could identify that man?"

"I have a vague recollection, but it wasn't something Marion was likely to do, so I never gave it much credence. I expect he was just asking for directions."

"What did you make of it when the police interviewed Simon Turner?" asked Lydia. "That must have surprised you when they found his fingerprints inside the Lexus."

"Not at all," said Theo. "I remember that stormy night, and Marion told me what had happened as soon as she reached home. Simon lives just up the road. It was the neighbourly thing to do. The poor chap didn't deserve the third degree for accepting a lift."

"That's all the questions we have, Mr Reeves," said Gus. "We may return in the future based on the answers we receive from the other names on our list."

"You plan to speak to Stephanie, of course," said Theo. "What about Martyn? Perhaps it would be best if you spoke to his manager, Arthur Jackson. He's nearing retirement, which is a shame. Martyn will miss him. He'll feel less threatened with Arthur in the room."

"You believe Martyn needs a responsible adult in attendance?" asked Lydia.

"Look, I'm not his favourite person after showing him the door," said Theo Reeves. "Arthur Jackson knows Martyn as well as anyone does. He'll help you get Martyn to answer any questions you have."

"Many thanks for your time, Mr Reeves," said Gus. "We'll let you get on with your day while we take a trip towards town and then onto the industrial estate."

Lydia and Gus walked to the front door. Theo Reeves followed them and stood by the door until they were inside Lydia's Mini and had pulled away from the kerb.

"What did you make of that then, Lydia?" asked Gus.

"I don't think Theo was hiding anything, guv," said Lydia. "I thought you gave him a hard time, but his story didn't waver from what he told DI Wightman."

"There was one thing Theo didn't comment on that suggests we're on the right track."

"Really, guv," said Lydia. "What did I miss?"

"I said our colleagues missed something during their initial investigation," said Gus, "and we needed to uncover what lay behind Marion's clandestine meeting on Monday morning."

"Do you think there was an earlier meeting on Sunday afternoon?"

"At the café? I'll reserve judgement on that. I reckon Marion met a friend or colleague who happened to be visiting the garden centre for the same reason."

"Where will this person Marion arranged to meet have come from, guv?" asked Lydia. "An old friend or colleague, a person Theo knew too. Could it be someone from Stephanie's school, a teacher or another parent?"

"I'm conscious we know little about Marion's life before 1990 when Theo bumped into her in the Haunch of Venison. Doesn't it seem odd that Marion never talked about her life with Graham Street?"

"I can understand why Marion might not want to tell Theo the gory details of their marriage," said Lydia. "Put yourself in Theo's shoes. Isn't it better not to know what a girlfriend got up to before you met? You can kid yourself that everything's new for both of you if the past is a closed book."

"Theo suspected Marion had a chequered past," said Gus. "So, he went along with the idea of only looking to the future to avoid having his nose rubbed in it."

"There will be dozens of couples out there who have done the same thing, guv," said Lydia.

"We're almost at the Churchfields Industrial Estate already," said Gus. "Find a place to park as soon as we get inside. We'll walk and talk for a while. What did you see between Oakley Road and here? Did you spot a place where Marion might have stopped?"

"Sorry, guv," said Lydia. "I was listening to you."

"I can't fault you for that, Lydia," said Gus. "Despite the rumours, we men can multi-task when required."

He referred to his notebook and translated his unique shorthand notes.

"We left Oakley Road and proceeded along The Avenue, slightly above the speed limit," he said. "On either side of the road were small housing estates, a training centre, and various business premises where Marion might have stopped. Once we turned onto the A36, we soon reached the Wilton House Garden Centre on our right. I'm surprised you didn't drop in for coffee since we didn't get offered one by Theo Reeves."

"I saw the sign, guv," said Lydia, "but once you've seen one Garden Centre, you've seen them all."

"You should have listened to Blessing when she told us the dimensions of the Wilton House estate," said Gus. "Moving on, there were several shops on our left on the A36 before a signposted junction to Netherhampton Road, with access to Quidhampton."

"Netherhampton Road was the eastern boundary of the estate, guv," said Lydia.

"You were listening, well remembered, Lydia," said Gus. "We also passed the Cricket Field Hotel on our right before you turned off the A36 down Cherry Orchard Lane and negotiated the mini-roundabout that brought us onto Brunel Road, where we are now parked. Any of those places could have been where Marion picked up a passenger or spoke to someone on her mobile phone, confirming where and when they were to meet. So let's take a walk."

Chapter Six

"WE'VE BEEN PARKED on Brunel Road for three minutes, guv," said Lydia. "I have seen no security staff patrolling the estate. Nobody has approached us to ask what we're doing here."

"That's unlikely to happen, Lydia," said Gus. "I guarantee any security this site has is confined to hours of darkness. Look at the number of premises surrounding us and the variety on offer. Major car dealerships operate alongside artisan craft outlets. Parking bays dotted here and there, larger lay-bys for trucks. There's even a snack van with a permanent pitch a hundred yards ahead. They don't need security during the day with hundreds of employees milling about the place, plus the constant stream of traffic."

"Maybe that's why Marion's car escaped notice, guv," said Lydia. "Her Lexus was just one vehicle among hundreds. So why would anyone stop to look inside?"

"Did you notice the large board near the entrance showing the site layout and a list of names of the businesses?" asked Gus.

"You can't miss it, guv," said Lydia. "I expect you'll say I was travelling too fast to read what it said."

"I wouldn't expect you to catch every name, Lydia," said Gus. "I was trying to see a light engineering firm next door to a fitness centre. I might have missed it, of course."

"Theo Reeves told us this site was still a hive of activity, but the businesses might have altered over the years. Brunel Road is the major thoroughfare; we need to move to the edges of the estate to find the spot where Marion Reeves parked her car, Was the name of the street given in the murder file?"

"It didn't register, Lydia," said Gus. "My mistake. I should have made a note. Call Luke Sherman and get him to dig it out, please. While you're on the phone, ask him to follow up on Marion's mobile phone. Is that still in evidence? Why didn't we see a call history from that phone? I can't imagine Billie Wightman and Matt Price didn't get details of every call to and from that mobile from Marion's service provider."

Lydia stepped away from Gus to call the office. Gus tried to determine whether it was quicker to return to the car and start again or head towards the Salisbury side of the estate and hope for the best. He elected to wait.

"Stephenson Road, guv," called Lydia. "It's on the edge of the estate on the Salisbury side."

Five minutes later, they stood on Stephenson Road, and Gus pointed to the name of a small engineering firm on a board near the pavement.

"No job too small," said Gus. "I reckon this must be the place. Marion parked between this firm and the next unit along, which was the gym back then."

"Today, it's a funeral home, guv," said Lydia.

"It's quieter this side," said Gus. "I wonder whether that's why they chose it?"

"Hardly the dead centre of the estate, guv."

"Look around us, Lydia; what do you see?"

Lydia checked her watch. It was early afternoon already. Time flew by when you were working on a case with Gus Freeman. Lydia wished Gus hadn't mentioned the snack van. A drink and a bite to eat would be most welcome right now.

"It's almost one o'clock," said Lydia. "I can hear the bustle of activity inside many of the premises close by. But there's not much traffic on this side street. Twenty vehicles are parked on either side of the road, which I can see from this spot. Foot traffic is non-existent. Apart from us two, of course."

"A second vehicle parked next to Marion's car wouldn't cause major concerns, would it? If the traffic volume was similar seven years ago on this side street."

"What about when you consider what was happening inside Marion's car, guv?" asked Lydia.

"As you pointed out, standing in the open air, we can hear activity from inside the buildings on either side of the road. The sound of machinery, forklift trucks, and the odd yell of a name or laughter. Would any of those people hear an argument from inside the car? Some of them will wear ear defenders for protection. Would they even hear screams?"

"I can hear music, guv," said Lydia. "That car repair and MOT garage across the road has a tannoy system tuned to Heart Radio. Perhaps we've got it wrong. This side street was an ideal spot to commit murder."

"In plain sight, with enough background noise to mask the sounds of the attack," said Gus.

"Luke said he needed to contact DCI Wightman about that mobile phone, guv," said Lydia. "Although it was in Marion's handbag that morning, it doesn't appear to get mentioned again in the murder file. That's odd, isn't it?"

"I'll talk to DI Matt Price at Portishead when we get back to the office. He's too good a copper to miss something significant in an investigation. It's more than odd, Lydia. This case is taking strange turns, so we need to keep our wits about us. I wonder whether anyone is working at the funeral home. It's tranquil. Perhaps they just store corpses here, then collect them on the way to the church or crematorium."

"Don't joke, guv," said Lydia. "That's creepy. No, they have their offices here too."

"Right, let's find out when they moved in. In seven years, there might have been more than one change of use."

Gus and Lydia followed the footpath to the side of the building and found a glass-partitioned door giving full details of the company. Lydia rang the bell. A tall, thin, bespectacled man in a dark suit opened the door. Gus sensed he would launch into his usual sombre greeting for grieving relatives and got in quick with his own spiel.

"Good afternoon," said Gus. "We're from Wiltshire Police. Can you provide us with information, please? You are?"

"Maurice Duffield, funeral director."

"When did your firm take over these premises?" asked Lydia.

"We've been here for five years. It was a gym before we took over. We needed to make alterations and repairs, of course. The place had suffered during the time it was unoccupied."

"Had the gym been trading for long?" asked Gus.

"Oh yes," said Maurice Duffield. "This industrial estate has existed for over fifty years and has had many corporate occupiers: BT, Wessex Water, and the Audi dealership. The gym opened in the late eighties and was a thriving concern for over a decade, but the original owner retired. After that, several inexperienced people tried to revive the place without success. They kept a hardcore clientele that enjoyed lifting weights, but the modern trend was a more varied form of exercise. The owners didn't have the capital to invest, so their equipment became worn out. The central heating and air-conditioning fell into disrepair. This building was in a sorry state when we moved here."

"How long did it remain unoccupied?" asked Gus.

"Two years," said Maurice Duffield, "and it was closed more than it was open during the previous eighteen months."

"Thanks for the information, Mr Duffield," said Gus. "We'll let you get on with your day."

"Would you like one of our brochures as you're here?"

"Not today, thank you," said Gus, making a sharp exit.

"Did that information on the gym help, guv?" asked Lydia when they reached the pavement again.

"It might explain why nobody noticed Marion's car from this stretch of road. The place was on its last legs, and there were probably no sweaty clients coming and going."

Gus set off towards the end of Stephenson Road, where it joined Churchfields Road. He was heading for the car. Lydia eased the Mini into the steady stream of afternoon traffic on the A36 twenty minutes later.

"Home, Lydia," said Gus.

"I'm still enjoying that greasy burger, guv," said Lydia.

"Mmm, that will repeat on me all afternoon. It wasn't

the best coffee I've ever tasted, either. Jeff's Diner will wait a long time before they get return business from me."

"I was hungry," said Lydia. "I couldn't wait until we got back to the office, even for the Gaggia."

"We must get everything we gathered into the Freeman Files," said Gus. "Meanwhile, Luke needs to arrange meetings with Graham Street and Stephanie Reeves. After what we learned today, I reckon they will be the best people to speak to."

"Setting up a meeting with Arthur Jackson and Martyn Street might be awkward, guv. Do you think we'd get permission to interview them at their place of work?"

"You think the titled folk who employ them might take issue with the local plods invading their space? Tough. We'll talk to Martyn when it's convenient, not to him or his employer. We can take Martyn Street to the custody suite in town if necessary."

Lydia noticed Gus was resting his eyes on the way back to the office. She wouldn't dare accuse him of nodding off, but while she was alone with her thoughts, she tried to make a list of genuine suspects for Marion Reeve's killer. Then, as she drew up alongside Blessing Umeh's car in the Old Police Station car park forty minutes after leaving Brunel Road, she had to admit defeat.

Gus opened his eyes as Lydia switched off the engine.

"Is it safe to look now?" asked Gus.

"Cheeky," said Lydia. "I was very careful driving back, honest."

"Upstairs then," said Gus. "Let's hear what Luke uncovered."

They travelled up in the lift, and the first words they heard were from Neil Davis.

"Heaven knows where that leaves us," he said.

"Problem, Neil?" asked Gus.

"Graham Street, guv," said Neil, "He suffered a heart attack during the night. Unfortunately, the hospital isn't sure he will make it."

"Where did they take him?" asked Gus.

"The main Salisbury hospital, out at Odstock, guv," said Neil.

"How old is he?" asked Lydia.

"Early seventies," said Neil. "Street had no underlying health problems before last night. He didn't even know the name of his GP. A lady friend called the ambulance at around one o'clock."

"Was he doing something strenuous?" asked Alex.

"The poor man," said Blessing.

"If Street doesn't survive, it will make solving the Marion Reeves' case that much harder, won't it, guv?" said Luke.

"Just when I thought it was as tough as it could get," said Gus. "Get hold of Stephanie Reeves, Luke. Can you arrange for me to speak to her tomorrow, please?"

"She works as a teaching assistant at a local primary in Downton, Luke," said Lydia. "We learned that from Theo Reeves this morning."

"Stephanie can take time off work," said Gus. "I don't do evenings."

The team could tell Gus wasn't in the best of moods. It was time to keep their heads down and wait until the storm blew over.

Gus grabbed the phone and called the Avon and Somerset Police HQ at Portishead.

Reception kept Gus on hold for several minutes, which didn't improve matters, but eventually, they connected him to DI Matt Price.

"Matt, it's Gus Freeman here. Congratulations on your promotion. Well deserved, I'm sure. Yes, I expect it will be a surprise to hear from me. Several months ago, I came out of retirement to work with a Crime Review Team. They're rough around the edges, but I'm doing my best with them. I'm sure you recall the Marion Reeves case out at Wilton. Yes, a messy business. We've got the murder file in our office, and I spoke to Theo Reeves, the victim's husband, this morning. The murder file lists a mobile phone as being among the contents of Marion's handbag. What work got carried out on that phone? Unfortunately, we can't find any details of her call history."

Everyone in the room listened in on the conversation. The pause while Gus listened to Matt Price's explanation seemed to last forever.

"Who handled the items from inside the Lexus, Matt?" asked Gus. "Hold on, do you mind if I put you on speakerphone?"

"No problem, Gus," said Matt Price. "We were at Bourne Hill nick when we got the call to attend an incident at Churchfields. Billie Wightman drove us to the end of Churchfields Road, where it joins Stephenson Road. We reached the outer cordon at twenty past twelve. Uniformed officers were already on the scene and following standard protocols as far as possible. For the young uniforms on-site that day, it was the first major incident they had attended. Sergeant Phil Youngman ran the show. He'd arrived with a female PC a few minutes before noon and soon realised they needed extra pairs of hands to secure the crime scene. Phil's reinforcements cordoned off access to Stephenson Road and evacuated as many personnel as possible from the nearby units. You can imagine how many people that meant; it was chaotic. Forensics and the police surgeon had beaten Billie and me to Churchfields by a matter of minutes. We were at least one hundred yards from the white tent Crime Scene Investigators erected over the victim's car. Even from that poor vantage point, Billie muttered that she thought there were far too many bodies milling around. She yelled at a PC wandering around with a roll of crime scene tape to get us booked in and escorted to the business end of operations."

"How good a job had Phil Youngman done as First Officer Attending in securing the crime scene and preserving evidence?" asked Gus.

"Phil Youngman must have been at Bourne Hill when you worked there, Gus," said Matt Price. "He was a safe pair of hands and had been in the job for years. Phil would never fly higher than a Sergeant, but you could always rely on him to perform well."

"Mister Dependable, yes," said Gus. "If anyone dropped the ball on this, it was unlikely to be Phil. Did an experienced forensics team attend the murder scene?"

"The Scene of Crime Examiner that day was Warren Baker. Thirty years experience."

"I don't think I ever met him. Had he been at Bourne Hill long?"

"Baker moved back to Salisbury from Southampton early in 2010. He was born in Bemerton, went to university in Winchester, and then joined the forensics team at Southampton. Warren has continued to live in Salisbury throughout his career. He married a local girl from Bemerton. They never had kids, and the scuttlebutt around the nick was that they had a certain circle of friends. Neither of them was easy to get to know."

"A certain circle of friends?" asked Gus. "That's an odd phrase. Was Warren Baker a Mason?"

"I don't believe so, Gus," said Matt. "Warren was an odd character. There were rumours when he first arrived at Bourne Hill."

"Rumours suggested he left Southampton under a cloud," said Gus.

"Something which never resulted in a censure that appeared on his record. We wouldn't have employed him if it had. The younger female uniformed officers and forensic staff avoided getting left in a room alone with him. Nobody ever made a complaint, but Billie overheard comments in the ladies' toilets that Warren gave them the creeps just by how he looked at them."

"How did he relate with the guys at the station?" asked Gus.

"Warren kept himself to himself. He never socialised with anyone from the station during my time at Bourne Hill. He was peculiar; Warren would collar a married officer in the canteen and show him photos of his wife on his mobile phone. She wasn't much to look at, but Warren doted on her and thought she was beautiful. He'd ask whether the bloke had a photo of his wife he could see. It could have been innocent enough, but after a while, the blokes were doing the same as the young women and keeping their distance."

"What happened after you and Billie arrived at the white tent?" asked Gus.

"The Crime Scene Manager fetched us from the external cordon. We'd already suited up while we were waiting. He took us to the tent, and we found Warren Baker and two of his forensic team gathering evidence. The police surgeon leaned in from the driver's door, carrying out his black arts on Marion Reeve's body. We heard him detailing every step as he went. His recorder sat on the dashboard."

"Had forensics removed evidence from inside the car already?" asked Gus. "Could you see the victim's handbag?"

"I couldn't see much because the police surgeon was in the way. Billie moved to the passenger side for a better look at the body. I couldn't get further than the bonnet for a while because one of the forensic guys was still working there. When I joined Billie, the only thing left inside the Lexus was Marion's dead body."

"Someone removed the handbag before you reached the murder scene. Was it properly bagged and recorded, with separate bags for each item?"

"Everything was by the book according to the crime scene logs we studied later."

"When was the last time anyone saw the phone?" asked Gus.

"We never saw it, Gus," said Matt Price. "The Crime Scene Manager's logs listed everyone in or near that car from the second Phil Youngman and his PC arrived. As Billie remarked when we stood at the bottom of Stephenson Road, when you added up the uniformed officers, Baker and his forensics people, and the police surgeon, there were a lot of people in the vicinity."

"So, the handbag and its contents supposedly got entered into evidence and stored away at Bourne Hill," said Gus. "When did you realise it was missing?"

"I don't need to tell you what it's like to work on a murder case such as that, Gus," said Matt. "You get on with interviewing people connected to the victim as soon as possible. Forensic analysis can take hours, days, or even weeks, so you concentrate on what you have at hand. When results started filtering through later, Billie queried why there was nothing on the phone's call history. We sent a young Detective Constable to the evidence room, and he spent hours hunting for that phone. It wasn't where it was supposed to be, but time is always against you. We couldn't leave the guy there opening every box looking for a phone that got misplaced. It could still be there, for all I know. We didn't find it before getting assigned to a new case. That was five or six weeks later."

"When did you and Billie Wightman stop working together?"

"She moved to Gablecross after her promotion came through at the end of 2015. My elevation to DI came through in May 2016, and I secured a post here at Portishead."

"The rumours suggest you haven't stopped smiling since," said Gus.

"Billie had a rough deal with her husband, Gus. It became tough to work alongside her. I was always walking on eggshells in case I said something to set her off."

"Did either of you review the case before you left Salisbury?" asked Gus.

"We had another stab at it together in 2014. That would have been in the summer, June, or July. We couldn't dent any of the alibis we got during the first investigation. The evidence, or lack of it, didn't point us towards having missed an obvious suspect. So we spent two or three days on it and moved on."

"What did you make of Martyn Street when you interviewed him in 2014?" asked Gus.

"He wasn't much help on the original investigation nor the review. His alibi was rock solid. Martyn is a bit backward, if that's the right term to use these days. He answered our questions with as few words as possible. Martyn looks like the strong, silent type. The sort that many women might go for until he opens his mouth. Sorry if we've left you an even harder nut to crack by losing that mobile phone, Gus. I hope you and your team find something we missed."

"I don't blame you or Billie, Matt. Let's hope the phone is misplaced and not lost. Thanks for your time."

"That didn't sound good, guv," said Neil after Gus ended the call. "Do you think Marion Reeves's phone got lost in transit?"

"Before they had the chance to retrieve the call history, which could have identified our killer," said Blessing.

"Losing evidence is rare, thank goodness," said Alex.

"Unfortunately, it's not always human error," said Luke. "It makes you wonder whether everyone who handled that evidence was trustworthy."

"I'll pass the information on to DS Mercer," said Gus. "He can investigate whether there was foul play or just carelessness. It's not something I can tackle myself. If the phone's gone for good, we'll need to manage without it. I can't deny it's a body blow."

"As big a body blow as perhaps losing Graham Street, guv?" asked Neil.

"Get to the hospital, Neil," said Gus. "I want you there in case he comes around long enough to talk. Luke, or Alex, will relieve you at midnight."

"I'll go," said Luke. "Alex can take over at eight in the morning."

"We should know one way or another by then," said Neil as he headed for the lift.

"Where do we go from here, guv?" asked Lydia.

"We stick to the schedule I had in my head, but Graham Street is on hold until we hear from the hospital. So, Stephanie Reeves is up next, followed by Martyn Street. For the benefit of the rest of you, Arthur Jackson is Martyn's line manager at Wilton House. Theo Reeves suggested his name as a responsible adult to sit in on our meeting. Martyn has a few issues. Theo Reeves talked about his stepson being a slow learner. Theo didn't want Martyn in the house after Marion died. We'll learn more when we speak with Stephanie, but Theo suspected Martyn had acted inappropriately with Stephanie. He might have taken advantage of her when she used alcohol to blot out the trauma of losing her mother."

"We don't have confirmation of that," said Lydia. "It could be Theo was over-protective of his daughter. Although Theo said he was happy to take on Marion and another man's child at the start of the marriage, the issues Gus mentioned proved too hard a burden to carry."

"Did you do a walkabout?" asked Blessing.

"We did," said Gus. "I wish I could tell you it was informative. Without seeing the industrial estate, I thought it impossible to drive there and park the car for almost two hours, and a vicious stabbing could occur without someone noticing. Lydia and I found a quiet spot on the edge of the estate on Stephenson Road. No foot traffic, hardly any passing vehicles, but two dozen cars and vans parked on either side of the road. Every unit was in operation, with factory noise, music, and people moving about their business inside the premises. A nuclear bomb could have exploded, and nobody would have poked their nose outside to see what was happening. Perhaps they'll rewrite the manual on how to commit the perfect murder. Find a quiet corner in a busy place all year round, and you've got every chance of getting away with it."

"We asked a funeral director about the gym that used to operate out of the premise they now occupy," said Lydia. "It was a run-down shell of a place when they took it over five years ago. At the time of the murder, there was every chance it was closed for maintenance."

"The light engineering outfit next door is still going strong," said Gus. "I can visualise the Lexus and its surroundings now, but that's about it. We don't know whether Marion met someone on Stephenson Road at nine-thirty. I had hoped to learn something from her mobile phone."

"Who do you want to speak to after the children, guv?" asked Luke.

"Milligan and Preston, the builders," said Gus. "Other than that, I can't see anyone from Marion's printing firm or Theo's design company offering up a suspect."

"I suggested we look at the schools, guv," said Lydia.

"A long shot," said Gus. "No, we must concentrate on Graham Street. Even if we can't talk to him, we can still learn a lot by talking to his friends and colleagues. We might learn even more by having a word with his enemies. I want to know what makes that guy tick."

Chapter Seven

GUS DROVE HOME to Urchfont after a busy but frustrating day. The last thing he'd done before leaving the Old Police Station office was to call Geoff Mercer.

"Did Matt Price think it was possible someone tampered with evidence in the Marion Reeves case?" asked Geoff. "Why didn't he flag it up at the time? Why wait seven years?"

"Matt was still a Detective Sergeant back then, Geoff," said Gus. "It was his DI, Billie Wightman, who should have pulled the trigger."

"What do you think happened?" asked Geoff.

"Because of the number of people clambering over the crime scene, it's possible the phone didn't make it back to the evidence room. Maybe it got mislaid between the car and the forensics vehicle assigned to transport everything collected from the murder site. Or the switch occurred in the evidence room itself—human error. If we had a month of Sundays to spare, we could keep opening every box in the evidence room until we found it. A job you could assign to Grace Packenham to get her out of everyone's hair."

"Grace is far too busy. The other alternative doesn't bear thinking about, does it?" said Geoff.

"Someone close to the case put the phone in their pocket?" said Gus. "I didn't ask Theo Reeves whether his wife had a top-of-the-range smartphone or something basic but serviceable. Marion kept the same number from her first-ever mobile by the sound of things, so it's hard to tell which model she owned."

"Many people hold on to the same number," said Geoff. "It saves the hassle of having to notify people of a new one every couple of years. Let alone try to remember it when people ask. Theft wasn't the alternative that concerned me. What if someone removed it because they feared Marion's phone held information that could incriminate them?"

"That's a stretch, Geoff, surely?" said Gus. "Did any police or forensic people working there that afternoon even know Marion Reeves? Apart from the fact that we know she was married before she met Theo Reeves, we've got nothing to suggest Marion ever got involved in any dodgy business before she met Theo."

"Check with Theo Reeves," said Geoff. "Show him a list of names without revealing the background, and check whether he recognises someone Marion mentioned. Was there anything else?"

"You mentioned Marion's first husband," said Gus. "Neil Davis told me when we got back from Wilton Graham Street suffered a heart attack last night. So it's touch and go. Neil has gone to Odstock to see if we can question Street if he pulls through. Neil will stay with Street until midnight. My other two lads will cover the following sixteen hours.

The doctors told Neil the next twenty-four hours were critical."

"Why do you need to speak to Graham Street, anyway?" asked Geoff. "He wasn't on the scene when Marion died, was he? They got divorced twenty years earlier. Did the investigating team even check whether he had an alibi for the time of the murder?"

"Billie Wightman and Matt Price never found a viable suspect with the evidence they uncovered," said Gus. "I believe the answer lies in Marion's past; therefore, it could revolve around her relationship with Graham Street. The murder file held practically no information on Street. Perhaps you're right. Billie Wightman didn't bother with Graham Street because she thought he was old news and irrelevant. I'll call Neil and tell him to watch the situation and report back. We'll hold off on interrogating the guy as soon as he regains consciousness."

"I'm glad to hear it, Gus," said Geoff.

Gus had prepared everything for their meal when Suzie arrived home.

"You've got time to shower and change," said Gus. "Have you changed your mind about the grilled cheese?"

Suzie wrinkled her nose and went into the bedroom.

"All the more for me then," said Gus, putting the steaks onto the grill.

After they had eaten, they spent an hour relaxing in the back garden.

"Next summer, this will be a glass of wine rather than lemonade," said Suzie.

"I'm enjoying my lemonade. Did you hear from Vicky Bennison yet?" asked Gus.

"Not yet," said Suzie. "I plan to call her before the

weekend if she doesn't get back to me. So how did it go in Wilton?"

Gus outlined the various meetings and conversations he'd had during the day

"What did you think of Theo Reeves' behaviour towards his stepson?" asked Suzie.

"It might seem harsh," said Gus, "but we don't know the full story between Martyn and Stephanie. I found Theo's account of their first meeting of interest. What did you make of that?"

"What, because Marion didn't want to give Theo an insight into her failed marriage?" said Suzie. "I can understand that. She didn't hide the fact she had a child by marriage, though, did she? Theo knew what he was taking on from the off. He could have walked away."

"From what he told us this morning, Theo didn't realise Martyn would pose the problems he did," said Gus. "After twenty years, perhaps he'd had enough. Theo couldn't face dealing with it after losing his wife and seeing his daughter suffer a breakdown."

"No matter how we view the way matters got handled after Marion's murder, I can't see how Theo, Martyn, or Stephanie could figure in it. They had solid alibis, but what possible motive did they have? I haven't heard you say you've found evidence they weren't the happy family everyone saw from the outside."

"Apart from Theo's unproved suspicion over Martyn and Stephanie, Marion and Theo are squeaky clean. But, maybe when I speak to the builders, I'll discover the couple had a dark side."

"Neil didn't call with news on Graham Street," said Suzie. "What a terrible shock for his lady friend."

"Luke took over from Neil at midnight last night," said Gus. "Graham Street is ten years older than me. I've lived a sheltered life, and at my last medical, the doctor said I had the heart of a fifty-year-old."

"When was that?" asked Suzie.

"Just before I retired," said Gus.

"Idiot. Why did you say your life was sheltered in comparison, anyway?"

"Theo Reeves told us Graham Street had several children with different women. One might call his life unconventional; it certainly wasn't sheltered. But that lifestyle will catch up with you sooner or later."

"How do you plan to avoid that happening to you?" asked Suzie.

"I'll rely on you to help me eat well, restrict my alcohol intake, and have as many early nights as possible."

"Is it worth the risk?" asked Suzie.

"With you, always," said Gus.

Tuesday, 21 August 2018

THE ALARM RANG at seven o'clock, and Gus rolled out of bed. You can't beat a solid eight hours' sleep. As he stood in the shower, Gus heard Suzie moving around in the kitchen, Waffles for breakfast unless he was mistaken. He towelled himself dry and ticked off the list of questions he wanted to ask Stephanie Reeves.

"Coffee and waffles?" asked Suzie when Gus reached the kitchen.

"The perfect combination," he replied, "as long as they're separate."

They sat and ate in companionable silence. All was right with the world.

Gus knew on days such as this that things couldn't last. It had started too well.

Suzie was in the shower at a quarter to eight when the house phone rang in the hallway.

Gus prayed it was his old friend asking after Dorothy. No such luck.

"Morning, guv," said Luke Sherman. "Graham Street didn't make it. He passed away at around six-thirty this morning without regaining consciousness. I sent Alex a text telling him not to drive over from Chippenham. He'll be in the office at nine. Do you want me to hang around here to talk to the doctors or make a note of who they notified as next-of-kin?"

"No, don't bother, Luke," said Gus. "Get home to bed. We'll expect you in the morning. I want you with me when we interview Martyn Street."

"I slept for four hours after I got home yesterday after-noon, guv," said Luke. "I'll sleep until lunchtime, and then I'll be in the office by one or half-past. I've asked Alex to confirm those meetings for you today. See you later."

"Okay. Luke," said Gus, "further confirmation you're a team player. Much appreciated."

Gus ended the call. Suzie stood in the bedroom doorway wrapped in a bath towel.

"Bad news?" she asked.

"The worst," said Gus. "We must rely on others to tell us Graham Street's story."

They left the bungalow forty minutes later. Gus knew he had to rid himself of this sombre mood before speaking to Stephanie Reeves. The next few hours could be vital in this investigation.

Suzie had followed Gus through the gateway this morning for a change. She briefly flashed her headlights as she slowed to turn into the London Road car park. Suzie thought Gus needed a break tonight; perhaps an hour on the allotment and a meal in the Lamb would do the trick. It didn't pay to get too close to a case. You needed to step back to see the complete picture.

Gus followed the steady stream of traffic out of town and pulled into the Old Police Station car park at three minutes to nine. Another day, but would this one see another collar Neil Davis was so keen to quote?

Alex Hardy and Lydia Logan Barre had travelled together from Chippenham in her Mini. Blessing Umeh was still trying to master her reversing technique, so Gus waited and watched the fourth attempt at getting her Micra straight.

Gus spotted another car in his rear-view mirror. Neil Davis was another excellent team member. Neil had put in a long shift yesterday but was back for more today.

"Good morning, guv," said Neil as they eventually were able to park alongside Blessing.

"Not for Graham Street," said Gus. "Did Luke call you?"

"Luke sent me a text, guv, and told me he was letting Alex know the situation. But, when I left Odstock hospital last night, the mood around the place hinted that they expected the worst. Street died alone, guv. Whoever was with him when he had that massive heart attack never travelled in the ambulance. The staff told me they didn't get a single call for a report on his condition."

"All we can do is work with the living, Neil," said Gus. "We've got several witnesses directly connected to the case to interview, plus others with a connection to the victim that could prove invaluable. I want you to finish gathering the information on Graham Street you started yesterday."

"I'll give it my total concentration, guv," said Neil.

Blessing was waiting by the lift for Neil and Gus to join her.

"Morning, guv," she said. "Today will be a better day."

"Let's hope so," said Gus. They travelled up to the first-floor office together.

"Stephanie Reeves has taken this morning off work, guv," said Alex. "You know Downton village well, don't you? I've left a note of her address on your desk. Arthur Jackson has agreed to accompany Martyn Street to an interview this afternoon. He asked if they could meet you in the café at the Wilton House Garden Centre. Jackson said it would be less stressful for Martyn. He doesn't respond well to confined spaces or unfamiliar surroundings."

"We'll meet them there at three o'clock, Alex," said Gus. "I don't normally like witnesses setting the venue for meetings, but in this case, we can't afford to antagonise the person involved. We need Martyn Street to feel at ease and answer our questions. Matt Price told us yesterday Martyn said little when they spoke with him seven years ago. The questions I want to ask could require a more detailed response. Let's hope that's not beyond the young man."

"Who do you want with you this morning, guv," asked Lydia.

"My nerves wouldn't stand another trip in that Mini of yours, Lydia. Blessing, you can have a trip in my Ford Focus. I'll show you the delights of my old stomping ground of Downton."

"I can't wait, guv," said Blessing, collecting her notebook and pen from her desk.

Gus and Blessing were back in the lift less than two minutes after arriving in the office.

"I overheard you talking with Neil earlier, guv," said Blessing. "How sad that Marion's first husband died with no one to sit by his bedside. I hope that isn't what lies ahead for me."

"None of us knows what's in store for us, Blessing," said Gus.

"I'm sorry, guv. I forgot you couldn't be with your wife when she died."

"That's alright, Blessing," said Gus. "On balance, it's better not to know for both parties involved, isn't it?"

"When you're twenty-one like me, you spend little time thinking about the subject," said Blessing. "There I go again, putting my foot in it. I'll sit in the passenger seat and keep quiet."

Gus smiled as he unlocked the Focus. Blessing was a treasure they couldn't afford to lose. He drove out of the car park and was soon passing the junction to Crook Lane, which led to the shiny custody suite that replaced the Old Police Station.

"We should reach Stephanie Reeves's house in about an hour, Blessing," said Gus.

"Is it near the Abbey, guv?" asked Blessing.

Gus had to think for a minute what Blessing meant.

"That's a TV series, isn't it?" asked Gus. "I don't think there is such a place, Blessing. I talked to one of my friends from the village a month or two back. He was visiting Lacock Abbey with family members. That property was featured in the filming of Downton Abbey, along with other stately homes for different scenes. All that is on top of being the birthplace of photography. If you want to see that

Abbey, it's only three miles from our office. You could pop over in a lunch break."

"You learn something new every day, guv," said Blessing.

Gus was on familiar ground when they reached the village of Downton. It lay six miles southeast of Salisbury on the Hampshire border. Gus and Tess had enjoyed living on the doorstep of the New Forest. They had picnicked there and gone for long walks surrounded by trees and wildlife.

Stephanie Reeves and her partner lived in a three-bedroomed property close to the River Avon in Waterside.

"Not very imaginative of the planners, was it, guv?" said Blessing as Gus pulled up outside the house.

"They're not known for their imagination, Blessing," said Gus. "I haven't briefed you on how I plan to handle this meeting because I haven't got a plan. I'll ask a few general questions, and we'll see where that leads us."

"Got it, guv," said Blessing. "The practice I had on the way here will stand me in good stead. I'll sit and listen until you tell me to do otherwise."

"That's my girl," said Gus. He rapped the solid wooden door with the leopard's head door knocker. What a refreshing change from a UPVC and glass door and a battery-driven bell chime.

A tall, attractive young woman with long dark hair opened the door.

Blessing noticed the loose-fitting smock top and comfortable shoes; she guessed that Stephanie Reeves was around five months pregnant.

"Stephanie Reeves?" asked Gus.

"You must be the people from Wiltshire Police. Please, come in."

Stephanie led them through the hallway to a large farm-house-style kitchen at the rear.

"I've been baking," she explained. "I hope you don't mind the smell of fresh bread and cakes. Would you like a coffee? I was just about to make one."

"Mr Freeman takes his coffee, black without," said Blessing. "I prefer mine white with one sugar. Thank you, you're very kind. When's the baby due?"

Gus did a double-take. He'd been enjoying the smell of fresh bread and dreaming of Kassie Trotter's buns.

"Just in time for Christmas," said Stephanie. "Sit your-selves down anywhere you wish. What was it you wanted to know?"

"We should introduce ourselves first," said Gus. "DC Umeh works with me as part of a Crime Review Team. My name is Freeman, and I help the team review cases that were never solved in the weeks after they occurred. Your mother's murder occurred seven years ago, and her killer remains at large. We spoke with your father yesterday to check things he told the police in the original investigation and see whether he remembered anything new. He did expand our knowledge on various elements of the case. We're hoping you can also give us a fresh perspective."

"I'll try," said Stephanie. She placed a tray of drinks on the wooden table and sat beside Blessing. "Yours is at the front, Mr Freeman. DC Umeh and I have similar tastes."

"How long have you lived in this delightful property?" asked Gus.

"Five years," said Stephanie. "Danny and I moved in together in 2013."

"Danny?" asked Gus.

"Danny Ellis," said Stephanie. "He's a stonemason. Danny works at Salisbury Cathedral. He accepts private commissions too, but getting the contract for conservation work on the Cathedral was like getting the Forth Bridge painting contract. As soon as you get to the other end, it's time to start again. Our child will have a job if my scan is right and it's a boy. He can take over from where his father left off."

"Danny's a skilled craftsman," said Gus. "Where did you meet?"

"You've spoken to my father," said Stephanie. "There's no point denying I went through hell after Mum died. I drank to forget. That didn't work out the way I had hoped. Danny was often in the pubs I drank in; he was seeing another girl at the time. Someone I was at school with, and they both tried to help me stop punishing myself. I stayed with Dad for as long as I could stand it. Then Danny called to say he wasn't with Becky anymore. Would I like to go for a meal? I moved out of Oakley Road a couple of months later. We lived in Danny's flat in the city centre for eighteen months. Then we agreed to get a foot on the housing ladder. As soon as we saw this house, we knew it was a family home and would be perfect."

"Does Theo know you're expecting?" asked Gus.

"Yes, I called to tell him the news. Dad knows where we live," said Stephanie, "and we're happy. He always had different ideas about what I should do with my life. We'll let him see his grandson when the time comes, but he doesn't leave the house much since Mum died. He sits in that big house surrounded by memories."

"Theo didn't mention you were pregnant," said Gus. "He admitted it disappointed him you didn't go on to university and follow a professional career. But he also said Danny seemed a decent sort. Has your father not been to this house in the past five years?"

Stephanie shook her head.

"We invited him several times in the first year, but he could never make it. So in the end, we stopped asking."

"You work at the local primary school in the village, don't you?" asked Blessing.

"Yes, it's just across the road. I love it. The children are wonderful at that age. I can't wait to have one of my own. It's a shame they have to grow up, isn't it?"

"How's Martyn these days?" asked Gus.

"I wouldn't know," said Stephanie. "I haven't seen or spoken to him since Dad threw him out."

"Theo suggested he said it might be best for Martyn to move out," said Gus. "To throw him out sounds a touch heartless."

"As I said, Mr Freeman, it's a shame they have to grow up."

"I thought you and Martyn were close," said Gus. "Theo was proud of how you stuck up for Martyn when he got bullied."

"I was younger than Martyn by five years," said Stephanie. "He was slower than the other kids, and they never let him forget it. My parents did everything they could to help Martyn. They didn't need to spend as much time with me because I was bright for my age, or so the teachers kept telling them. I listened to Mum and Dad discussing Martyn at home, and nothing they did seemed to help. So I decided if I helped as well, it might be the extra push he needed. When that happened, I was about five. Five years later, I wished I hadn't bothered."

Gus looked at Blessing. She had been in the office when he ran through the chief things they had learned from Theo Reeves yesterday. They should tread carefully in the next few minutes. He hoped Blessing stuck to her word and kept quiet.

"Martyn was fifteen," said Gus, "and, physically, no longer a child."

"Mum was very protective," said Stephanie. "Although I was still only ten, I sensed her attitude towards Martyn was changing. She was less tolerant of his moods. Dad saw little of that because he worked long hours."

"Can you tell us how the relationship between Marion and Martyn changed?" asked Gus.

"Mum would take him to his room and lecture him for ages. I'd creep up the stairs to his bedroom door and try to hear what they said. I didn't understand much of it, not then. Then, I noticed that he got aroused when he greeted me after he got home from school. Martyn always wanted to cuddle me when we were younger, and I was happy he was in a good mood. It meant what we were doing must be working. Perhaps he wasn't a retard like the boys in the street said, but things changed. I was uncomfortable around Martyn because of the way he rubbed up against me. That's why Mum lectured him. She kept telling Martyn it was wrong, and he mustn't have those thoughts."

"Did it change his behaviour?" asked Gus.

"He couldn't understand why I didn't want a cuddle. Martyn thought he'd done something to upset me. Then I had my first period, and I got the lectures from Mum. It was a similar message. Don't let anyone touch you. It's wrong. It was my turn not to understand."

"Marion wanted to protect both of you," said Gus. "The number of teenage pregnancies has increased since Marion was a teenager. So, of course, she had concerns. What was it like when you had your first boyfriend?"

"A nightmare," said Stephanie. "I hadn't even kissed

him, and Mum panicked I would get pregnant. That relationship didn't last long. She frightened him away."

"Did you ever talk with your Mum about her childhood?" asked Gus.

"Only in general terms," said Stephanie. "She was born in Ringwood, across the border in Hampshire, and went to school there until she was fourteen. Then her parents split up, and her mother moved to Salisbury. My Mum rarely went to school once she got here. Instead, she played truant and went into the city centre. She started smoking and drinking before she was fifteen. Then, she met Martyn's Dad."

"Graham Street," said Gus. "A wealthy business person who was a good deal older than Marion. What did she tell you about him?"

"Nothing much," said Stephanie. "She said he ruined her, ruined her life. Mum didn't think she would have lived to see thirty if she hadn't met my Dad when she did. Graham Street sounded a horrible man."

"So, Marion met Graham Street in 1982," said Gus. "They were married until 1990, when your mother finally plucked up the courage to walk out. Theo and Marion met soon after and married the following year. You arrived in 1993. I wonder when they got married? Was it just before she had Martyn in 1988, or much earlier?"

"I don't know," said Stephanie. "Mum never spoke about that period of her life."

"Was there anyone she was still in touch with from that time?" asked Blessing. "Any girlfriends she made when she arrived in Salisbury?"

"Only Serena," said Stephanie. "Serena Campbell. She was Mum's best friend for years."

"Remind me again what you were doing on the Sunday afternoon before your Mum died," said Gus.

"I spent the afternoon studying in my room," said Stephanie. "Mum drove over to the garden centre."

"Theo told us she bought bedding plants but added he thought Marion visited the café for coffee and cake."

"That would have been with Serena," said Stephanie. "That's where they used to meet."

"Was it a regular thing?" asked Gus. "Theo wasn't aware of it."

"No, I got the impression Mum never wanted Dad to find out about Serena. I don't know why. She's posh. A couple of years older than Mum, but very attractive."

"Where can we find her?" asked Gus.

"At the café," said Stephanie. "She works there several afternoons each week."

"I've got several more questions," said Gus. "I'm afraid they might be less easy to talk about but bear with me. First, can we talk about the days leading up to your mother's murder?"

"You're going to ask about the money, aren't you?" asked Stephanie. "I was at school on Friday when Mum withdrew that cash. She said nothing that morning about needing to pop into town while at work. Because the builders were at the house daily, Mum started work later and only took thirty minutes for lunch. She hardly had time to eat the packed lunch she took every day and drink a cup of coffee. I never saw the money nor knew why she needed it."

"Was there anything you can remember that seemed odd on Saturday and Sunday?" asked Gus.

"Nothing. I was revising for my exams. I cycled to my friend's house to get away from the house for a while.

Martyn was his usual self, out drinking at lunchtime on Saturday, cooped up in his room in the evening. He had little imagination. It was the same routine every weekend."

"The builders worked on Saturday morning, didn't they?" asked Gus.

"Stuart and Derek," said Stephanie, "God's gift to women. Or at least they thought they were. Maybe they thought getting off with someone they did work for went with the territory. I wondered whether they'd tried it on with Mum before turning their attention to me."

"Was it anything more than innuendo?" asked Gus. "Did one of them touch you?"

"I never gave them a chance," said Stephanie.

"You had a lot to put up with during your teens, didn't you?" asked Gus. "Do you think you can tell us about Martyn now?"

"I told you what happened when he was fifteen. Mum must have got through to him because he kept his distance for the next three years. When he reached eighteen, Mum gave him some money from his father. She wanted Martyn to learn to drive, but he couldn't cope with the theory paper. He was working at Wilton House, walking back and forth every day, and some men he worked with suggested he meet them one Saturday night. They got him drunk, and I woke up at one o'clock to find Martyn climbing into bed with me. I screamed, and by the time Dad woke up and came to my rescue, he found Martyn standing by the doorway. Mum had followed Dad along the corridor, and she convinced him Martyn mistook the door because he was drunk."

"Did it happen again?" asked Gus.

"Dad fitted a lock on my door, so that was the end of that," said Stephanie.

"Did Martyn ever get accused of doing anything inappropriate at work?" asked Gus.

"He didn't go near the main house or the garden centre," said Stephanie. "Martyn worked with the ground staff. They took care of the lawns, trees, shrubs, and river banks. Martyn said he could go days without seeing a visitor to the estate."

"We know you were at school on the eighteenth of March," said Gus. "Let's talk about the aftermath of the murder. When did you start drinking?"

"A week later, perhaps. For days, the police kept coming to the house and asking Dad questions. They stressed they knew none of us was responsible but insisted we knew the killer. It had to be a man Mum knew. We didn't know anyone apart from those she worked with or those who worked with Dad. When they told us they had arrested Simon, it just seemed ridiculous. I went into town that night and kept drinking until I puked. That was the start of the downward spiral."

"How long did it last?" asked Gus.

"Months," said Stephanie. "Dad was suffering, Martyn too. We went to Centre Parcs at Longleat for a weekend break. It chucked it down with rain all the time we were there. I was never sober."

"Martyn made sure you got home safe from town when you were drinking, didn't he?" asked Gus. "Theo told us he was returning the favour for when you stood up for him when you were both younger."

"I was vulnerable," said Stephanie, "Danny and Becky could see that. So they saw off several blokes looking to take advantage of the state I was in. How I never got raped, I'll never know."

"What happened when Martyn carried you home on nights when you could barely stand?"

"He used to cop a feel," said Stephanie. "I'd slap his hand, and he'd laugh and do it again. The night Dad saw us by the front door, he thought something more had happened, but it hadn't. There was something wrong with Martyn. He was slow-witted; we knew that. You could tell him something once, and he'd remember it. Another time you could repeat it a hundred times, and it never sunk in."

"Do you think he took in what Marion told him?" asked Gus.

"He always listened to Mum," said Stephanie. "After his Dad disowned him, Mum was all he had. He used to tell her he trusted her to the moon and back."

"What did you mean when you said you left Oakley Road because you couldn't stand it any longer?" asked Gus.

"Dad was a mess. He wanted to get rid of Martyn as soon as he could after Mum died. Then I had my meltdown, which made Dad tougher to live with. Martyn had moved out. He was so confused. I'll never forget the look on his face when his boss picked him up to take Martyn to his new place. He couldn't understand what he'd done. Then there were the neighbours, who kept sympathising or crossing the road to avoid us. Finally, I just had to get away."

"What about the builders?" asked Gus.

"They were as lecherous as before, but only one day a week. They knew Dad wouldn't make a fuss, so they squeezed every pound out of the job they could. All the while, Stuart was trying to get me alone."

"Did anything happen you want to tell us about?" asked Blessing.

Stephanie shook her head.

"I think that's everything for this morning, Stephanie," said Gus. "Many thanks for the coffee. We'll be in touch if we need more information."

"One final thing, guv," said Blessing. "Stephanie, you said your mother took a packed lunch to work every day."

"She did."

"There wasn't a packed lunch in the car or her handbag, guv," said Blessing. "Did Marion Reeves know she wasn't going to work that day?"

Chapter Eight

"I ENJOYED your Lieutenant Columbo moment, Blessing," said Gus when they reached the car.

"Who, guv?" asked Blessing.

"A TV detective, way before your time, Blessing. It was a trademark move of his. But, just as the villain thought he was off the hook, Columbo asked a telling question."

"We don't believe Stephanie Reeves is a villain, guv, do we?

"Of course not, but the packed lunch could be a game-changer. Theo never mentioned it. It adds another item that requires an explanation. We already have a missing mobile phone. Did the same person remove them from Marion Reeves's car, and if so, why?"

"I wonder if the builders saw Mrs Reeves carrying it when she left the house that morning?" asked Blessing.

"I'll ask tomorrow," said Gus. "Along with questions about their behaviour while they worked at Oakley Road."

"They sound a couple of creeps, guv," said Blessing. "But because they took a close interest in everything Marion and Stephanie did in the months they worked at the house, those men can help check what we've learned from Theo Reeves and his daughter. Although they got distracted by the females in the property, they had a unique view of how the family interacted."

"That's an excellent point, Blessing," said Gus.

As he drove them back to the office, Gus thought listening to Milligan and Preston would be like watching a dreadful reality programme where the builders would be the camera. The Reeves family would become celebrities that were a complete mystery.

As long as it helped explain some remaining questions, Gus was happy to sit through it. But, unfortunately, that was tomorrow's torture; this afternoon, he had to face Martyn Street.

"I wonder whether Serena Campbell will be working this afternoon, guv?" said Blessing as Gus parked the Focus.

"I'll keep an eye out for the lady, Blessing," said Gus. "I need to concentrate on getting the most out of my conversation with Martyn Street. Luke's car is already here. I'll take him to Wilton later."

Gus and Blessing exited the lift and entered the office.

"Can we spend five minutes agreeing on our plan for this afternoon's meeting, Luke?" asked Gus. "I want you to prevent Arthur Jackson from contributing too much to the conversation. It might paint you as the bad guy, but I need Martyn Street to trust me throughout the meeting to get maximum benefit."

"I understand, guv," said Luke. "I'll drive to Wilton if you wish. We need to leave by a quarter past two. When do you want that five minutes chat?"

"Let's do it at two o'clock, Luke," said Gus, checking the clock on the far wall. "We'll update our files with what

Blessing and I learned from Stephanie Reeves this morning."

"What were the major points you took from the meeting, guv?" asked Alex.

"Stephanie has a lovely home," said Gus. "She and her partner are in full-time employment and doing well. She's five months pregnant. As for her relationship with her father, I would describe it as cordial. Stephanie is an independent young woman, with her drinking problem firmly behind her. Since Martyn moved into the flat near where he works, Stephanie hasn't seen or spoken to him. Despite Theo Reeves's concerns that something physical occurred while living under his roof, Stephanie denied it. I believed her."

"That was pretty comprehensive, guv," said Lydia. "You had a good morning."

"There's more," said Blessing. "Theo Reeves had two lecherous builders working at Oakley Road for months, and Marion Reeves was in the habit of taking a packed lunch to work every day."

"Do either of those things help identify Marion's killer, guv?" asked Neil.

"The deeper we delve into this case, Neil," said Gus, "I no longer imagine there's a magic bullet to blow everything wide open. Instead, we've uncovered these unimportant and unrelated scraps that will provide the solution. We just need to be patient."

"When do you want to go through my Graham Street background information, guv?"

"It will have to wait until tomorrow, Neil," said Gus. "Have you entered it into the Freeman files?"

"I'll do it this afternoon while you and Luke are in Wilton, guv," said Neil.

"What do I do about those two builders, guv?" asked Luke. "They're playing hard to get."

"That's easily sorted," said Gus, "Call Bourne Hill nick and book a room for tomorrow morning. We'll kill two birds with one stone. Ask Milligan to attend at ten o'clock and Preston at ten-thirty. If they say they're too busy, inform them that uniformed officers will collect them from whichever property they're working at and escort them to the custody suite for an interview under caution."

"Who do I contact to arrange that, guv?" asked Luke.

"Who said anything other than informing them?" said Gus. "I'm not running after these people. Our second bird is Warren Baker, the forensic guy. Arrange for Baker to be in whichever room Bourne Hill assigns us at eleven o'clock. I want to get to the bottom of this mobile phone fiasco."

"Got it, guv," said Luke.

Blessing was halfway through updating her digital files. Gus took a second glance at the clock and got his head down. He could still get his part done before he left for Wilton House. As he loaded the appropriate files, he had a thought.

"Lydia, are you busy?"

"If you need my help, I'll find the time, guv. What do you need?"

"Call DS Mercer at London Road," said Gus. "We need a photograph of everyone who entered that tent at the murder scene. Retrieve those names from the crime scene logs in the murder file. It will give exact times of arrivals and exits and should be comprehensive. Explain we must be discreet. I don't want Bourne Hill to know we're checking up on their people. Once you've got photos for the various disciplines that attended, call Theo Reeves, and tell him you're driving over straight away and need his help. Don't let him fob you off. We need to know whether one or more of those faces was someone Marion knew."

"Will do, guv," said Lydia.

Gus started typing. Around him, the team was hard at work. Were they making progress or just being busy fools? Gus wished he knew.

"Two o'clock, guv," said Luke. "Are you ready?"

"Two minutes, Luke," said Gus. "I could murder a coffee if you're not doing anything while I keep you waiting."

"On its way, guv," said Luke. He walked to the restroom and fired up the Gaggia.

Gus and Luke then made their preparations for meeting with Martyn Street and Arthur Jackson and travelled to the car park together in the lift. Lydia called after them to wish them luck. She was about to pick up the phone to speak to Theo Reeves.

"Lydia won't be far behind us, guv," said Luke.

"She'd better not overtake you, Luke," said Gus. "That girl is a crazy driver. Have you ever travelled with her?"

"Of course, guv," said Luke, "it's an experience and no mistake."

Gus relaxed in the passenger seat of Luke's car and thought about Serena Campbell. Stephanie hadn't known enough to tell them where Serena fitted into the life Marion lived before she met Theo Reeves. Perhaps, at last, he'd discover who Marion really was.

"This is a busy spot, guv," said Luke as he hunted for a parking space close to the Garden Centre café.

"I don't mind walking a few hundred yards, Luke," said Gus. "Leave the spaces closest to the café for the old folks."

"Sorry, guv," said Luke.

They entered the café at two minutes to three. Luke

spotted Arthur Jackson and Martyn Street in the far corner. Arthur had chosen well. Martyn had his back to the crowds, and a large table featuring upcoming events to their left meant they wouldn't get overheard.

"Far right-hand corner, guv," said Luke.

"I was checking name tags on the staff," said Gus. "They gave me a few odd looks. I think they thought I was staring at their breasts."

"Did you see anyone you recognised?" asked Luke.

"Not so far; perhaps Serena Campbell doesn't work on Tuesdays. To avoid getting thrown out, I'll ask Arthur Jackson if he knows."

"Did you want another coffee, guv," asked Luke.

"If you're buying, Luke," said Gus. "Let's get over to their table first. We don't want to unsettle Martyn by keeping him waiting."

As they moved between the tables filled with older people enjoying afternoon tea, they saw Arthur Jackson heading their way. A waitress was now sitting beside Martyn Street, holding his hand.

"Is Martyn okay?" asked Gus.

"Serena will keep him calm. She's known him since he was a baby. I just thought I'd put you in the picture if you aren't aware of how his condition affects him. Martyn's social behaviour is immature and unstable. He lacks judgement and can sometimes get aggressive over petty issues. So, we do our best to keep everything on an even keel. Martyn is self-conscious, so he prefers working alone. We can accommodate that here. Martyn has never enjoyed working in a group. His mood can change in a split second when we've tried it."

"Is he likely to become aggressive or violent during a simple conversation?" asked Gus.

"Not in my experience," said Arthur, "which stretches back to the first day he came here straight from school."

"You must be near retirement age," said Gus, knowing the answer already.

"I don't know how Martyn will cope," said Arthur. "Serena's good with him, but I very much doubt whether one of the younger managers could cope with his mood swings."

"What would happen to Martyn if they had to let him go after you retired?" asked Luke.

"I dread to think," said Arthur. "Perhaps his family will reconsider."

"Theo Reeves isn't a blood relative," said Gus. "Did Serena Campbell ever mention Martyn's father?"

"A bad lot, from what Serena told me," said Arthur. "He washed his hands of Martyn after he divorced poor Marion. How could anyone do that?"

"I'll tell you this in confidence, Mr Jackson," said Gus. "I'm sure it will soon be common knowledge, but Graham Street, Martyn's father, died in hospital last night from a heart attack. It's unlikely Martyn will benefit from Street's estate, but you probably know better than us how Martyn might react when he hears the news."

"Thank you. I'll keep an eye on the lad. Well, more than I do already. I still call him a lad, but he's thirty now. We'd better let Serena get back to serving tables. Martyn seems calm enough for us to make a start."

Arthur Jackson led them to the table where Serena stood beside Martyn with a hand on his shoulder. Gus couldn't hear what she was whispering to him. Serena turned away without looking towards the three men approaching and attempted to escape to the safety of the kitchen.

"Not so fast, Mrs Campbell," said Luke Sherman.

"Wiltshire Police, we need to speak to you later. So please don't leave the building. When we're ready, I'll collect you from the kitchen or the main hall."

"It's Ms Campbell," spat Serena Campbell.

Gus could tell she was annoyed at Luke for letting everyone within earshot know she was a person of interest to the police. Stephanie Reeves was right. Serena Campbell looked every inch a woman from an upper-crust background, with looks that, even at fifty, could see her gracing the catwalk at a London fashion show.

Serena Campbell disappeared, and Gus turned his attention to the interview. Luke was seated opposite Martyn Street and Arthur Jackson. Martyn watched every step Gus took as he walked behind Luke to take the remaining chair. His eyes never left Gus's face.

"Good afternoon, Martyn," said Gus. "Has Mr Jackson told you who we are and why we're here this afternoon?"

Martyn nodded.

"We want to ask you a few questions, Martyn," said Gus. "We'd like you to answer them as best you can. Of course, you might not know the answers, but that's okay. Just remember as much as you can and tell the truth."

"I should always tell the truth," said Martyn.

"Your parents raised you well, Martyn," said Gus, "Mr Jackson tells us you do a good job here, working on the grounds. What do you enjoy best about what you do?"

"I keep the lawns and the shrubs tidy so the visitors say how pretty the gardens are. I can't climb the trees like Ralph, but I clear away the branches he removes with the chainsaw. I enjoy that."

"Ralph Tucker is the tree surgeon we employ," explained Arthur, "He's worked on the estate since before Martyn started working here."

Gus saw the look Arthur gave Luke. There must be something Arthur wanted to add. Perhaps it was best to wait until later.

"What can you remember from the time you and Mum lived in Salisbury?" asked Gus.

Martyn looked confused.

"Do you remember living in another house before you moved to Oakley Road?"

"Mum didn't want me to talk about that," said Martyn. "I tried to forget like she told me, but I couldn't."

"You lived with your Mum and Dad in a big house, didn't you? Of course, you were only young, and perhaps you don't remember your Dad?"

"He hurt Mum," said Martyn. "I didn't like him. So we stayed with Serena after he hit Mum again, then Mum married my other Dad, and the hitting stopped."

"Theo Reeves, yes, we spoke to him yesterday. Theo raised you and Stephanie as brother and sister, didn't he? I expect you were happy living with Mum, Dad, and Stephanie?"

"I was happy at home but didn't enjoy going to school. The other children were nasty because I wasn't clever like them. I was glad when I left school and came here to work. I could be alone, and only a few people make fun of me. Nobody will bother me if I do what I get asked the best I can. That's what Mum said."

"A wise woman, your mother," said Gus. "You must miss her."

"Mum told me I mustn't do bad things. I mustn't hurt women like my Dad did. She always told me people shouldn't say one thing and do another."

Gus knew he was on dangerous ground. His open-ended questions might get a verbal response from Martyn, but if he pressed too hard on details surrounding Marion's death, Martyn would revert to nods and shake his head or shut down altogether.

"How did you feel after Mum died, Martyn?" he asked, knowing it was a risk.

"I was angry and sad," said Martyn, more animated now. "People asked questions about where I worked that day, and I couldn't remember. Mr Jackson told them I was mowing the grass between the fruit trees that morning. It takes a long time, especially the first time you do it in the spring. Loads of rubbish gathers on the ground over the winter. If you're not careful, you hit it with the mower. Mum said if you have a problem, it's up to you to fix it. It takes time to clear the ground before you start mowing."

"That it does," said Arthur Jackson. "Martyn is only one of a team of people we need to work on the fifteen thousand acres we have to handle here. He's the most conscientious worker I've got. Martyn spends as long as it takes to prepare the ground. He was working on the eastern side of the estate for over two days, getting everything ready for the first cut."

"Did you see him during the morning to check he was okay?" asked Luke. "Isn't it more usual to work in pairs for health and safety?"

"Rubber duck, rubber duck," said Martyn.

Arthur grinned. "We keep in touch via walkie-talkie because of the distances involved. All our ground staff carry them. So I contact them regularly throughout the day to check their progress or ask them to move to another job if required."

"Do you bring a packed lunch to work each day, Martyn?" asked Gus.

"No," he replied.

"I suppose you would have to make it yourself," said Gus. "But you used to bring a packed lunch to work when you still lived at home, didn't you? Mum made one for herself every day, didn't she?"

"Sometimes I was so busy I forgot to eat it. Mum would tell me off when I took it home again. She said people in Africa were dying of starvation. We mustn't waste food, she said. I always tried to do what she said."

"Do you miss not living in Oakley Road?" asked Luke.

"It wasn't the same," said Martyn. "Mum wasn't there, and Dad was always sad. Stephanie got drunk every day. Ralph and his friends got me drunk once. I didn't like how it made me feel. I worried Stephanie felt that way every morning."

"You remembered when Stephanie stood up to the bullies, didn't you, Martyn?" said Luke. "So, you helped Stephanie when she needed someone to make sure she got home safely."

"I wanted to help her. Mum said I should treat women with respect, but one time I got into trouble when I got Stephanie home. Dad said I was disgusting. I had done nothing bad. I couldn't understand what I did wrong. He wanted me to leave. That was when Mr Jackson helped me find my new place."

"Do you own a mobile phone, Martyn?" asked Gus.

"I don't need one at work," Martyn replied. "I've got my rubber duck."

Martyn pointed to the unit attached to his trouser belt.

"I need the toilet," he said.

"Off you go then, Martyn," said Arthur. "Remember to wash your hands."

Martyn moved quickly from the table to the toilets at the back of the room.

"Right, Mr Jackson," said Gus. "What was it you wanted to tell us about Ralph Tucker?"

"Martyn explained just now," said Arthur. "Ralph Tucker has worked here for years. He's a good tree surgeon, but he has a mischievous side. Ralph persuaded Martyn to join him and a few of the lads to go out drinking. That was several years ago now. I got the impression Ralph knew Marion before she married Theo Reeves."

Luke nodded at Gus. He'd already added the name to his list of people to contact.

"Was Tucker working here at the time of Marion's murder?" asked Gus.

"We use Ralph's services most in October, November and February," said Arthur. "Then he's back and forth between May and September. I doubt we had any work for him in March and April. There would be plenty of places near Salisbury that need his skills. Ralph doesn't stay idle for long."

"How do you think Martyn's holding up this afternoon, Mr Jackson?" asked Gus.

"He's remained pretty cool. Why? Do you intend to grill him for much longer?"

Gus smiled as Martyn rejoined them.

"Just one more question, and then we'll let you get back to work, Martyn."

Martyn sat and leaned forward, waiting for Gus's question.

"Did you know Stephanie was having a baby?"

"With Danny?" asked Martyn.

"That's right. Stephanie and Danny live in Downton, by the river. Why don't you speak to Stephanie, Martyn?"

"Danny got angry if people bothered Stephanie when

she was drunk. He frightened me. I only wanted to help her."

"Perhaps Mr Jackson can show you how to call Stephanie on the public phone on the wall over there."

Martyn's chair shot back as he jumped up. Gus had heard of people going from nought to sixty in seconds, but this was something else. He was glad there was a wide table between them.

"Calm down, Martyn," said Arthur Jackson. "Come on, son; you don't have to do anything you don't want to do. Mr Freeman didn't mean any harm. It was just a suggestion."

"I was alone in a strange place," Martyn shouted. "Nobody came to ask how I was, only Mr Jackson and Serena. They looked after me. Mum said families should stick together. Everybody lied to me except them."

Arthur Jackson had risen from his chair and did his best to stop Martyn from lashing out. Serena Campbell ran across the hall to comfort the well-built young man who towered over her.

"Now look what you've done," she snapped at Gus and Luke. "You and your questions. How can Martyn help you solve my best friend's murder? Theo, Stephanie, and Martyn were never suspects after Marion died. So how can Martyn help you find who did it now, seven years later?"

"We didn't mean to upset him," said Gus. "We've spoken to Theo and Stephanie already. However, it's fair to say they've added little to the knowledge gathered in the earlier investigation. We hoped to learn more by chatting with Martyn. Once Mr Jackson has taken Martyn back to work, we'll speak with you, Ms Campbell. Who knows how significant the few scraps we gather from you might be in solving this case?"

"I need to tell my supervisor," said Serena, "can you let me have fifteen minutes?"

"We'll find something to occupy our time," said Gus. "I've heard that coffee and cake is a popular afternoon pastime here. So join us as soon as you're free."

Arthur Jackson had led Martyn Street to the nearest exit. Martyn was confused and upset that the café's customers seemed to stop talking, and stare, as he passed their table.

"I didn't expect *that* to happen," said Gus. "What did you make of it, Luke?"

"I can understand how tough it must have been for Martyn in the months after his father essentially threw him out," said Luke. "He turned to the two people who still believed in him, Arthur and Serena."

"Martyn had lost his mother in tragic circumstances, then his sister went off the rails," said Gus. "It was interesting how often Martyn referred to 'rules to live by' his mother instilled in him. For example, Stephanie told us that Marion took Martyn into his bedroom to lay down the law on how to treat Stephanie as she matured. Theo's reaction only months after Marion died flew in the face of how Martyn understood the family unit, as did Theo's outburst when Martyn carried his sister home late at night. Martyn believed he was doing what his mother wanted him to do. No wonder he got confused."

"What was behind the packed lunch question, guv?" asked Luke.

"I was only getting independent confirmation of Marion taking a packed lunch to work. Stephanie is the only person to have mentioned it. Theo told us he parked in the centre of Wilton, bought a newspaper and grabbed a sandwich as he walked to the office on the morning of the murder. I think we can assume that was what he did on days when he wasn't wining and dining clients. Like most teenage girls, Stephanie either had school dinners or starved herself during the day."

"The frequent communication between Arthur Jackson and his team puts more than Martyn Street in the clear, guv," said Luke. "Not that we know whether any ground staff knew Marion Reeves. But, even if they did, then none left the estate long enough to get to Churchfields to kill Marion and then get back again."

"Ralph Tucker wasn't working on the estate that day," said Gus. "I wonder whether he drives a pick-up truck. As soon as we get back to the office, you need to get hold of him and arrange a meeting."

"Yes, guv," said Luke. "Shall I get our coffee and cake now?"

"I thought you'd never ask," said Gus. "Anything but a lemon drizzle cake."

Chapter Nine

SERENA CAMPBELL JOINED the pair after three o'clock. Gus enjoyed his slice of fruit cake and finished his cup of coffee.

"I'm sorry if we got off on the wrong foot, Ms Campbell," said Gus. "My name is Freeman, and my colleague is Detective Sergeant Sherman. Wiltshire Police asked my team to take a fresh look into Marion Reeves's murder. Her daughter, Stephanie, gave us your name this morning. It explained something her father had told me yesterday. Theo said Marion came here on the Sunday afternoon before she died to buy bedding plants. When she returned home later than expected at four o'clock, Marion explained she'd visited the café for coffee and cake. When Stephanie told us how close you and Marion were, it seemed obvious it was with you she shared afternoon tea."

"We met here from time to time," said Serena. "I doubt Marion mentioned me to Theo. Marion would have said she sat alone."

"Why was that Ms Campbell?" said Gus. "Stephanie

said much the same thing. She thought Marion kept your friendship a secret from Theo."

"I met Marion a few months after she moved to Salisbury to live, Mr Freeman. We were both fifteen years old and attended different schools. My parents paid an exorbitant amount each term for my schooling, while Marion went to the local comprehensive. Yet, within weeks we found we were kindred spirits with a rebellious nature."

"You both started smoking and drinking," said Gus. "You skipped school and mixed with people who get young girls into trouble."

"A rather old-fashioned attitude, Mr Freeman," said Serena with a mocking smile.

"When did you meet Graham Street?" asked Gus.

"Graham spotted us drinking in pubs where we had no right to be," said Serena. "He spent time and money on us, and it flattered us."

"Street groomed you, is that right?" asked Luke.

"We were having fun," said Serena. "Graham knew so many people. Some were older than him, but they had one thing in common. They had plenty of money. It was obvious from the moment we met him that Graham fancied Marion, even though he knew we were both under sixteen. I felt left out, but Graham was so keen to get Marion alone he introduced me to Dave Francis when we were in a nightclub. Dave was an antique dealer and auctioneer. After that night, we went around in a foursome."

"Did you have sex with this man Francis before you reached sixteen?" asked Gus.

"What do you think?" replied Serena. "Marion and Graham were at it too. We were having fun, mixing with a group of grown-ups. Several drinks gave us a pleasant buzz every night without ever having to pay for them. We thought it would last forever."

"Marion married Graham Street," said Luke. "What happened to you?"

"Campbell is my maiden name," said Serena. "I married Dave Francis. Marion was eighteen when she and Graham got married. Dave had proposed to me on my seventeenth birthday. We married in a registry office two months later."

"So, Marion and Graham married in 1984," said Gus. "They had Martyn four years later. Yet, by 1990, Marion had left her husband and taken Martyn to live with you. Have I got that right? Martyn mentioned your name earlier this afternoon when I asked if he remembered the house he lived in when he was a young child."

"I had split from Dave the year before," said Serena. "I reverted to my maiden name as soon as possible. I didn't want to be associated with that man any longer than necessary."

"Things turned sour," said Luke.

"Things couldn't have been hunky-dory, Luke," said Gus. "Can you explain something to me, Ms Campbell? Do you believe Graham Street and Dave Francis married for love?"

"I don't think either man knew the meaning of the word, Mr Freeman," said Serena. "Marion and I were naïve and gullible from the outset. Two stupid young girls besotted with older, wealthy lovers. You continue to see that lethal combination around the world today. Nothing changes. The men have the money and power; the women are playthings to be enjoyed on a whim and cast aside when a prettier face with a younger body arrives on the scene. Graham and Derek had a slight variation on that routine. They married us to give them an extra element of control. We didn't realise it at first because we were so pleased that someone well-connected wanted to make us their wife."

"When did events take a turn for the worse for you?" asked Gus.

"Before the wedding," said Serena, "I know how stupid it sounds, but I loved Dave and would do anything for him. Marion felt the same way about Graham. We lived in flats they owned in the same building in the city centre. They picked us up one night, and we drove into the country to a quiet village pub. Graham bought a round of drinks and introduced us to his friends. After the pub shut, we went to a party in a big house outside the village, miles from anywhere. Four men and four women were in their late thirties or early forties. The person who owned the house kept topping up our wine glasses. I saw Dave dancing with a woman on the other side of the room. She was touching him. I saw Graham leave the room with another woman. Marion wanted to go after him, but Dave grabbed her arm and told her to behave. Dave said it was just fun and it meant nothing. We should go with the flow and enjoy something different."

"That was the first party of many, I presume?" asked Gus.

"Every weekend, those two organised parties somewhere in or near Salisbury. When I told Dave I wasn't happy going with yet another man, he told me not to be so parochial. That was just three weeks after we'd got married. He thought my upbringing should have let me know what to expect. So why worry, he said. You've got me to yourself Monday to Friday, and I'm asking that you're good to my friends at the weekend. A few men I slept with were gentle, but others were gross. I complained to Dave once more, and he suggested that if the husband turned me off, why not sleep with the wife?"

"Did Marion complain to Graham about what was happening?" asked Gus.

"Marion soon learned to hold her tongue," said Serena. "Dave Francis was a swine, but he never struck me. I saw the bruises Graham left on Marion's face and body. He was a sadistic devil, but Marion forgave him every time. She knew she should leave, but where could she go? She was trapped, the same as me. Everything I had, Dave had given me. We used to go to one another's flat, cry our hearts out, and wonder how to escape."

"Then Marion got pregnant," said Gus.

"And got another beating," said Serena. "Graham wanted her to get rid of the baby. How could she go to parties if she was expecting? His reputation relied on delivering an attractive young woman to wherever his friends held the next party. By this time, I had had enough of Dave. I discovered he saw other women during the week and shared my body around at the weekend. I rang my mother for the first time in six years, and my father drove to Salisbury within the hour to collect me. They didn't judge. They dropped everything and took me in without question. Dad helped when I said I wanted to divorce Dave. After the nightmare ended, Dad found me a cottage near Bemerton Heath. I still live there to this day, and after several jobs working with horses and flowers, I came to work here. It took many years to be comfortable among people again. Marion had told me Martyn worked on the ground staff. He remembered me from the old days. Martyn's slow on the uptake, Mr Freeman, but he's got a heart of gold."

"How did Marion escape Graham Street's clutches?" asked Luke.

"Oh, it wasn't as difficult after I'd left Dave as we believed," said Serena, "Graham was ready to move on from Marion too by the time Martyn was two years old. Graham didn't want his friends to know he'd fathered a less-than-perfect child."

"We heard there were other children by different women. Is that correct?" asked Gus.

"I don't know exactly how many," said Serena. "Three, maybe four. I could make a guess at who gave birth to one of Graham Street's children, but don't hold me to it."

"What proved the final straw?" asked Gus.

"Marion refused to participate in an extreme sex game Dave had dreamt up one Sunday night, and Graham punched Marion so hard and so often she had to go to the hospital. She called me while she waited for the ambulance, and I looked after Martyn at my place until Marion took him back."

"We saw no mention of your name in the original investigation," said Gus. "If you were one of Marion's best friends, how did the police not interview you?"

"You look an intelligent man, Mr Freeman," said Serena. "How can you ask such a dumb question?"

"Are you saying a senior police officer was a member of the group of people that Graham Street and Dave Francis called friends?"

"Swingers come from every level of society, Mr Freeman," said Serena. "The higher you climb, the further you have to fall. There's no limit to what they might do to prevent that happening."

Gus could have kissed Serena Campbell. It would have been no hardship; Serena was an attractive woman.

At last, they had uncovered a different aspect of this case. Gus had always hoped to find something in Marion

Reeves's past that contributed to her murder. This could be it.

"What's Dave Francis doing these days, Ms Campbell?" he asked.

"He's serving a custodial sentence in HMP Winchester," said Serena, with a hint of a smile. "Items Dave Francis catalogued as eighteenth-century porcelain from the Qing dynasty were fresh off a container ship from Shanghai. An expert from a TV programme spotted the minute differences between the copies and the genuine article when he viewed them in Dave's saleroom. My ex-husband sold one vase for three-and-a-half million pounds, which cost him less than two hundred. Men like Dave Francis and Graham Street can never have too much money. Greed drives them to do foolish things."

"My colleague, DS Sherman, was at Odstock hospital last night, Ms Campbell," said Gus. "An unidentified female had alerted the emergency services from an address in Salisbury early yesterday morning. Her partner had suffered a heart attack."

"Where were you between nine o'clock on Sunday night and four o'clock on Monday morning, Ms Campbell," asked Luke.

"At home, or in bed, alone, during that time," said Serena. "Why, what is this?"

"My colleague, DS Davis, sat beside the patient's bedside until midnight, and then I took over," said Luke. "The patient never regained consciousness, and doctors declared him dead at six-thirty this morning. Graham Street died from a massive heart attack. Unfortunately, his mysterious companion was unwilling to explain what Mr Street was doing before he suffered the attack. Indeed, she refused to travel with him in the ambulance and never contacted Odstock for an update on his condition."

"I won't shed any tears over that devil's death," said Serena. "Street must have been in his early seventies by now. It sounds as if he was still grooming impressionable young women. But, even at that age, his money talked."

"When was the last time you saw Graham Street?" asked Gus.

"I avoided him and Dave Francis like the plague as soon as I reached the safety of my parent's home," said Serena. "I doubt I've laid eyes on either of them more than a handful of times in over twenty-five years. I never spoke to them, nor did Marion, to the best of my knowledge. She would have told me if one of them got in touch,"

"I might be asking another dumb question, Ms Campbell," said Gus, "but once the two of you were free of your ex-husbands, why didn't you report the abuse you suffered to the police? Sex with someone under the age of consent is rape. Criminal charges would have followed for how Street and Francis used coercion to get you to perform various sexual acts with men and women at those weekend parties."

"My association with Marion and the swingers group got swept under the carpet seven years ago," said Serena. "The man responsible was at that first party in the country house. I'll never forget the look on his face when he realised Marion was his for the night. He attended most of the parties for the first three or four years. I hated every second I had to spend with him on future occasions. Then his wife died of cancer. Graham and Dave didn't invite anyone who didn't have a wife or partner willing to participate. Marion and I were fearful that even though he wasn't on the scene any longer, that man would still have the power to squash any investigation. What happened after Marion's murder proved how right we were."

"Why not give us his name this afternoon?" asked Gus. "We can check officers serving in the city when you and Marion attended those parties. If that man's wife died from cancer in the mid-eighties, we're detectives. We'll soon find him, anyway."

"I warned you this goes deeper and higher than you can imagine," said Serena. "I can't prove they murdered Marion because they feared she was about to name and shame someone, but they are more than capable. You'll have to find that man without my help. Why didn't we act sooner? Marion was too scared of how Graham would react if she spoke out. He threatened to get rid of her and the baby she refused to abort. She had other reasons too."

"Such as," asked Luke.

"Remember what I told you that Dave said when I first complained," said Serena. "He was mine during the week, and being with someone at the weekend meant nothing; it was just a bit of fun. I soon discovered that he saw other women who had nothing to do with the parties. That convinced me I'd been a fool and should do what I could to escape him. With Marion, it was different. She had lovers during the week, but they were men she'd slept with at parties. I only found that out after we were both single again. I called her to ask if she wanted to meet for a coffee. There was another man with her at the flat."

"The flat she had before she married Graham?" asked Luke.

"I moved in with Dave when we got married," said Serena, "Dave rented the flat out to another girl; no doubt she was another of his conquests. Marion moved in with Graham in '84 when they married, and he did the same thing, rented the flat out after she left him. When they finalised the details of their divorce, Graham gave Marion the flat plus a cash sum he described as being for Martyn. Marion said Graham wanted to make sure she didn't reveal anything of what happened during their relationship. So she lived in that flat until she married Theo Reeves."

"Did Marion hang onto it?" asked Gus.

"You've seen their home in Oakley Road," said Serena. "Marion sold the flat when she and Theo married. The money gave them a brilliant start to married life. The mortgage they took out was a fraction of what most couples who moved into those new builds needed."

"Theo didn't mention that," said Gus. "Did he know where the money came from?"

"Marion told him her grandfather had left her the money. How could Theo check? Before they met in the Haunch of Venison, Marion's life was a closed book."

"Can you give us the names of Marion's lovers?" asked Gus.

"Did she continue to see them after she met Theo Reeves?" asked Luke.

Serena shook her head.

"No, Marion wanted to put her past life behind her for good. So Marion severed all links with anyone she met between arriving in Salisbury and the night she met Theo. A clean break and a fresh start. That was how she described it the first time we met for a chat after they met."

"What did you talk about on the Sunday afternoon before she died?" asked Gus.

"We sat over there by the window," said Serena. "I could tell straight away something was troubling her."

"Was it to do with Theo or the children?" asked Gus.

"Or was it something from her past she was desperate to keep hidden?"

"An ex-lover was blackmailing Marion," said Serena. "She received an envelope in the mail Thursday morning at the print firm where she worked. The envelope contained photos of Marion taken at several of the parties."

"Intimate photos?" asked Gus.

"Marion's face was in every photo, but the faces of the men and women had been pixilated to hide their identities."

"Where is that envelope now?" asked Gus. "What did Marion do with the photos? Was there a note inside demanding money?"

"The only thing Marion had received before we met on Sunday afternoon was the envelope and those pictures."

"Had you arranged to meet here that day?" asked Luke.

"No, Marion called me on her mobile on Thursday afternoon. We met as often as we could without raising Theo's suspicion. Weekends were best because Marion could drive here to chat with me, knowing Martyn wouldn't suddenly walk in and see us together."

"Martyn likes you," said Luke.

"I know," said Serena, "but we couldn't risk him saying something at home. Martyn didn't understand the meaning of keeping something secret."

"Did Marion tell you she had withdrawn six thousand pounds in cash on Friday?" asked Gus.

"She told me on Sunday afternoon. I asked her how and when the blackmailer had contacted her. I warned Marion that the blackmailer would keep coming back for more unless she got every available copy and the negatives. Marion told me nobody had contacted her yet, but she had no money left from the divorce settlement. So she hoped to persuade them to take the six thousand and walk away."

"Did Marion show you the photos?" asked Gus.

"Heavens, no," said Serena.

"Did she describe them in any way?" asked Luke.

"I told you earlier that Dave was into extreme sex games, and the longer the group stayed together, the more the boundaries shifted. Graham was into role-playing and BDSM. We both hated what we had to submit to, but we went along with it and pretended to enjoy it to please our husbands. I can imagine how distressing it must have been for Marion to see those photos turn up after over twenty years."

"Have you ever received any blackmail demands, Ms Campbell?" asked Gus.

"No, thank goodness. Marion didn't tell me who she thought was behind it, but I guess someone she met at a party she later took as a lover. Perhaps they wanted the liaison to continue, but Marion ended the affair, stuck to her guns, and stayed loyal to Theo."

"Did you hear from Marion after she left here on Sunday afternoon?" asked Gus.

"Only a text on Monday morning," said Serena. "The blackmailer must have waited until Theo and the children left the house and contacted Marion on her mobile."

"Marion kept the same number regardless of the handset she bought," said Gus. "So it could have been from someone she met twenty years ago."

"What did the text message you received say," asked Gus.

"The caller must have been waiting close to her home," said Serena. "They called while the builders were reversing their van onto the drive. They mentioned that, and they'd seen Stephanie cycle to school. So they told Marion to drive to the Churchfields Industrial Estate. She was to park on Stephenson Road and wait until they arrived."

"They could have done a circuit of the estate first checking for a police presence," said Luke. "Was there any sign whether the blackmailer was a man or a woman?"

"None," said Serena. "Whoever they were, they must have killed Marion."

"Why, though?" asked Gus.

"They could have argued over the money," said Serena. "When Marion told them the six grand was all she had, they could have flipped," said Serena. "Surely, that's the logical explanation? Or the ex-lover wanted to pick up where they left off, and Marion refused. That could have triggered a violent assault if the person was obsessed with Marion."

"Did Marion ever mention someone from her past who threatened her when she ended their relationship?"

"Marion didn't tell me the names of the men she saw," said Serena. "I might have recognised their faces if I'd seen them together. I could have been with them myself at a party. But, unfortunately, we didn't make a habit of exchanging names, addresses, and telephone numbers, so I couldn't help you identify them."

"Who do you know that owns a pick-up truck?" asked Gus.

"You'll find a dozen outside in the car park this afternoon, Mr Freeman," said Serena. "In a rural area like this, it's all 4x4s, Land Rovers, and pick-up trucks. Why do you ask?"

"Eyewitnesses said Marion talked to the driver of a pick-up truck in Wilton on Friday afternoon. She was on the pavement outside the bank where she'd just withdrawn the six thousand pounds."

"You think they were stalking Marion, checking she did as they asked?" asked Serena.

"The blackmailer didn't demand money at any point, Ms Campbell," said Gus. "Even the last text message Marion received only gave her instructions about the meeting place. There was never any mention of a sum of money."

"So, how relevant is that truck driver, guv?" asked Luke.

"We can't discount the driver yet, Luke," said Gus. "The eyewitnesses thought Marion knew the man. Perhaps it was Ralph Tucker, our mischievous tree surgeon. Arthur Jackson told us he would have been doing odd jobs around the local area."

"Ralph drives a monster truck," said Serena. "Well, he would, wouldn't he? It suits his personality. Arthur told me Ralph tormented Martyn when he started work here. A crowd of Ralph's cronies got Martyn drunk and made fun of him. Ralph's a nasty individual, but he's too young to have been to any of the parties. He might earn a comfortable living, but he wasn't in the same league as the pixilated faces in those photos."

Another potential lead quashed, thought Gus. What was it with this case? One by one, any possible suspects vanished before their eyes.

"When did the bullying stop?" asked Luke. "Was it before you started work here?"

"Oh, gosh, yes," said Serena. "Arthur put a stop to that nonsense. I watched what was happening earlier when Martyn jumped out of his chair. Something you said struck a nerve. That's typical of his behaviour. Calm as you like for weeks, and then the slightest thing can make him explode. I could tell you were wary of what he might do. He's such a big man. That was Arthur's doing. Martyn was never a seven-stone weakling, but when Ralph and his friends picked on an eighteen-year-old Martyn, Arthur lent a hand. He got Martyn involved in weight training by persuading the lad he needed to improve to enable him to carry out his work here better. So, Martyn went at it full-tilt, like everything else he does here. One of Ralph's mates nudged Martyn in the back while trimming the edges of the lawn. Arthur wanted the finish to be as neat as possible. Martyn strode after the chap and shoved him face-first into a firethorn hedge. They kept their distance after that. He had the strength to go with his already size-able frame."

"Where did Martyn do his weight training?" asked Gus.

"You would have to ask Arthur," said Serena, "I'm not a huge fan of such places. However, I enjoy swimming to keep fit, and as long as I can lift a glass of wine, that's good enough for me."

"I've made a note of it, guv," said Luke.

"Will we be much longer?" asked Serena. "I've missed the rush hour sitting here with you. My supervisor will land me with the washing-up."

"I don't think there's anything we haven't asked, Ms Campbell," said Gus. "If you change your mind about giving us those names, please call me on this number.

Gus handed her a card.

"There was one thing," said Gus, taking a leaf out of Blessing's playbook. "You said you could take a stab at the names of women who might have had children by Graham Street. Can you write the most likely women on the back of that card? I'll give you another one. I've got plenty."

Luke stayed at the table while Serena Campbell scribbled three names. Gus visited the toilets before the trip back to the office.

"An afternoon of surprises, Luke," said Gus when they were in the car motoring on the A360.

"We should get back to the office in forty minutes, guv," said Luke. "Just enough time to brief the team on the highlights before they head home."

"How many places in the Wilton area offer weight training facilities, Luke?"

"I'd need to check that one, guv. If you're after a men-only, serious weights type of club, then one or two. Women lift weights, too, as part of a structured fitness regime. There could be half-a-dozen businesses covering all aspects of well-being."

"Can it be a coincidence Marion Reeves died on Stephenson Road, only forty yards from a gym?"

"The blackmailer told Marion to park on Stephenson Road, guv," said Luke. "They didn't specify where, and from what you and Lydia said about the size of the site, Stephenson Road covers a lot of ground."

"We need confirmation from Arthur Jackson," said Gus. "He's four years older than me. Even twenty years ago, when Martyn started adding muscle to his enormous frame, I can't picture Arthur Jackson renewing a gym membership yearly."

"What did you make of Serena Campbell's story?" asked Luke.

"I see no reason not to believe the lady," said Gus.

"Why are young women so gullible?" asked Luke.

"I'm sure there are a dozen reasons, Luke," said Gus. "In Serena and Marion's case, look at their family lives. Marion arrived in Salisbury from Ringwood after her parent's marriage ended. Marion had no father on the scene in her early teens. How did her mother cope with the split and a growing daughter? Why didn't her Mum intervene when Marion played truant from school? Where was she when Marion stayed out late or came home drunk? Did she report Marion missing when she started staying the night at Graham Street's place? We don't know; there could have been a combination of things to explain that. The same applies to Serena. Her parents came up trumps a decade after Serena left home, but what were they doing when she started smoking, drinking, and skipping school at fourteen? Serena slept with Dave Francis when she was fifteen. I hope I'd better protect a child of mine from evil men like Street and Francis."

"I bet you don't regret not having kids, guv," said Luke. "They must be a constant worry for parents."

"But then I look around the Old Police Station office and look at the five of you. Despite the grey hairs that you caused your parents, you've turned out okay. Although, some days, I wonder whether they've passed that worry onto me."

Luke thought of the arguments he had with his father when he first came out and thought Gus would have handled it better.

147

Chapter Ten

"RIGHT," said Gus when he and Luke arrived back in the office. "Listen up; it's twenty minutes before the end of play for the day. I hoped to have time to give you extended highlights of our meetings with Martyn Street and Serena Campbell, but time is tight. So how did you get on with Theo Reeves, Lydia?"

"I showed him photos of Billie Wightman, Matt Price, Phil Youngman, Warren Baker and an assortment of uniformed officers and forensics people, guv. There was nobody among the list that didn't at one point set foot inside the tent."

"Good. How did Theo react?"

"Theo Reeves recognised Wightman and Price at once. He said they were the detectives who visited him frequently after the murder. I watched as Theo scanned the array of photos. I'd swear he wasn't trying to pull the wool over my eyes, guv. He said he didn't recognise any of the others. He shrugged when I asked whether he thought Marion might have known them."

"Did you ask him to explain?" asked Gus.

"Of course, guv," said Lydia. "Theo said that he'd questioned just how well he had known Marion over the past seven years. He was positive he'd seen none of those faces during their twenty-three years married. If she knew one, or more, of those people, it was before they met."

"Did you stay with Theo long?" asked Gus.

"He offered to make me a cup of coffee, guv. I reckon he's lonely."

"I'm sure you got him talking, Lydia," said Gus. "Don't keep us in suspense."

"I didn't tell him the real reason for the visit, guv. Theo thinks it was for clarification only. He asked why the lady who spent the most time at the house wasn't among the people on my list."

"Family Liaison Officer, guv," said Neil. "Had to be. She would have looked after Stephanie and perhaps kept Martyn calm while Wightman and Price interviewed their father."

"Get me the name of that woman first thing in the morning," said Gus. "Let's get off home. I sense tomorrow could be our breakthrough day.

"Can't you give us just one highlight, guv?" asked Blessing.

"They serve an excellent fruit loaf in the garden centre cafe, Blessing," said Gus.

He was in the lift and making for the Ford Focus before anyone could ask another question.

"Come on, Luke, spill the beans," said Neil. "We've got fifteen minutes before we leave."

"The news of Graham Street's death hadn't reached Wilton," said Luke. "Neither of the three people we spoke to this afternoon was aware he was dead. We didn't inform

Martyn Street because Arthur Jackson told us we couldn't predict his reaction. They prefer to keep him on an even keel. Nobody mentioned whether Martyn takes any medication to assist in that process. We learned from Arthur Jackson that Ralph Tucker, a tree surgeon, was behind the drunken night and the frequent bullying Martyn suffered after he started work on the estate twelve years ago. Unfortunately, Tucker wasn't on-site that day, nor was he the truck driver Marion Reeves saw in Wilton on Friday afternoon. He might be worth an interview, but we're still hunting that pick-up driver."

"If Tucker wasn't working on the estate, then he could have driven to the industrial estate," said Alex. "Has Gus ruled him out?"

"Not yet," said Luke. "Gus can't see how the guy could have a motive. Tucker knew Martyn, but nobody has ever said he knew Marion Reeves. Serena Campbell told us Tucker was too young to attend the parties, anyway."

"Hang on," said Neil. "The parties? What parties?"

"I'll get to that later, Neil," said Luke. "Martyn told us Marion wanted him to forget about his father and their time living in his house. Martyn tried but said he couldn't. Street hit Marion frequently, even when she was pregnant with Martyn."

"That fits with the picture I got when I delved into his background, Luke," said Neil. "A nasty piece of work, who convinced wealthy, important people he was a decent bloke."

"Arthur Jackson confirmed that on the day of the murder, he kept in contact with Martyn and the rest of the ground staff via walkie-talkie. Each employee carries a unit with them throughout the day. Because of the distance they have to cover, it's the sensible way to check their progress and move them around if an urgent repair crops up."

"That means nobody working in the grounds of Wilton House could have been the killer," said Lydia. "Did Gus think someone there wanted Marion dead? If so, why?"

"Gus is keeping our options open at present," said Luke. "As he said to Serena Campbell before we started our conversation, we didn't learn many additional facts from Theo or Stephanie. Likewise, this afternoon we added precious little from our chat with Martyn. Gus hoped that what Serena added to our scraps of information would gel into a giant arrow pointing at the killer."

"Forever the optimist," said Neil.

"Gus's last question caused Martyn to explode with rage," said Luke. "Gus went as white as a sheet. I thought Martyn would throw the table across the room to get at him."

"What did he ask him?" asked Alex.

"Theo and Stephanie didn't get in touch with Martyn after Theo insisted he leave Oakley Road. Gus told Martyn his sister was expecting a baby with Danny Ellis. He suggested Martyn phoned Stephanie for a chat."

"That caused him to go crazy?" said Neil.

"Martyn said he was alone when he moved into his new place. The only people who cared were Arthur Jackson and Serena Campbell. He felt abandoned. His Mum had stressed the importance of family, and Martyn got upset because he said everybody lied to him, except Arthur and Serena."

"We've read the Freeman Files and the report Gus and Blessing added relating to this morning's meeting with Stephanie Reeves," said Alex. "So, we know Serena was

Marion's best friend. I assume the parties you referred to were where the two met?"

"They met soon after Marion moved to Salisbury from Ringwood," said Luke. "Marion and Serena fell into the clutches of Graham Street and a guy called Dave Francis. Those two characters procured attractive young women, some underage, and introduced them to a group of wealthy people who enjoyed weekend sex parties."

"Gross," said Blessing.

"Dave Francis and Serena married two years after they met. She was just seventeen. Graham Street married Marion soon after. That was in 1984. Four years later, she gave birth to Martyn, much against her husband's wishes. She was no good to him if he couldn't take her to these parties and share her among his friends."

"We know Theo met Marion while she was getting divorced from Street," said Neil. "What happened to Serena?"

"She left Dave Francis, returned to her parents, and divorced him. Marion walked out on Graham several months later. Two things we learned from Serena this afternoon. One, Marion got the flat Street set her up in as part of the divorce settlement. Two, Marion sold it when she married Theo and convinced him the money she suddenly had available was a windfall from a dead grandparent. Oh, and there was one more thing added to the divorce settlement. Marion agreed never to reveal anything that happened when she knew Graham Street."

"A non-disclosure agreement?" said Blessing. "Doesn't something else apply to a married couple?"

"It's complicated, Blessing," said Alex, "but they were no longer married. Street had total control over Marion during the relationship, and he would not relinquish that when she walked away. He knew what trouble she could cause him if she talked."

"The original investigation couldn't find a connection between Street and Marion's murder," said Blessing. "They uncovered nothing related to these sex parties either. So why didn't they interview Serena Campbell or Dave Francis? Their names aren't in the murder file."

"Excellent spot, Blessing," said Luke. "Serena Campbell told us this swingers group, or whatever you want to call them, was well-connected. A high-ranking police officer and his wife attended these parties in the early years. Serena claimed he steered the murder investigation in a different direction. Gus believed her. We know Marion's mobile phone went missing too, and the forensics guy, Warren Baker, could be responsible for its disappearance. We don't yet know whether he was a participant in the parties or acted on orders from above, we don't yet know. Finding the name of that police officer will be another job for first thing in the morning. As Gus said, tomorrow should be interesting."

"Blimey," said Neil. "This group must have clout if they've kept a lid on goings-on such as that for over twenty years. My Dad never heard a whisper. You know how close Dad had his ear to the ground."

"Someone broke ranks seven years ago, Neil," said Luke. "Serena told us that Marion Reeves received intimate photos of her at these parties. There was no note, no demand. The envelope arrived on Thursday, and on the following day, she withdrew the cash. On Saturday, she called Serena, and they arranged to meet in the café the following afternoon. That was when Serena learned what had happened. On Monday morning, Serena received a text message from Marion saying the blackmailer wanted to meet her on Stephenson Road at Churchfields Industrial Estate. As Gus pointed out, at no time was any sum of money ever mentioned."

"If Marion Reeves had six grand in her handbag, why did she die?" asked Alex. "It makes little sense."

"Even if her killer was angry that six grand was everything Marion had that day," said Lydia. "Most blackmailers keep the victim on the hook and squeeze them for money any way they can."

"What happened to the photographs?" asked Blessing.

"They never found them," said Neil. "Perhaps Marion Reeves had already destroyed them; if she had them in the car, her killer would have taken them, plus the money. They could destroy the photos whenever they wished."

"What happened to the lunchbox then?" asked Blessing.

Lydia laughed.

"You won't forget that lunchbox, will you, Blessing? Are you hungry?"

"We only had Stephanie's word that her mother took a packed lunch every day," said Alex.

"Not now," said Luke. "Martyn Street confirmed Marion gave him a packed lunch every day before she died. It's another gold star to Blessing. So why *didn't* they find it in the car?"

"I can't wait until tomorrow," said Blessing.

"You can help me first thing in the morning, Blessing," said Luke. "Serena Campbell gave us the names of three women who may have given birth to a child by Graham Street. I'm not sure of the relevance yet, but Gus wanted to check them out."

"It's time we disappeared, folks," said Neil. "We've had

more than enough highlights for one day. Anyone fancy a party?"

"Gross," said Blessing.

AS HIS TEAM made their way down in the lift, Gus Freeman drove past Wadworth's brewery in Devizes. He wondered whether he would see Suzie pulling out of the car park as he made his way along London Road. There had been surprising developments today and yet more setbacks. It still wasn't clear who had the opportunity to murder Marion Reeves. Indeed, Gus wasn't sure he understood the motive.

If Graham Street was so concerned with what Marion knew about his past, why wait twenty years to take action? The same went for Dave Francis. Serena walked away and divorced him without the golden handshake of a free flat or a cash settlement. Serena had mentioned no document she signed swearing not to talk of the sex parties and who attended. So why didn't Francis take the same precautions as Street? Gus wondered if he was wrong to take everything Serena said as gospel. Had her good looks blinded him to the fact she was as much a threat to Francis as Marion was to Graham Street?

Gus continued to mull this over as he drove into Urchfont. Finally, he parked the Focus beside the bungalow and went indoors. Gus had been so engrossed in his thoughts that he'd forgotten to look towards the Wiltshire Police HQ. Less than a minute after he hung his jacket on the back of a kitchen chair, Suzie breezed through the front door.

"I was two cars behind you from the car park to the junction," she said. "Didn't you see me waving and flashing my headlights?"

"I was watching the road ahead," said Gus.

"I'll bet," said Suzie. "My money is on that case of yours. You're stuck, and it's occupying your every waking minute."

"As it happens," said Gus, "we might make a break-through in the morning. I can't deny I wasn't considering the case on the way home, but I can't tell you too much, I'm afraid."

"Now you've got my interest," said Suzie. She closed the distance between them and held him close. "Are you sure there's nothing you want to tell me?"

"If what Luke and I learned this afternoon is true, then if word gets out that we're pursuing a particular line of enquiry, it could put us in danger. The fewer people that know, the better."

"I don't like the sound of that, Gus," said Suzie. "Why can't you get a simple murder case to solve? You've survived an assassination attempt from Albanian gangsters, brought a dirty cop to justice, and rescued me from Terry Davis's killer. What have you got mixed up in this time?"

"Weekend parties that featured extreme sex games, BDSM, and several TLIs," said Gus.

"I've read about BDSM," said Suzie, "but it's never appealed. As for TLIs, I can't imagine what deviant behaviour is involved there.

"Nor can I," said Gus. "But so many things are covered by three-letter initials these days, I threw it in to cover every-thing that might have gone on."

"You never change, do you," said Suzie. "You use humour to convince me there's nothing to worry over. So be careful, darling, please."

"Are we staying here moulded together the whole evening?" asked Gus.

"No, you need to shower, get changed, and get to your allotment. You can have an hour's gardening while you plan how to avoid getting hurt, and then I'll join you. We're eating in the Lamb tonight. Our table's booked for eight o'clock."

"Fair enough," said Gus. "I've only eaten a slice of fruit loaf since breakfast. I could eat a horse."

"I didn't hear that," said Suzie. "Get in the shower."

A few minutes after six, Gus walked through the gateway of the allotments and scanned the area for fellow gardeners. He'd checked his maths as he walked along the lane. Suzie had said an hour on the land, and they were eating at eight o'clock. Something was going on.

"Good evening, Gus,"

Clemency Bentham was kneeling by her rows of lettuces, radishes, and other salad crops.

"Trouble, Reverend?" asked Gus. "Do your plants need heavenly help? They look fine from where I'm standing."

"I got down here to avoid bending for an extended period, Gus. Although my diet has had limited success, I cannot get back to my feet without outside help. Prayer won't help me. Can you give me your arm, please?"

Gus helped the Reverend back to her feet without comment. He knew when words weren't necessary.

"Thank you, Gus," said Clemency. "Is Suzie still coming along later?"

"Still?" asked Gus. "I'm guessing this is something you two are aware of, but I'm to be kept in the dark."

"We're hoping there will be an announcement at seven o'clock in the Lamb," said Clemency.

"Has Bert Penman been here today?" asked Gus.

"I haven't seen him," said the Reverend. "Now I'm back

on my feet; I'll cycle home and get ready to get to the pub later. Bye for now."

With that, she was off. Gus opened his garden shed, found the required tools, and set to work. Whatever was happening at seven o'clock, he couldn't waste time thinking about it now. His vegetable patch needed work.

Suzie strolled up at a few minutes to seven, looking as fresh as a daisy.

"What's going on?" he asked.

"Not much, by the looks of it. I thought you would have done more in an hour," said Suzie.

"Am I okay to visit the pub in this state?" asked Gus, returning his tools to the shed.

"You'll be alright for ten minutes," said Suzie. "then you can dash back to the bungalow, shower and change while I enjoy a cold drink in the beer garden with the Reverend."

"You've got it worked out, haven't you?" said Gus.

"Someone has to. It wouldn't get done if we left it to you men."

Gus bought the drinks and followed Suzie outside into the beer garden. Clemency was already there with Brett Penman. They both look pleased with themselves. Gus wondered whether they were making the announcement. An engagement, perhaps? They hadn't been seeing one another long, but who was he to judge?

"Hello, you two," said Brett. "Glad you could make it."

"Making it wasn't a problem," said Gus. "Understanding why we're here is another matter."

Gus and Suzie took a seat next to Brett and Clemency.

"Busy day?" asked Brett.

"Challenging," said Gus.

"Mr Freeman, Miss Ferris. I hoped you would be here."

Bert Penman's voice rang out from the pub doorway.

Gus couldn't be confident from this distance, but Bert appeared to be wearing a suit. When his old friend finally walked outside into the sunlight, Gus saw that Irene North had joined him. She must have dug deep in her wardrobe to find a dress he'd never seen her wear. It knocked ten years off her.

Bert carried the tray with their drinks to the table, and when he and Irene were seated, Bert cleared his throat.

"We thought you four should hear the news from us before anyone in the village starts talking," he said, taking a large sip of his pint of cider. "Irene agrees with me. It's daft keeping two properties going when we spend so much time together. My place is big enough for two good friends to live under the same roof."

"What other people think of what we plan to do doesn't concern us," said Irene. "We'll save money, and we're both sensible enough to realise that having someone around the place will benefit us when one of us doesn't feel so good."

"It's a great idea, whoever first thought of it," said Gus. "I wish you both health and happiness. Then, when the time comes, and you need someone to lend a hand, you know who to call."

"We're not staying after this drink, Mr Freeman," said Irene. "There's a programme on TV that Bertie and I want to watch."

"I'll walk up the lane with you," said Gus. "I'm under orders to shower and change before they let me inside to eat."

Bert never took long to demolish a pint, so Gus was on his way to the bungalow in a matter of minutes. Brett and Clemency agreed to keep Suzie company until he returned.

"We'll cycle home at eight o'clock when you go for your meal," said the Reverend. "I've got two eulogies to prepare

for funerals tomorrow afternoon. So don't worry, Gus. I'll
be extra careful not to mix them up."

Wednesday, 22 August 2018

GUS AND SUZIE left the bungalow at eight-thirty. After
Brett accompanied Clemency to the rectory, he and Suzie
went inside to eat. When Gus went to the bar at the end of
the evening, the landlord told him Bert and Irene had left
enough money behind the bar to cover the bill.

"Don't know what's got into Bert," the landlord said.
"He didn't seem himself tonight."

"It was the suit," said Gus. "The only time he's worn it
was at Frank North's funeral."

"No, not the suit. Bert's usually cadging drinks off the
likes of you, Mr Freeman, not putting his hand in his
pocket."

Gus smiled to himself as he stood by the Focus.

"See you at the usual time tonight, darling?" asked
Suzie.

"No reason to be later than half-past five," said Gus.

"Remember what I said. Take care," said Suzie.

Gus followed Suzie along the lane, past the Lamb,
and eased the Focus into heavy traffic on the main road.
They moved slowly onto London Road before Suzie
turned into the Headquarters car park, and then Gus
watched traffic thin out as he reached the top of Caen
Hill. With a following wind, he should be in the office
before nine o'clock. Gus realised he hadn't given the
Marion Reeves case a second thought since he drove
home last night.

The team was already hard at work when Gus exited the lift at one minute past nine.

"Did those temporary traffic lights at Redstocks catch you, guv?" asked Neil.

"They did. What are the Highways Department digging up the road for now?" asked Gus.

"It's on the schedule for this week, guv. They don't need a reason."

"Everyone has things to do," said Gus. "I need to update my files with what we learned yesterday afternoon. When do you want to hear the highlights?"

"Luke went through them last night after you dashed away, guv," said Lydia.

"Right, well, I'll carry on then," said Gus.

"Before you get stuck in, guv," said Neil. "Luke's doing the same as you, updating his files. Alex is arranging the next set of interviews. Blessing is finding Graham Street's children and Lydia's tracing that Family Liaison Officer. I'm hoping to identify the senior police officer that could have attended those parties from 1980 to 1984."

"It sounds like you got most things covered," Gus said. "Luke, if you get a minute can you check on that gym with Arthur Jackson, please?"

"I haven't forgotten, guv," said Luke.

Gus had finished updating the Freeman files by ten o'clock. When he glanced across the office at Luke, he was on the phone. Neil Davis looked puzzled while Blessing and Lydia were in the restroom. Gus hoped it was coffee time for everyone. He was right. The restroom door opened two minutes later, and the girls returned with drinks.

"Your turn tomorrow, guys," said Blessing.

"Luke, did you speak to Arthur Jackson?" asked Gus, taking a sip of a well-earned coffee.

"Just got off the phone, guv. Arthur introduced Martyn Street to the gym owner on Churchfields Industrial Estate. Arthur's son, Keith, was a keen bodybuilder. Martyn joined the gym in 2006 and continued to use the gym once a week for three years. The original owner had sold up by then, and their maintenance problems started soon after the new people took over. Martyn had cut back to training once a month but got frustrated with arriving to find a notice telling him it was closed for repairs. Arthur said Martyn didn't renew his membership in 2010."

"I'd get frustrated if I walked from his flat to the gym and found it closed," said Neil. "How far is that, anyway?"

"It overlooks the Wilton House estate," said Luke. "It's the same distance Martin used to walk from Oakley Road to work. That took him thirty minutes."

"An hour's exercise without needing to pay for a gym membership," said Neil. "That works for me."

"Thanks, Neil," said Gus. "A coincidence, I suppose, that the blackmailer chose Stephenson Road and a spot close to a building associated with the victim's mother."

"We discussed this yesterday, guv," said Blessing Umeh. "You and Lydia agreed the killer chose to meet there because of its position. The length of the road and the number of vehicles present meant the two cars that arrived at half-past nine that morning were hiding in plain sight. So the premises on that road don't necessarily have any relevance."

"I stand corrected, DC Umeh," said Gus.

"I still want to know what happened to the lunchbox, guv," said Blessing. "If we can explain that, our view of where the cars parked could change."

"Have you put in for your Sergeant's exam yet, Blessing?" asked Gus.

"No guv. I'm not twenty-two yet, and if my father gets his way, I'll marry someone I don't know before getting promoted."

Gus made a mental note to make sure he kept the best people where he could see them. This team would inevitably attract others across the county and beyond in time. But, unfortunately, he'd lost several excellent Detective Sergeants before he retired. His superiors told him it was his fault for training them too well.

Gus had told them if a job's worth doing, it's worth doing well, but their decisions never got reversed, and he had to start over again with another raw recruit. Enough was enough. Time to dig his heels in. When they solved this case, he would plant the seeds in Kenneth Truelove's head that if anyone came poaching his team, the Chief Constable had two choices. Tell them to take a running jump or look for another mug to come out of retirement to handle those cold cases piled high on his swish new desk.

"Everything alright, guv?" asked Lydia.

"Everything's fine for the time being, Lydia. I was planning my next move."

"I've found the Family Liaison Officer who spent so much time with the Reeves family, guv. Unfortunately, she's left the job since 2011, but we can still interview Genevieve Harding. Ms Harding lives near the Hampshire border, on the outskirts of Salisbury."

"Alex, can you add the lady to our list, please?" said Gus. "How old is Genevieve? Do we know?"

"Forty-eight, guv," said Lydia.

"Three years younger than Marion Reeves at the time of the murder," said Gus. "Interesting. Have you got a schedule yet for my interviews, Alex?"

"The two builders are first on the list, guv. They're

working on a small housing estate in Bemerton Heath. Your invitation to attend Bourne Hill nick did not attract them. They preferred to make themselves available first thing after lunch today. We can drive over to talk to them at one o'clock."

"Is there anyone I can fit in this morning?" asked Gus.

"Phil Youngman is retired these days. I can ring him now if you wish."

"Give me his number, and I'll make the arrangements," said Gus. "Who else?"

"I thought it made sense for you to get an overview of how they handled the murder scene before you spoke to Warren Baker, guv. Phil Youngman should remember who did what, when, and where on the day. He was in charge of most of it as he was first on the scene."

"That makes perfect sense, Alex. Good thinking. When can I get to Warren Baker?"

"I'll set it up for first thing tomorrow, guv. You can drive straight to Bourne Hill and speak to him before forensics receive their first call. When I contacted them yesterday, they said that Baker and the rest of the crew spend most of the day out of the office."

"How long do you think we'll spend with Milligan and Preston?" asked Gus.

"They will want to get back to work, guv," said Alex. "Who did you think we could catch later this afternoon?"

"The tree surgeon, Ralph Tucker," said Gus. "I'm prepared to accept Serena Campbell's word he wasn't the truck driver talking to Marion Reeves outside her bank, but he could have been at Churchfields on Monday morning."

"Arthur Jackson told us they used Tucker on the estate between May and September, guv," said Luke. "Ralph should be there tomorrow. Bemerton Heath to Wilton

House is only a brief trip. Gus should be able to meet him by three o'clock at a push."

"Thanks, Luke," said Alex. "I'll get onto it."

Alex handed Phil Youngman's phone number to Gus and called Ralph Tucker's mobile number.

Gus called Phil Youngman.

"Phil, it's Gus Freeman here. Remember me?"

"Blimey, you're a blast from the past. Did I hear you went back to work after Tess died? I was sorry to hear about that, by the way."

"Yes, it's been a long time, Phil," said Gus. "I sat on my allotment with nothing positive to think of for three years until Ken Truelove called me. We're reviewing unsolved murders now. I'm sure you remember the Marion Reeves case?"

"Hard to forget the inside of that car, Gus. It was too much for the young PC I had with me that morning. She left the force after a couple of months. What did you want to know?"

"Can I drive over and have a chat now?" asked Gus. "I should reach you in an hour."

"I'll have the kettle on," said Phil. "Coffee?"

"Black with no sugar, Phil," said Gus. "How's retirement, anyway?"

"Always under the wife's feet. I get tired quicker than I used to when the grandkids are here, and I can't pick up the local rag without seeing another old colleague who's dropped off the perch. There is an upside to it, of course."

"A lot less paperwork," said Gus.

"You got it," said Phil. "See you in an hour."

"Are we good, Alex," he said.

"I fixed the meeting with Ralph Tucker for three o'clock this afternoon, guv. Warren Baker will be in his Bourne

Hills office at nine o'clock. He can't think why you need to speak with him."

"An interesting start to the day, then," said Gus. "Send directions to the housing estate on the Heath to my phone. Then, I'll drive to meet you for our meeting with MP Builders at one."

"Will do, guv. Have a pleasant trip."

Gus was already striding towards the lift. Alex believed Gus was right. Today was a breakthrough day.

Chapter Eleven

GUS ARRIVED in Downton and weaved his way towards Greenacres. He knew the village well because he and Tess had lived not half a mile from where Phil Youngman was spending his retirement. Gus had heard his phone 'ping' when Alex sent a message while driving along the A338. Plenty of time to check the directions later.

As he stood outside the compact semi-detached house, Gus admired the garden. Someone had green fingers. The flowers that bordered the lawn looked magnificent. Finally, a short, grey-haired lady answered the doorbell.

"Mrs Youngman?" said Gus. "Can Phil come out to play?"

"Och, get away with you, Gus Freeman. You'll never change. And it's Phyllis, as you well know. I worked in the back office at Bourne Hill when you were just a young whippersnapper in uniform."

"That's more years ago than I care to remember, Phyllis," said Gus. "Somehow, you don't look any older than when you left to have your first child."

"If only; Phil's in the front room. He put the kettle on as he told you, but I still have to pour the coffee for you both."

Phyllis scuttled along the hallway to the kitchen, and Gus joined Phil.

"Good to see you again," said Phil, shaking Gus warmly by the hand.

"You might revise your opinion on that when I tell you why I'm here," said Gus.

Phyllis appeared in the doorway with two large mugs of coffee and a plate of biscuits. Gus could tell Phil hoped this chat would fill a quiet morning.

"Has something turned up after all this time?" asked Phil.

"You were first on the scene with that unfortunate PC you mentioned," said Gus. "Let's start from there. It's not what we found that concerns us."

"Headquarters received a call from a member of the public," said Phil. "A bloke who worked out at the industrial estate at Churchfields. We arrived on Stephenson Road to find him standing several yards away from a parked car. Vehicles drove past in both directions, and parked cars and trucks were on both sides of the road. On the right-hand side, the nearest car was about forty yards further up the road. As soon as I got out of the car, I could see where the bloke had puked on the grass verge. He was in shock and just pointed to the Lexus."

"You did everything by the book as far as we can tell, Phil," said Gus. "Did anyone go near the car before the forensic team arrived?"

"I got close enough with my PC to see inside the car, Gus. There was blood everywhere. The driver, later identi- fied as Marion Reeves, slumped over the steering wheel. We didn't touch the car, and there was no point in checking for

signs of life. She was gone. I called for more uniformed officers because of the size of the site and the many access
points to Stephenson Road. It was lunchtime, and everywhere we looked, there were vehicles on the move and
people milling around close to premises on both sides of the
road. Somehow, we preserved the immediate area. As soon
as I had more people available, we cordoned off the murder
scene, plus an exclusion zone that allowed us to evacuate as
many people as possible. I had to be on my toes that morning, Gus."

"So, you're positive nobody tampered with the Lexus at
any point between you arriving on scene and the forensic
team taking over and erecting their white tent."

"Positive," said Phil. "One hundred percent. Why do
you ask?"

"When Billie Wightman showed Theo Reeves a list of
the contents of his wife's handbag retrieved from the Lexus,
he confirmed nothing was missing. Her purse, bank cards,
keys, and mobile phone were present and correct. But,
when Matt Price and Billie did a brief review of the case a
couple of years later, there was no sign of the mobile phone
in the evidence room."

"What, someone nicked it from the evidence room?"
asked Phil.

"Not according to Matt Price. The phone could have
provided vital information, and after tagging and bagging it
at the scene, it should have been available for the service
provider to give a detailed history. Instead, Billie Wightman
concentrated on the family, work colleagues, and neighbours while waiting for forensic test results to get returned
to her. Billie had a bee in her bonnet."

"The killer had to be a man, either the husband or a
lover," said Phil. "I remember Billie. She was a good detec-

tive until her old man cheated on her, and then she lost the plot."

"Agreed, but the clock is always against you on a murder case. Billie and Matt pursued every line of enquiry they could before their superiors dragged them away to another urgent case. Billie had queried why the mobile phone results were still pending, but she had another case file on her hands before she knew it. When Billie and Matt did the follow-up review, they sent a DC into the evidence room to hunt for the missing phone. He didn't stay long enough to search every box, but he had no luck before getting moved to something else."

"That suggests the mobile phone got mislaid earlier in the piece," said Phil. "Am I right?"

"We're assuming someone removed it after it got tagged and bagged. There are several questions that possibility raises. Who would have wanted to take it? What did they know or suspect on that phone that could prove incriminating?"

"You would know better than me, Gus," said Phil. "The murder file lists every person who entered the tent."

"We've analysed the list, Phil," said Gus. "Did you spot any suspicious behaviour when you went inside?"

"I was in and out at the start of the forensic team's work, Gus. Then again, as things were winding down, Matt Price asked me to remove the external cordon. I doubt I spent two minutes inside the tent, all told. I certainly didn't touch the car or get close to getting inside it. PC Gupta didn't even go near the tent. As for anything suspicious, no, I can't say I noticed that."

"Did the car's contents stay inside the tent until the forensic team left?"

"They set up a small table by the door, Gus," said Phil.

"Somewhere to label and pack items after they got removed. They stored things in large plastic boxes under the table. There wasn't much room inside the tent for people to move around. So, people like Matt and the forensic crew stepped outside often to allow a colleague better access to whatever they were swabbing and photographing."

"Is it possible someone removed a bagged item from the box under the table and slipped it into their pocket or wandered outside with it beyond the inner cordon?"

"There were times it was chaotic that day, Gus," said Phil. "If you had asked me that question seven years ago, I would have said, never, but I don't know now, looking back. Maybe it slipped through the net. Why, though? Do you think the killer was inside the tent? A copper or someone working with the forensics team?"

"We've learned much more about this case since we first discovered the mobile phone was missing," said Gus. "I can't say much, but Marion Reeves had lived another life before meeting her second husband, Theo. It's possible the phone disappeared to prevent a search of its history. The details of names, numbers, times of conversations, and text messages could have incriminated important people."

"Blimey, it was a brutal murder, but I never imagined anything such as this being behind it."

"Did you ever meet FLO Genevieve Harding?" asked Gus.

"Of course," said Phil, "she worked in Salisbury for twenty years. A good lassie. Why?"

"Did you ever see her talking to Warren Baker?"

"The creepy forensics guy, I would hope not. Genevieve was a curvy, attractive woman who kept herself to herself. There were rumours she was seeing a married man, but I didn't find out who he was while I still worked there."

171

"A married police officer?" asked Gus.

"Who else are we going to meet, Gus? I wouldn't have met Phyllis if she hadn't been in the back office. In my view, when you're both in the job, the relationship has a better chance of success. Civilians don't understand us."

"That's enough background for me, Phil. You didn't see anyone slipping that phone in their pocket, and with the many comings and goings, someone might have got away with it with no one being the wiser. We'll keep searching. Thanks for your help. Thank Phyllis for the coffee and biscuits, won't you? Take care, both of you."

Phil saw Gus to the front door. Phyllis joined him on the step, and she waved at Gus as the Focus slowly pulled away from the kerb. Gus stopped in the nearest layby and studied his phone. Sarum Close, just off the A360. Twenty minutes drive at this time of day. Gus realised he had thirty minutes to kill before Alex arrived. This layby was as good a spot as any to mull over what they'd learned since yesterday.

After five minutes, Gus had a thought. He called the Old Police Station office to speak to Neil Davis.

"Alright, guv," said Neil. "Did you get lost?"

"Not a chance, Neil. I'm on familiar ground. How did you get on identifying that senior police officer?"

"Crashed and burned. I dug out the family tree for every station across the force area for the years we were interested in. It would surprise you how many names there were, guv. Of course, you remember the officers who stick around for years, like yourself, no offence. But then, officers are just passing through, people on temporary secondments, and those who retired through ill health."

"Skip to the bottom line, Neil," said Gus.

"I couldn't find anyone whose wife died of cancer during the years I checked."

"Perhaps Serena Campbell got the dates wrong," said Gus.

"I thought of that, guv, and extended the period by two years on either side. Perhaps Ms Campbell got the whole thing wrong, guv. The man at the parties wasn't a senior officer."

"Serena Campbell convinced me she was telling the truth, Neil," said Gus. "Okay, we'll need to grill the woman again. Why don't you and Luke get onto that?"

"Will do, guv. Is that all?"

"Can I speak to Blessing, please?"

"Yes, guv," said Blessing, "How can I help?"

"Have you linked the names from Serena Campbell with Graham Street, Blessing?"

"Kathy Mellor gave birth to a son in 1972. She named him Derek. Kathy married John Preston earlier in the same year."

"Derek Preston, the builder, is one of Graham Street's children? John married Kathy when she was pregnant by another man. Did he know? What a tangled web we have before us, Blessing."

"It gets better, guv, or worse, depending on how you look at it. Sonya Tucker had a baby by Graham Street in 1968. Ralph Tucker, the tree surgeon, is another half-brother of Martyn Street."

"Don't tell me," said Gus. "The third woman's maiden name was Milligan, or she married someone of that name."

"No guv," said Blessing. "Maureen Glendenning had a child, name and whereabouts unknown. She may have put the baby up for adoption. Maureen disappeared soon after the birth. Nobody has seen or heard of her since 1968. She's believed to be living in Spain."

"Many thanks, Blessing," said Gus. "I'm glad I spoke to

you before I met two of Graham Street's children this afternoon. This case was strange at the beginning. Now it's getting surreal."

"Good hunting this afternoon, guv," said Blessing. "Alex should reach Bemerton Heath in fifteen minutes."

Gus ended the call and spent the next fifteen minutes revising every opinion he had of anyone connected to this case. As the clock on the dashboard ticked closer to one o'clock, Gus drove to Sarum Close. Alex had already parked outside the house where MP Builders were working. The van was a giveaway.

Gus parked the Focus and crossed the road to join Alex Hardy.

"Have you heard from Neil, Alex?" he asked.

"We spoke before I left, guv. It frustrated Neil not finding the name of the senior officer."

"Did Blessing share her findings with the rest of you?" asked Gus.

Alex grinned.

"We could tell what Blessing was finding was dynamite, guv," said Alex. "It was as if Ted Hastings was in the room."

"I know what you're on about for a change," said Gus. "Suzie never misses an episode of Line of Duty, although I can't imagine Blessing using the language that character does."

"Not quite," said Alex, "but 'Holy Moly' and 'Heaven help us' told us she'd found something juicy."

"Theo Reeves told us Graham Street fathered children with several women. Until I heard from Blessing thirty minutes ago, I never imagined so many of them connected to the case. It has to be significant, surely?"

"Two conversations this afternoon could give us the

answer to that one, guv. Shall we get Stuart Milligan out of the way first?"

Gus nodded his agreement. They walked up the driveway to where the builders had parked their van. Derek Preston sat inside, eating his lunch. Stuart Milligan stood on the doorstep watching them.

"The owners are at work," he said. "We can do this inside. I'm painting the lounge, so let's use the kitchen."

Gus and Alex followed Milligan along the hallway into the kitchen. The pair had been working here installing a fitted kitchen. He preferred the rustic look of his kitchen at the bungalow. That looked as if its owners used it regularly. This room was more for show than anything else: white goods and chrome everywhere, but no warmth or soul.

"What did you want to ask me?" asked Stuart Milligan.

"Tell us about the Monday morning of the murder," said Gus. "Leave nothing out."

"I arrived at the Reeves's house in Oakley Road at eight-fifteen. As I reversed the van into the corner of the driveway, Theo Reeves was leaving for work. Marion came out of the house to chat with me for a minute, then went back indoors. I started fetching my tools from the van and transferring them to the rooms inside the house where we planned to work that day. Steph, the daughter, was eating breakfast in the kitchen when I passed the door. I said hello; she nodded and carried on eating. Steph cycled to school at around twenty-five past eight, the same time as normal. I heard a mobile phone. It must have been Marion's, but she wasn't talking to anyone. I asked her if everything was okay as she rushed out of the house. She was later than usual; it was after nine. Marion left here fifteen minutes earlier than that every weekday we'd worked here; until that morning."

"Where was Derek while this was going on?" asked Alex.

"Derek was here, moving the gear around and preparing to start work."

"Derek's sat in the passenger seat of your van today," said Alex. "Do you drive everywhere, or do you take it in turns?"

"We've taken it in turns for the twenty years we've worked together. Derek drives his car if he needs to go to the bank or when one of his kids had football practice a few years back. Something which meant he needed to leave his job early. Our kids are old enough to make their own way anywhere these days."

"What about the Monday morning of the murder?" asked Gus. "Was Derek in the van when you arrived?"

"Derek drove his car that day," said Stuart Milligan, "He wanted to bank several cheques that arrived in the post on Saturday. Money was tight, and suppliers were putting pressure on. We need to bolster our bank balance to ensure none of our cheques bounced."

"When did Derek leave the house to visit the bank?" asked Gus. "How long was he away?"

"It was after Marion left. No later than a quarter past nine. I wasn't checking the clock, but he must have returned before ten."

"Are you certain of that?" asked Alex.

"How long does it take to drive into town, pay in a few cheques and drive back?" said Stuart. "Ask him when you finish talking to me."

"According to Theo Reeves," said Alex, "who did that journey every day, it took four or five minutes to reach the town centre. The banks opened at nine, so even with an early morning rush, Derek would have been in and out of the bank in five minutes. So if Derek left no later than nine-fifteen, he should have gotten back here in around fifteen minutes, twenty minutes tops. You said he *must* have returned by ten. Why are you so sure of that?"

"We have the radio on while we're working. There was something on the news bulletin on the hour that we laughed about. I remember what it was. Our kids were young then, and we took them to a Lapland-style theme park in Hampshire just before Christmas. It was a rip-off, and loads of parents complained. They jailed the brothers who set it up for a year that day."

"How can you be sure it wasn't the eleven o'clock news bulletin?" asked Gus.

"If I'd heard it on my own at ten, I would have told Derek when he got back, wouldn't I? But, as I said, check with Derek. See if he remembers what we heard."

"When did you hear about the murder?" asked Alex.

"We'd stopped for lunch," said Stuart. "Theo came home in a state, told us to pack up, and he'd be in touch when he needed us again. A police officer in a uniform arrived as I was driving the van off the driveway. Theo let her in straight away. I knew something serious had happened but didn't find out Marion died until later that day. I thought Steph had got knocked off her bike while cycling to school. Something like that. You never think it will be murder, do you?"

"And Derek?" asked Gus.

"He was still walking to his car. I was going in the opposite direction, so we didn't speak until I rang him later that evening to talk about Marion. We saw her every day; she was a good person."

"You didn't see Stephanie or Martyn?" asked Gus.

"No, I don't know how they got home. I guess the police

collected Steph and Martyn from school and work, then brought them back. The woman I saw arrive in her car was there for that reason."

"A Family Liaison Officer," said Alex. "Yes, that's normal procedure. Did either of you recognise the woman?"

"I'd never seen her before," said Stuart, "Derek was on the pavement walking to his car as she arrived. She was behind him; he might not even have seen her. So I never mentioned her when we spoke later."

Gus tried to make the numbers work while Stuart spoke with Alex. Derek Preston was one of Graham Street's children. Did he know that, or had John and Kathy Preston kept it from him? Could Derek Preston be the killer? That was impossible if he was here with Stuart at ten o'clock.

Time of death could only be one hundred percent accurate when a skilled medical practitioner was present at the exact moment it occurred. So perhaps Marion Reeves died at nine-thirty? But, no, that didn't work either. Serena Campbell told him the text message she received from the blackmailer said they'd seen the builder's van reversing onto the drive and Stephanie leave for school.

Derek Preston was at Oakley Road at nine twenty-five. Stuart Milligan was inside the house, getting ready to start work. The pair weren't together. Derek had arrived in his car and transferred his gear from the van to whichever room in the house he was due to work. Derek could have sent that text message.

Derek Preston left Oakley Road to visit the bank but took a detour to Churchfields.

"I think we're ready to speak to Derek now," he said.

Alex left the kitchen and walked to the front door.

"The van's gone, guv!" he shouted.

"Call it in to Bourne Hill, Alex," said Gus, dashing into the hallway. "Get a general alert bulletin issued to every officer in the area. Preston can't have got far. You know the colour and make of the van, and the signage is a giveaway. Get the registration of the van from Milligan. Ask him for details of the car Preston drives. Send uniforms to his home address as a matter of urgency in case he switches cars. Arrest Preston, and get him into custody. He's wanted in connection to a crime."

"Is Preston our killer, guv?" asked Alex.

"Can't be sure," said Gus. "But everything points to him being our blackmailer."

"I can't believe it," said Stuart. "You must have got it wrong. I've known Derek ever since we were at school."

"Did you know John Preston wasn't his father?" asked Gus.

"You're kidding?" said Stuart.

"Think back to the week after the murder," said Gus. "Did you get a phone call from your bank?"

"Not that I can remember. Why?"

"If you've still got statements going back seven years, I should check Derek paid in those cheques on Monday morning. I bet those statements will show he went to the bank in the days following the murder when you two took time off. Theo didn't want you here until after the funeral. Unless someone had an urgent job to offer you, you had nowhere to go. Am I right?"

"I did a few jobs at home," said Stuart. "What they say about builders is spot-on. Our wives get no running repairs done, even though they've got experts on hand. My wife had nothing to moan about after the ten days to a fortnight I spent ticking off items on her to-do list. I don't know what Derek did while we waited. We went to Oakley Road as soon as Theo called to say we could start work again. It wasn't the same, though. He wasn't that interested in getting it finished. Steph and Martyn were in bits."

"Theo has a slightly different view of that time," said Gus. "He thought you hung around longer than necessary. Theo told us you only went there one day a week. Sometimes you left things unfinished for several weeks."

"Things are making sense now," said Stuart. "Derek was the one who didn't want to go there to work. He said it made him feel uncomfortable. I was also uneasy, so I went along with what he said."

"Where would Derek run to?" asked Alex, who had returned to the kitchen and had heard the latter part of the conversation.

"No idea," shrugged Stuart. "He must have panicked. His wife works in Salisbury, and the kids are at school. Derek wouldn't leave them behind."

"Are his parents still alive?" asked Gus.

"John, his father, well, I always thought he was his father, was a lot older than Kathy. It would have been 2009 when he died. Kathy died in January, a couple of months before Marion's murder."

Gus was happier with the numbers now. They still had a significant problem to solve, but there was light at the end of the tunnel.

Chapter Twelve

GUS AND ALEX left Stuart Milligan at the house on Sarum Close and drove in convoy to Wilton House. They had an hour, at least, before meeting Ralph Tucker. The fruit loaf at the Garden Centre café was an enormous temptation.

"What do you think Stuart Milligan will do, guv?" asked Alex as they found a seat in the café.

"We warned him not to contact his partner," said Gus. "Milligan seemed a decent sort. I imagine he's wondering how much it will cost to get the van signage altered. If he gets it back in one piece."

"We need to speak to Derek Preston's wife, guv," said Alex. "Milligan didn't think Preston would do anything stupid, but you never know. Preston knows what he's done. He might think it's the only way out."

"I don't believe Preston is our killer, Alex," said Gus. "The timing doesn't fit, nor would a blackmailer kill the goose that laid the golden egg. But, of course, Marion Reeves may have died earlier than the time in the murder file. Milligan swears his partner returned to the house well before ten o'clock. What didn't he say?"

Alex looked puzzled for a second and then snapped his fingers.

"Milligan didn't say Preston had changed his clothing or was covered in blood when he returned. So why did he run if he didn't do it, guv?"

"If Preston admits he was in the car, demanding money from Marion Reeves in return for intimate photos, he believes nobody will accept his story she was alive when he left her."

"The sooner we find him and get him into custody, the better, guv," said Alex. "Derek Preston has a lot of explaining to do, but he could provide us with vital information."

"There's a good chance Preston saw the killer between getting out of the Lexus and walking to his car, you mean?" asked Gus.

"We might get lucky, guv," said Alex.

Gus tucked into his extra-large slice of fruit loaf and looked around the room. Serena Campbell wasn't working this afternoon. Gus tried to think what they'd forgotten to ask her. The untraceable senior police officer was a nuisance. Gus put that part of the enquiry on hold until they homed in on the major prize. The person who murdered Marion Reeves.

"The guy just walking into the café could be our tree surgeon," said Alex.

"I never met Graham Street," said Gus. "Tough to tell whether there's a likeness between Ralph Tucker and his father. Can you see anything in the three men we've identified as Street's children to suggest they were related?"

"Martyn Street is much taller than the man I'm looking

at, guv, but physically they're similar. We haven't met Derek Preston yet, except for a brief sighting of him munching on a sandwich in the van."

"I'm in the right place, aren't I?" said Ralph Tucker. "You two are the police officers I'm supposed to meet."

"Sit down, Mr Tucker," said Gus. "I'm Gus Freeman, and this is DS Alex Hardy from Wiltshire Police. We have several questions relating to Marion Reeves and Martyn Street."

"I remember Marion Reeves," said Ralph, shaking his head. "Nasty business, that. You didn't find who did it, did you?"

"We haven't given up hope yet," said Gus. "We're getting closer every day. When did Sonya, your mother, tell you about your father?"

"I don't understand what that has to do with anything," said Ralph. "But when I reached sixteen and left school, I told her I'd decided I wanted to work in forestry. Climbing trees in the open air every day appealed to me. My mother never mentioned my father's name before that day. I hoped to take a full-time course and aim for Level Three qualifications, but my mother said she couldn't afford to support me. So I had to start work straight away. Graham Street had never acknowledged me as his son. He wouldn't give her a penny to help. So, I started at the bottom until I could get enough wiggle room to work four days a week and set one aside for college."

"You made it to the top with no help from Graham Street," said Gus.

"It took me ten years longer than it should have," said Ralph.

"So, when Martyn Street started working here, you decided to get your own back on a lad you discovered was another of Graham Street's children. That was what was behind the bullying."

"I couldn't understand why Martyn had Street's name. So I did some digging and learned that Marion used to be married to my father. Graham Street couldn't bring himself to marry my mother. What was wrong with her? Then I heard a rumour Martyn had money waiting for him from his father as part of the divorce settlement. I wasn't happy and took it out on the lad."

"Martyn fought back, didn't he?" said Alex.

"That one doesn't realise his own strength," said Ralph.

"Arthur Jackson told me one of Martyn's favourite jobs was helping you. He enjoys clearing the debris from the ground as you clamber in the upper branches with your chainsaw. A job the two of you carry out in the Spring to allow the mowing season to begin."

"Martyn said that?" said Ralph. "Well, I never. I misjudged him. Many people make that mistake because they think he's backward. He's slow on the uptake, not stupid."

"What vehicle do you drive, Mr Tucker," asked Gus.

"A Chevrolet truck, Mr Freeman. It's a large unit with huge tyres."

"A lady who works here, Serena Campbell, described it as a monster truck," said Gus.

"I wish," said Ralph. "My truck's big, but not that big. It's ideal for the work I do."

"Do you take Martyn in your truck to carry out this Spring clean operation?" asked Gus.

Ralph Tucker roared with laughter.

"I thought you were detectives," he said. "Any ground staff who need to be in that part of the estate make their own way. Often they need to ferry heavy equipment to the far corners of the estate. Arthur Jackson's team has six quad bikes at their disposal, plus several Ifor Williams Trailers for their gear and any rubbish they take back to base. Arthur keeps in contact with them by walkie-talkie. Is that news to you as well?"

"No, we heard how Arthur kept tabs on where everyone was," said Gus. "When we spoke to Theo Reeves, he said Martyn walked everywhere because he couldn't pass the theory element of the driving test."

"That's what I mean about misjudging the lad," said Ralph. "Martyn would never pass a test to get a licence to drive on public roads, but he can bomb around the wide-open spaces of the grassland and forest on a quad bike. I doubt Arthur has seen him. There's plenty Arthur doesn't see these days. He's happy to sit in his office, checking where everyone is on his two-way radio. Arthur moves his crew around a map on the wall like moving chess pieces."

"Where were you on the day of Marion Reeves's murder?" asked Gus.

"Steeple Langford," said Ralph. "A village six miles from here. A farmer had a couple of ash trees that needed felling. Unfortunately, they were infected with this ash dieback fungus. The farmer wanted to leave them alone, but they stood on a public footpath. I spent Monday and Tuesday there. I can give you the farmer's details if you want to check."

"We may need to check later, Mr Tucker," said Gus. "When you were digging around for information on Martyn Street, did you discover any other children Graham Street fathered?"

"You think I've got more half-brothers and half-sisters living nearby, do you? No, I was only interested in Martyn because he worked here."

"When did you learn your father was dead?" asked Alex.

"I was in the Greyhound last night," said Ralph. "People were talking."

"A massive heart attack," said Gus.

"My father was in his seventies," shrugged Ralph. "He never acknowledged I was alive. Don't expect me to care he's dead. The man brought it on himself from what I heard in the pub. Chloe Zafferelli was her name, the woman he was in bed with at the time. I hadn't heard the name before. Bill, the landlord, told me that was because she was a high-end call girl who charged at least two grand a night for her services. How Bill knew, I didn't ask. He reckoned there was nothing normal about the services she provided. It takes all sorts, doesn't it?"

Gus and Alex had to agree that it did. Neither of them could think of a good reason for speaking to Ms Zafferelli that could be argued was part of the case they were investigating. It was time to move on.

"Something else I can help you with?" asked Ralph Tucker.

"Did you ever ask your mother how she came to know Graham Street in the first place?" asked Gus.

"My mother was just sixteen when she met him in town," said Ralph. "Street was twenty-one. He wasn't the wealthy man he became in later years. I like to believe they had genuine feelings for one another. But he did the rounds, didn't he? The only woman he married, though, was Marion. Martyn was the only child carrying the Street name, and because the lad wasn't perfect, Graham Street cast him adrift just as he had me, and heaven knows how many others. My Mum is sixty-six now and not in the best of health. I think it's best to draw a veil over the entire episode as if it never happened."

Gus and Alex sat at the table and watched Ralph Tucker walk to the café door.

"Do we drive back to the office now, guv?" asked Alex.

"Call Bourne Hill first. Then, let's see if they've caught Derek Preston."

Alex made the call while Gus visited the toilet. When he returned, he saw Alex giving him the thumbs-up.

"Police caught Derek Preston queuing for the Isle of Wight ferry in Portsmouth, guv."

"That's a relief," said Gus. "I admit, I was concerned he might do something stupid. Why the Isle of Wight, I wonder? There aren't any extradition problems I don't know about, are there?"

"Hardly, guv," said Alex. "He just wasn't thinking straight. We can interview him in the morning at Bourne Hill."

"Right, you can head back to the office and get your files updated. Keep the rest of the team in the loop. I need to find a quiet spot to plan my questions for Preston. Oh, Alex, ask Luke to tell Warren Baker to be in his office at lunchtime tomorrow. We'll talk to Preston first, and then I want to revisit the Churchfields Industrial Estate."

"Are you not following me back, guv?" asked Alex.

"No, I'm driving to Urchfont. Sherlock Holmes used to describe a tricky case as a three-pipe problem. My allotment stands next to a church with an organ that boasts many more pipes than that. Yet, I still don't think it's enough."

Alex left Gus standing by his Ford Focus, staring into the distance. He left the Garden Centre car park and took the A360 back to the Old Police Station office. It appeared Gus was formulating those questions already.

Thursday, 23 August 2018

GUS ROLLED out of bed at half-past seven. Suzie stirred but resisted the temptation to join him. They had spent two hours yesterday evening on the allotment before a meal at home and an early night. Conversation was at a minimum. Suzie allowed Gus to do the pondering he needed. She sensed he was ready to feel the collar of another killer. Whether he shared his thoughts with her before he left for Salisbury was a mystery.

Gus had showered and dressed when Suzie finally lifted herself from the tangled sheet covering her. As she padded softly to the bathroom, Gus called out:

"Coffee and cereal?"

"Fine," she replied.

Gus was sitting at the table, toying with a piece of sausage, trying to soak up the remains of the yolk from his fried egg. The concentration on his face caused Suzie to burst out laughing.

"Are you still struggling with getting your ducks in a row, darling?" she asked.

"When we left the allotment last night, I thought I had it," said Gus. "Then, in the night, I started having doubts and lay there for ages going through my thought processes. The result was different every time. I'm missing a vital piece of my jigsaw, Suzie. I think I know where to find it, but part of me hopes I'm wrong."

"You can't have the answer you want, Gus," said Suzie. "You must accept the answer the facts prove. You know that better than anyone."

Gus swallowed the final tasty morsel, drained his coffee cup, and sighed.

"It will be strange visiting Bourne Hill nick today," he said. "I spent many happy years there, but many faces have disappeared."

"Derek Preston is first on your agenda, isn't he?" asked Suzie. "Are you certain he's not your killer?"

"I asked myself whether Stuart Milligan had a reason to lie about when Derek Preston returned to Oakley Road. They were friends from school and had worked together for twenty years. Of course, he may have lied to protect his friend and their business, but my hunch is quick cash was the only thing on Preston's mind that morning."

"What if Marion Reeves wasn't the only partygoer his mother, Kathy, kept photos of from her time in the group?" said Suzie.

"That was a question I added to my list at around four this morning," said Gus. "Marion may not have been the first blackmail victim. A thorough analysis of Preston's financials now in custody will reveal the truth. The team at Bourne Hill will already have searched his house, car, and the firm's van. If Preston took Marion's photos away with the six grand in cash ready for another sting, they'd find them."

"You need to leave, darling," said Suzie. "It's a quarter past eight. I've got time for a slice of toast before I leave for London Road."

Gus kissed Suzie on the top of her head and collected his car keys from the hall table.

Forty-five minutes later, he was standing in Reception at Bourne Hill, waiting to suffer the usual nonsense of getting past the desk sergeant. He needn't have worried.

"Mr Freeman, we were expecting you."

The fresh-faced youth was far too young to have been

here when Gus was a serving officer. Yet, somehow, he'd made a sergeant. Gus wasn't sure that he'd started shaving.

"Am I first to arrive?" asked Gus.

"DS Sherman arrived five minutes ago, sir. He told me you were on your way."

That explained a lot, thought Gus. He signed in, accepted the shiny Visitor's badge, and listened intently to the directions provided by the desk sergeant. Gus didn't tell the youngster he'd interviewed a hundred criminals in that interview room before he was born.

He found Luke Sherman standing in the corridor outside the room.

"We tossed a coin, guv," said Luke. "There wasn't much difference in distance to travel between Neil and me. I hope you don't mind?"

"The more, the merrier, Luke. Neil hasn't been out of the office on this case, but there's still time. The advantage of those digital files is that everyone on the team is singing from the same hymn sheet. I'll show you my list of questions while we wait for Preston to appear with his escort. Chip in if I've missed something."

"Got it, guv," said Luke. "I spoke to the custody sergeant soon after I arrived. Preston will be with us in the next two minutes."

Gus and Luke entered the interview room, and Luke checked the recording equipment. Everything was set. A knock at the door heralded the arrival of the forty-six-year-old builder, Derek Preston. If he slept last night, it didn't show. He wore a grey sweatshirt and jogging bottoms, and trainers with no laces.

Luke went through the preliminaries while Derek Preston studied the tabletop.

"Good morning, Derek," said Gus. "You know who I

am. Gus Freeman, the man you agreed to meet for a chat yesterday afternoon at a house on Sarum Close. While I was indoors chatting to your friend and colleague, Stuart Milligan, you sat outside in the van eating lunch. So what possessed you to dash off to the Isle of Wight? Don't answer that. We know about the photographs."

Derek Preston lifted his head, and Gus knew they didn't have to suffer a series of no comments. The dam was about to burst.

"My life has been a mess since my Dad died," he said. "John Preston was the only father I knew. Growing up, it didn't register that my Dad was much older than my Mum. When I took Ellie, my girlfriend, home to meet my parents, she said she was surprised, but that was the last time she mentioned it. We've been married for eighteen years this year. Nine years ago, Dad passed away. John never had cancer or heart problems, he was eighty-eight, and everything just shut down. After the funeral, Mum told me a man called Graham Street was my father. She'd got pregnant soon after leaving school. Mum worked in a tobacconist's shop, and John was the owner. His wife had recently died of a heart attack in her early forties. They had no kids. Mum and John married in 1972, three months before I was born."

"How old was your mother?" asked Gus.

"They married on her seventeenth birthday," said Preston.

"A marriage of convenience?" asked Gus.

"At the start, maybe," said Preston. "As a child, I never doubted they cared for me. How they felt about one another, I couldn't say. Mum missed John; I know that."

"Did you know Graham Street?" asked Luke.

"Only by reputation," said Preston. "Loads of money.

He liked to flaunt his wealth. When Stuart and I were old enough to drink, we saw him in pubs and clubs in Salisbury on weekends. Street went nowhere alone, and there were always young women hanging on his every word and a gang of rich friends in tow. I knew he had once been married to Marion, which made Martyn some relation to me."

"Did Kathy tell you how they met?" asked Gus.

"After John died, she just told me she had been a foolish young girl, flattered Graham Street had noticed her among the many pretty girls in the city. I knew how good-looking my mother was when I was a teenager. All my mates, including Stuart, fancied her. Mum didn't add to what she told me after John died; the following summer, she fell ill. Typical of Mum, she'd suffered on and off for a couple of years without bothering the doctors. She died in January, just two months before Marion Reeves's murder. The solicitor told us they found complications when they read her will. I never understood it, but they warned us it would take time to get probate agreed upon. We had a huge mortgage and three kids who never stopped growing, and we were desperate for that cash. Mum and John lived in a two-bedroomed bungalow that needed work. I kept promising to spend time on it but never did. I knew the money it raised would get us out of trouble, but we needed something immediately."

"You found the photos when you cleared their house?" said Gus.

"They were in a small case just inside the loft," said Preston. "It was locked, and I couldn't find a key. When I prised the lock open with a screwdriver, I had the shock of my life. I recognised Marion Reeves straight away. There were dozens of pictures of people doing all sorts of things.

I'm broad-minded, Mr Freeman, but it turned my stomach."

"Why do you think Kathy had these photos?" asked Luke.

"I didn't know the full story before I found that case. At work, I saw Marion every day. When I saw those photos, I knew someone had taken them long ago. She looked so young. Eighteen or nineteen, maybe. I couldn't talk to Stuart, but I couldn't look Marion in the eye after that."

"You mentioned people," said Gus. "Does that mean Marion wasn't the only woman in the photos? Did you recognise anyone else? The men, perhaps?"

"I was relieved not to find any of my mother, Mr Freeman. Although, from what I learned later, she must have destroyed them. Somebody took them twenty-five years before I found them. So many of the men and women in the photos would be dead or aged so much I couldn't identify them."

"Did you doctor the photos featuring Marion Reeves to mask the identity of the others involved?" asked Gus.

"I did that on my computer at home. It wasn't difficult. I thought if Theo and Marion Reeves could afford eighty grand to spend on tarting up their house, another ten grand wouldn't be hard to find. I knew Marion wouldn't want those pictures to see the light of day."

"When did you approach Marion to tell her what you had found?" asked Luke.

"I sent her copies in an envelope in the post," said Preston. "I'd done nothing like it before and realised it was stupid as soon as I put the envelope in the post box. So I wrote the address myself and even licked the stamp."

"How much money did you ask for?" asked Gus.

"I hadn't thought that far ahead," said Preston. "I sent

the photos, nothing else. Then, on Monday, I arrived on Oakley Road a few minutes before Stuart. I watched Theo leave, and Stuart reversed the van into the driveway. Stephanie cycled away on her bike, and I called Marion's mobile when I reached our van. Then, as I started unloading my gear, I sent Marion a text, hinting that I was watching the house, and told her to meet me on the industrial estate."

"Why there?" asked Gus.

"If we'd gone to a secluded spot, you could guarantee someone would pop up from nowhere and remember seeing two cars. On the other hand, places such as Churchfields are always busy, so two more parked cars wouldn't catch anyone's attention."

"What time did you reach Churchfields?" asked Luke.

"Half-past nine or just after. I was two cars behind Marion on the main road. She had just pulled up by the kerb when I entered Stephenson Road. I parked in front of her, got out and walked back. I'll never forget the look of embarrassment on her face when she realised it was me. When I sat beside her, I apologised for what I'd done. It sounds crazy, but I liked Marion. She was a lovely woman. I told her I was desperate for money. She handed me an envelope filled with cash. I asked how much it was, and she said six thousand pounds. Then Marion started crying. She said she had no more money. Marion told me it was what remained of the money Graham Street gave her when they divorced. I asked her if she knew my mother. Marion nodded and said Kathy and John were regulars at parties she attended. I was ten years old and spent weekends with my grandparents when those photos got taken. We were both in tears by then. I wanted to hand back the cash, but Marion insisted I take it. I gave Marion the originals and the negatives of every photo I found in that case. She told me Graham Street was an evil man with friends in high places. Marion begged me to steer clear of him and not say anything about what I'd found. Despite what had just occurred, we hugged one another, and as I got out of the car, Marion said something odd. Remember Maureen Glendenning. I didn't have a clue who she meant. I walked to my car, drove to Oakley Road, and parked up the road from the house because I needed five minutes to get myself together."

"What time did you go inside the house?" asked Gus.

"Ten to ten, or thereabouts," said Preston. "I made a brew and chatted to Stuart before we got stuck in. He had Heart FM on the radio, and we listened to the ten o'clock news headlines. We cheered when the piece about the Lapland experience came on. The two blokes got sent to jail. Quite right, too; Ellie and I were gutted for our kids when we saw how little they were getting for the money we paid."

"What did you think had happened when Theo arrived home from work later?" asked Gus.

"I didn't have a clue," said Preston. "Stuart worried his precious Steph had got knocked off her bike. Then the police lady arrived, and Theo bundled us out of the house. He said he'd let us know when he needed us again. When the news filtered through later in the day, I knew I was in trouble. Marion was alive when I left her, Mr Freeman. You must believe me. I didn't kill her."

"No, I don't believe you did, Mr Preston," said Gus. "Just a couple more questions, and we'll let you get back to your cell. What did you do with the cash?"

"I paid it into our joint account in Barclays on Tuesday morning," said Derek Preston, "and walked over the road to

Lloyds to bank our business cheques. The ones I told Stuart I was going into town to do the day before."

"When you got out of Marion's Lexus, did you see anyone near the car?"

"Several vehicles passed me in both directions," said Preston. "I didn't see anyone walking, if that's what you mean."

"Thank you, Mr Preston. It's been most enlightening," said Gus.

Derek Preston looked confused.

"Is that it? What happens now?"

"The CPS will consider what charges you will face, Mr Preston. However, that's none of our concern. We'll carry on looking for Marion's killer."

When Preston left the room with his escort, Luke sat back in his chair.

"That sounded convincing, guv."

"It confirmed what we already knew, Luke. The field is narrowing with every person we interview. So let's visit Churchfields once more. I've got questions that need answers."

"That John and Kathy Preston were involved in those parties must have come as a shock to Derek Preston, guv," said Luke.

"John was the cameraman," said Gus, "unless I'm much mistaken. Serena Campbell warned me this affair went deeper and higher than I imagined. I wonder what Marion Reeves meant by her last comment to Derek Preston?"

"Blessing told us people believed Maureen Glendenning moved to Spain, guv. She had a child by Graham Street in 1966, six years before he got Kathy Mellor pregnant. Nobody has seen Maureen since 1968."

"We'll look into it once we've solved Marion's murder," said Gus. "I'll leave my car here. You can drive, Luke."

WHILE GUS and Luke listened to Derek Preston's story, the rest of the team had work to do. Neil arrived at the Old Police Station office at nine o'clock.

"I wondered who would get the gig with Gus to interview Preston," said Alex.

"Luke asked me to call heads or tails," said Neil. "He reckoned it was heads, so he's gone to Bourne Hill to meet Gus. We should get on with talking to Genevieve Harding and Serena Campbell."

"What did Luke do about Gus's meeting with Warren Baker?" asked Alex.

"Luke called him to delay their meeting until lunchtime. Why?" said Neil.

"Genevieve Harding lives on the other side of Salisbury, doesn't she?"

"Redlynch," said Blessing, "a village several miles further from Downton, where Gus used to live."

"What are you thinking, Alex?" asked Lydia.

"If we've got to go that way, why don't *we* speak to Warren Baker?"

"Another coin toss?" asked Neil. "One where I can check the result."

"No need. You can go to Redlynch and back to Bourne Hill, Neil," said Alex. "You haven't left the office on this case yet. Take Blessing with you, as she did the work of finding the lady. Lydia and I will follow up on Serena Campbell. She lives near enough to Salisbury for the four of us to keep in touch and then meet up at Bourne Hill later."

"When we've got something to pass to Gus and Luke, we can call them," said Neil.

"It beats sitting in the office waiting for news," said Blessing.

Neil contacted Genevieve Harding and said they were leaving right away.

"We'll get to her place by half-past ten," said Neil. "Alex, can you call Baker and tell him we'll be at Bourne Hill for noon? Let their desk sergeant know to expect DS Davis and DC Umeh."

"No worries, Neil," said Alex. "Good hunting."

Neil and Blessing headed for the lift and were soon out of town.

Lydia's phone call found Serena Campbell at home in Bemerton Heath, Serena told Lydia she was working in the café this afternoon, but if they needed an hour of her time this morning, she would stay home until they arrived.

"If I drive via Devizes, we should get to her cottage by ten o'clock," said Lydia.

"I'll drive," said Alex. "There's no rush."

Lydia and Alex took the lift to the ground floor, and Alex drove them towards Devizes. It was a team effort, after all.

Chapter Thirteen

NEIL AND BLESSING arrived in Redlynch at twenty past ten.

"This village is like Mere, isn't it?" said Blessing. "Lots of old buildings, a small population, and houses dotted around that are way out of my price range."

"If the rumours concerning our former Family Liaison Officer are correct, Genevieve could live with someone who can afford to buy a decent house here," said Neil. "We won't find many priced at less than half a million."

"This is it," said Blessing, "well, it's got kerb appeal. Roses around the door, well-kept gardens. How old do you think this house is, Neil?"

"The earliest parts of the house are from the nineteenth century, and someone has extended and improved it several times. The satellite dish has only been on the roof for two decades."

Blessing giggled.

"You knock, Neil. I can't see a doorbell."

Neil knocked on the solid wooden door, and Genevieve Harding answered.

The Freeman files showed that Phil Youngman had described the former FLO as curvy and attractive. Neil had to agree, and at forty-eight, she left him tongue-tied.

"DS Davis, I presume?" said Genevieve.

"Yes," said Blessing. "And I'm DC Umeh. We need to talk to you about the Marion Reeves murder case."

"Come in, please," said Genevieve. "Excuse the mess; the dogs were frisky this morning after I took them for a walk. I've shut them in the conservatory, or else you wouldn't get a second's peace. We can talk here in the living room."

"The dogs must be splendid companions," said Blessing. "Do you live here alone?"

"I do these days," said Genevieve, "Tom, my partner, died eighteen months ago."

"We're sorry to hear that," said Neil. "We hoped to speak with him. Where did Tom work before he retired? Sorry, I assumed he was older than you. Perhaps our information was incorrect."

Genevieve sighed and sat in a chair beside the inglenook fireplace. Neil and Blessing stepped around cushions and newspapers the dogs must have disturbed when they got back indoors to sit on dining chairs beside a small oak table.

"It was inevitable someone would ask me about this in the end," said Genevieve. "Tom did everything he could to keep a lid on it. So when I heard of Graham Street's death, I thought it might be over at last. So what do you want to know?"

"Where did Tom work?" asked Neil. "What was his name? Unfortunately, we didn't find anyone in the county who matched the description of the mystery man we uncovered during our case review."

"Tom Kellett worked in Winchester," said Genevieve. "It's a thirty-five-minute drive from here. He retired as a Detective Superintendent with Hampshire Constabulary. Tom always worked in Hampshire, and he and his wife lived closer to Southampton for many years."

"When his wife died of cancer in the early Eighties," said Blessing, "were you already seeing one another?"

"Heavens, no," said Genevieve. "I was seeing someone else then."

"A married man?" asked Neil.

"Yes," said Genevieve.

"How did you and Tom meet?" asked Neil.

"What have you learned so far?" asked Genevieve.

"We're asking the questions, Ms Harding," said Blessing.

"Graham Street invited me to a party in the country in 1984. I was seventeen. I met Marion that night. She and Graham had only been married six months."

"Did you know what you had agreed to?" asked Blessing.

"Oh yes," said Genevieve. "I was looking forward to it. I'm sorry if that shocks you, but I couldn't get enough of what I enjoyed with any of the young men I met. My married lover didn't go to the parties, but he had whet my appetite. Graham Street and Dave Francis showed me there were places I could go to satisfy my urges. Tom's wife died, which would have meant he couldn't get an invitation to the parties anymore. We spent time together that first night, and I knew we were compatible. So I said yes when he called to ask if I'd accompany him the following weekend. We moved in together soon after and enjoyed the scene for another fifteen years at least. The repercussions of getting found out increased and bothered him as the years passed. He'd worked hard to get as high up the ladder as he had."

"Let's talk about the eighteenth of March in 2011," said Neil. "Where were you when you got the call to drive to Oakley Road?"

"At Bourne Hill," said Genevieve. "I told you I met Marion in '84. Over the next four or five years, her relationship with Graham deteriorated. Marion wanted out, but Street was a nasty piece of work. I was happy for her when she finally walked out on him. Marion met Theo Reeves, and I learned they got married. So, when I received the name and address, I realised the incident at Churchfields involved Marion. I called Tom right away. He said he'd deal with it."

"What did you think that meant?" asked Neil.

"Whatever it took to keep our names out of the case," said Genevieve. "Tom had been involved in things from the beginning. He felt he owed some loyalty to Street and Francis, but most of all, he wanted to protect the others we met with most weekends."

"The rich and famous who Street and Francis rubbed shoulders with," said Neil.

"So, you do know something of what went on."

"A friend of Marion Reeves gave us details of these parties but was afraid to give us names."

"Serena," said Genevieve. "That makes sense; they were close. Serena and Dave Francis were married for a while."

"Who did Tom call after you rang?" asked Blessing. "We have his name. You might as well confirm it for us now. We'll interview him later today."

"Tom's biggest fear was Marion's mobile phone. Although she had left the scene by 1990, Tom knew the phone numbers of two dozen founder members were on that phone in the late Eighties. He couldn't risk the police getting hold of it, so he called Warren Baker. Tom knew what a sleaze the man was; they'd worked at the same police station in Southampton. Tom was his superior officer and covered up an incident involving a Portuguese cleaner. On that Monday morning in 2011, Tom called Baker and reminded him he owed him one. Baker made sure the mobile phone didn't reach Bourne Hill."

"That confirms what we knew," said Neil. "Thank you. Did Tom do anything else to influence the original investigation?"

"Billie Wightman needed little convincing," said Genevieve. "Tom steered her away from anyone who could connect the case to the sex parties. Matt Price wanted to speak to friends of Marion, like Serena. I worked with Billie on several cases, Tom drove into Salisbury the day after the murder, and I arranged for us to bump into Tom casually. He asked how the enquiry was going. Billie was looking at Theo and the other men in Marion's life. When Billie told him Matt's idea, Tom suggested she stick to her guns. The killer was a man Marion knew, he said. Why interview a girlfriend she might only have known for a few years?"

"A month later, the detective team hadn't uncovered a single suspect," said Neil. "The case went cold. So Billie Wightman, Matt Price, and the rest of the team moved on to a new case."

"Can I get in trouble for what I did?" asked Genevieve.

"Tom Kellett used his position to pervert the course of justice," said Blessing. "He'll never face charges now. Warren Baker tampered with evidence, which is a serious charge. All you've admitted to was making a phone call to your partner. We'll be back if we find you played a more significant role."

The barking from the conservatory grew louder. Genevieve stood up and followed Neil and Blessing to the front door.

"How long do you think it will be before the story hits the newspapers?" she asked.

"I don't know whether the whole story will ever come out, Ms Harding," said Neil. "Many people who attended those parties have died in the past forty years. You told us earlier you and Tom stopped going fifteen years ago. Will there be a party somewhere this weekend?"

"Where there's a demand, there's always someone willing to supply, DS Davis," said Genevieve. "After Dave Francis went to prison and Graham Street dropped off the scene, everything fizzled out, as I understand it. I've no way of checking."

Neil and Blessing drove back from Redlynch to Salisbury and parked in the Bourne Hill police station car park. Neil called Alex Hardy for a catch-up on their meeting with Serena Campbell.

"THIS IS LIKE THE OLD DAYS," said Lydia as Alex drove them towards Devizes. "Gus keeps us apart, doesn't he?"

"The Trudi Villers case, you mean?" said Alex. "Yes, we did several interviews together back then. Gus wants to make sure the top brass at London Road doesn't think one of us should get moved out of the CRT. We wouldn't want that, would we?"

"No way," said Lydia. "I enjoy it too much."

Alex soon found Serena Campbell's tiny cottage on the Heath, and he and Lydia walked along the cinder path to the door. The doorbell gave a half-hearted ring when Lydia pressed it. The bell sounded as tired as the decorative order of the house it belonged to.

"We keep meeting, DS Hardy," said Serena. "Who have you got with you this time?"

"Lydia Logan Barre," said Lydia. "We're colleagues serving on the Crime Review Team with Mr Freeman."

"Of course, you are, dear," said Serena. "I never smiled at my colleagues as you did as you walked from the car."

"When we spoke with you the other afternoon," said Alex, ignoring Serena's comment, "you said a senior police officer attended parties when you and Marion were young women. However, we can't trace anyone on the Wiltshire force matching your description. Why is that?"

"He lived in the county," said Serena. "Perhaps he worked over the border in Hampshire. I didn't ask; I just knew he was a high-ranking officer. Dave Francis encouraged me to ask the man what he wanted me to do for him, not find out what he did for a living."

"Have you thought any more about revealing the names of people involved in these parties?" asked Lydia.

"Not a chance, dear," said Serena. "Since Mr Freeman started poking around, more attention has focussed on me than I would prefer. I've kept a low profile for years, and nobody here knew anything of my past. Marion and I were careful when we met not to get tongues wagging. Yesterday evening I had a call from Ralph Tucker. He wanted to know if I remembered his mother, Sonya. Of course, I didn't. Graham Street started fathering kids before he dreamed up the idea of the parties. Then Tucker mentioned the police arrested a builder called Derek Preston. He asked whether I knew his father. What could I say? I denied knowledge of having heard the name. Was it Preston who killed Marion?

As soon as Tucker said the name, it fell into place. John Preston took his young wife Kathy to parties. He got off seeing her with other men. John always had a camera with him. Derek wasn't his son, though. I remember Kathy Mellor with Graham when she was fifteen or sixteen. Tucker wanted to check if Derek was another of Graham's kids. I didn't give him the satisfaction. If you've got your man, why do you need to ask me about that senior police officer?"

"We like to corroborate evidence we gather from various sources," said Alex. "We can't rely on people telling us the whole truth."

"I must get ready for work now," said Serena. "Have you got what you need from me?"

"If we think of something else, we'll drop into the café this afternoon," said Lydia.

Serena closed the door firmly behind them as they left her cottage.

"We've got lots to tell Gus," said Lydia. "He's going to get a surprise."

"We won't know until we catch up with him later whether we're one step ahead of him or two steps behind," said Alex.

"Spoilsport," said Lydia.

Ten minutes later, they arrived at Bourne Hill police station.

"It's barely eleven o'clock," said Alex. "Neil won't be here yet, and Warren Baker isn't expecting anyone until twelve. So we shouldn't have any problem getting through Reception. When I called, I gave our names to the desk sergeant to tell him Neil and Blessing would be in later."

"We could get a coffee," said Lydia. "I promise not to look at you too affectionately. But, in case word gets back to London Road, we're an item."

"I'd rather call Warren Baker to see if he's here. If so, we'll crack on with the interview and wrap it up before Neil and Blessing arrive."

Alex was right about the desk sergeant. There was no problem getting signed in and issued a Visitor's badge. It took longer for Lydia; of course, the desk sergeant was only human.

"Can you tell me whether Warren Baker is in the building?" Alex asked as Lydia donned her visitor's badge.

"He's in the forensic department, DS Hardy. The map on the wall will guide you to where you want to go. I'll phone Mr Baker to tell him you're on your way."

"Don't," said Lydia, "we'd like to surprise him."

"Yes, miss. Whatever you say."

THE FIVE-MINUTE DRIVE from Bourne Hill to Churchfields hardly gave Luke's car time to warm up. As he entered Stephenson Road at a quarter past ten, he wondered where Gus wanted to stop.

"Shall I park where Marion Reeves did, guv?" he asked.

"No," said Gus. "We're visiting the light-engineering firm on the left. No job is too small. So that's our first port of call. Then we'll walk to the funeral directors to chat with Maurice Duffield."

Luke decided it was best to let Gus take the lead. He wasn't altogether sure how this visit could help matters.

Gus led the way through the works entrance. A man in a hi-viz jacket was leaving a Portakabin ten yards inside the compound on their left.

"Can I help you, gents?" he said.

"Wiltshire Police," said Luke. "We need to speak to someone in charge, please."

"That'll be me. Bob Frisk. This is my business."

"Have you been here long, Mr Frisk?" asked Gus.

"Call me Bob. The Grand National jokes have worn thin over the years."

"Have you, Bob?" asked Gus.

"I opened this place in 1990. Okay, let's get it out of the way. That was a good year for people called Mr Frisk, wasn't it?"

"It won't heal if you keep picking at it, Bob," said Gus. "Can we discuss the eighteenth of March, seven years ago? The day a woman died in her car, not forty yards from where we're standing. Were you here that day?"

"I was," said Bob. "The police evacuated eighty percent of my workers and asked each of us if we'd seen anything. Of course, nobody saw a thing."

"Did you have many visitors that day?" asked Gus.

"We don't keep a log," said Bob. "We offer a service that appeals to the businesses on this site. People are always popping in with an urgent job. They might want a replacement part for a vital piece of kit they use or a simple repair. So, our gates are always open. We could survive with the work this site generates, but we don't turn away jobs for private individuals or businesses from anywhere in the city. We've got an excellent reputation for efficient service."

"Have you ever done work for the Wilton House estate?" Gus asked.

"I don't recall them approaching me," said Bob Frisk. "It wouldn't do any harm to add them to our clientele. Almost like having 'By Royal Appointment' on our letter heading."

"Although you don't log visitors in and out, surely you record the jobs you've done to raise invoices?" asked Luke.

"You need to speak to Jasmine in Accounts. Don't

worry; it's not far. She's in the Portakabin. Second office on the right."

Gus watched Bob and his hi-viz jacket disappear into the machine shop to their right. No wonder nobody heard anything that day. There was a high level of activity inside.

Gus and Luke walked up the steps to the portacabin and went inside. Luke knocked on the second door on the right.

"Jasmine?" he said as he opened the door.

Luke had expected a younger woman.

"Yes, dear?"

"Bob said you could help us trace invoices for work done in 2011," said Luke.

"Did he now?" said Jasmine. "It depends on who's asking."

"We're from Wiltshire Police," said Luke.

"I knew he couldn't get away with it forever," sighed Jasmine. "I prayed it wouldn't come out until I retired in three years."

"Jasmine," said Gus, "we're the police, not HMRC. Our case doesn't concern the cash-in-hand jobs Bob does for friends on the site. We won't breathe a word, honest."

"Right, so when did you say it was?"

"Monday, the eighteenth of March in 2011," said Gus.

Jasmine pushed herself from her chair and walked to a rank of grey metal filing cabinets.

"It's always the bottom drawer," she complained. Luke could tell that bending over to retrieve the correct folder could prove difficult and embarrassing.

"Let me help, Jasmine," he said. "How are the folders labelled?"

"You're a lifesaver, young man. Are you married?"

"I am," said Luke.

"Just my luck. March 2011 should be the fifteenth file back."

Luke found it in seconds and handed it to Jasmine.

"The eighteenth, you said. We were busy that day. What name are you looking for?"

"Street," said Gus.

"Nothing under that name," said Jasmine, flicking through the folder. "Any idea what type of job it was we did for this firm?"

"Were there any running repairs for a private individual?" asked Gus.

"A Mr Jackson wanted a replacement part for a ride-on mower," said Jasmine. "The customer brought the damaged item in on Friday. The machine shop supervisor decided he couldn't salvage it, so we made a new part. It was a simple job; we charged the customer fifteen pounds. They paid in cash when they collected it that day."

"I don't suppose the file mentions the time they collected their order?" Gus asked.

"No, we wouldn't record that detail."

"Let me return the file for you, Jasmine," said Luke.

"Bless you, dear. Is that all I can do for you both?"

"You've been a great help," said Gus. "Many thanks."

Gus and Luke left Jasmine in Accounts and walked back outside. Bob Frisk wasn't in sight.

"Onwards to Duffield's Funeral Home, Luke," said Gus.

"Arthur Jackson, guv? Could it be him?"

"Patience, Luke. Let's see what Maurice Duffield has to say first."

They walked to the next premises on Stephenson Road.

"This used to be a gym?" asked Luke.

"Hard to imagine, isn't it?" said Gus. "The offices are around the side."

Maurice Duffield looked up when they walked through the door. He didn't look pleased to see them. Gus thought that was just as well. If they had come here to arrange a funeral, it wouldn't do for Maurice to jump out of his chair with a beaming smile.

"Was there something else we can help you with, Mr Freeman?"

"You've made significant changes here since you took over, Mr Duffield," said Gus. "Can you recall the security arrangements when it was a gym?"

"They had a five-digit entry code on the front door members received to enable them to enter," said Maurice. "Each member had an individual locker assigned to them, accessed by a key. The showers and changing rooms were at the rear. The lockers were on either side of the building. Gym equipment was scattered throughout the centre of the main room."

"Who was the first person to visit this building after you took it over?" asked Gus.

"I came with my brother," said Maurice. "There was a good deal of detritus that needed clearing. Much of the gym equipment had gone by then. The lockers remained. Several were locked, and we had to check there was nothing inside them of any value. The tiled ceiling in the shower area was on the floor; frozen pipes, I imagine. Why the water and electrics weren't cut off as soon as the gym ceased trading, I don't know."

"Two years before you took over, it was closed for maintenance from time to time," said Gus. "If they didn't shut off the utilities, I don't suppose they bothered when the business closed. So what else did you find lying around?"

"Someone started a fire over there by the lockers on that side. They left a pile of ash scattered across the floor. The lockers themselves revealed little. A few pairs of trainers, t-shirts, shorts, hats, gloves, and boxes. We had the place cleared within two days, ready to convert to its new usage."

"Boxes?" asked Luke. "Did you find a lunch box by any chance?"

"An empty one, yes, I believe we did."

"Many thanks, Mr Duffield," said Gus. "DC Umeh can sleep easy tonight."

Gus and Luke walked back along Stephenson Road to the car.

"It will be noon before we get to Bourne Hill, guv," said Luke. "What did you want to do after we've spoken to Warren Baker?"

"When we get to the car park, we'll call the office. They might have found a fresh lead. Unless they've been sitting on their hands throughout the morning."

Luke called the office as soon as he parked the car.

"No reply, guv," he said.

"Try Alex's mobile," said Gus.

"Alex, it's Luke. Where are you? You're kidding. Okay, we'll see you in a minute."

"Are they inside?" asked Gus.

"Alex said they used their initiative. Neil and Blessing interviewed Genevieve Harding. He and Lydia talked to Serena Campbell, and because that conversation ended abruptly, they came here and waylaid Warren Baker."

"What did he have to say?" asked Gus getting out of the car. "Come on. We're missing the fun."

"Baker denied everything at first," said Luke. "Blessing told him Genevieve Harding had confessed everything. DS Tom Kellett had something on Baker and used it to get him to lose Marion's mobile phone."

"The FLO had nothing to confess," said Gus. "She

phoned her lover to warn him his links to the sex parties could surface *if* Marion's phone held incriminating evidence. Blessing was fishing. A smart girl, that one."

"Baker took the bait, guv. He started singing like a chorister in Salisbury Cathedral. Neil found the missing phone in the evidence room tucked into a box relating to a death in custody from decades ago."

"Excellent choice," said Gus. "No copper would open that box again unless he had to. It will be fascinating to learn what information Marion's phone held."

"After what we've uncovered today, guv, does it hold the name of our killer?"

"I'm confident it does, Luke," said Gus.

Epilogue

Friday, 24 August 2018

GUS ARRIVED at the Old Police Station office at a quarter to nine. He and the team had spent yesterday afternoon pulling together the results of the different conversations that had taken place across the southern end of the county on Thursday morning.

By four o'clock, everyone agreed they had identified the killer.

A thorough search of Derek Preston's property uncovered the remaining photos taken by John Preston when Kathy was a young woman. Derek had hidden them in a compartment he had fashioned in the boot of his car. Gus asked Neil and Blessing to transfer the photos to Divya in the Hub at London Road.

"I'm sure Divya understands the need for discretion," said Gus. "Make sure she's the only person who handles them."

"Understood, guv," said Neil.

Police had recovered Derek Preston's phone when they arrested him in Portsmouth. A quick analysis confirmed the content and timing of the message he sent Marion Reeves.

Marion's phone stayed at Bourne Hill for a complete analysis of its contents and call history. The phone wasn't password-protected, nor did she attempt to hide the real names of her contacts. DS Tom Kellett had been right. Although Gus didn't recognise many names on the list, it would be simple to compile the network of partygoers Graham Street and Dave Francis had assembled.

Combining the information gathered from the photos and the mobile phone would take time. But Gus was confident they could identify locations and dates. Gus knew the Chief Constable had to set up a specific task force to carry the case forward. Kenneth Truelove would ensure it got handled better than Operation Conifer.

Luke Sherman returned to the room that Bourne Hill had set aside for the team.

"Do you have good news, Luke?" asked Gus.

"Arthur Jackson will be here in the morning with his solicitor, guv. The interview room is booked for noon."

"Alex will accompany me here to Bourne Hill," said Gus. "Luke, I'd like you to start the search for Maureen Glendenning tomorrow. Lydia, Blessing, and Neil can assist you once they've updated their digital files with today's events."

"Got it, guv," said Lydia.

"The three of us must find time to update our files on Friday. This time tomorrow, I want to be ready to hand the final Reeves case data over to the Chief Constable."

"Okay, guv," said Alex.

"No problem," said Luke.

Gus had driven to Urchfont and parked outside the bungalow before half-past five.

Suzie arrived ten minutes later and listened to the evidence they had gathered as they sat on the patio.

"I didn't see that coming," she said after he'd revealed the killer's name.

"It's been a long, tiring day," said Gus. "I need a quiet evening and a good night's sleep."

When he awoke this morning, Gus felt refreshed and ready for another gruelling day. The rest of the team was hard at work. Gus had just started updating his section of the Freeman files when his phone rang.

"The DNA results are back, Gus," said Geoff Mercer. "They confirm Jeff Cummins is Rachel's biological father."

"Thanks, Geoff," said Gus. "We've been expecting them. I must inform the family."

Gus picked up his car keys and headed for the lift. First, he had to inform Rachel Cummins, Sean, and Byron Hogan that Gerry's death was a tragic but genuine mistake.

"Everything alright, guv?" asked Alex.

"Best laid plans, Alex," said Gus. "At least we can tie the Hogan case in a bow now. Then, I'll drive to Bourne Hill from Trowle Common. Meet me there before twelve."

The lift doors closed before Alex could answer. It was all-systems-go this morning.

At noon, Gus and Alex entered the interview room. Alex had already checked everything was ready. He went through the preliminaries while Gus studied the people on the opposite side of the table.

"I thought it best to employ the services of a solicitor," said Arthur. "This gentleman is Mr Edward Vince."

"Thank you, Mr Jackson," said Gus. "Let's begin. My first question concerns the ride-on mower you use when mowing the grass between the lines of fruit trees on the Wilton estate. When and how did it get broken?"

"I thought we'd cleared away every piece of rubbish that fell from the trees over the winter. Then, the mower hit something hard on Friday afternoon, and a piece almost snapped in half."

"You took that broken part to Frisk Engineering, didn't you? The firm on Stephenson Road on the Churchfields Industrial Estate, next to the gym."

"The sign says no jobs too small. I knew we needed the mower on Monday. They couldn't repair it straight away. I had to go back."

"How did you get to Churchfields on Monday?"

"I took one of the quad bikes. I had to get there and back as soon as possible."

"What happened when you came outside with the new part they'd made?"

"I took off my fleece because it was hot in the building. I put it on the quad bike. When I looked up, I didn't understand why the cars were there."

"You saw Derek Preston, one of the builders, didn't you, Martyn?"

"The man sat in the car with Mum. They were hugging each other. I didn't like it. The man got out and went back to his car. I waited until he drove away and asked Mum why she wasn't at work."

"Did you sit next to her?" asked Gus.

"I had to move things first. There were photos on the seat. The lady looked like Mum in the pictures but was naked and doing dirty things. I can't remember what happened after that."

"Did you carry your walkie-talkie with you that morning?" asked Gus.

"Mr Jackson called me first thing; then he said he'd call again at lunchtime."

"Do you carry a knife with you when you're working?"

"Yes, but it's always in the sheath on my belt. It's sharp."

"You say you don't remember what happened after you saw those photos. What do you remember about what you did later?"

"Mum told me it was wrong to have feelings for someone else when you were married. She said the family was everything, yet she lied. She was with that man. I couldn't even be friends with Stephanie; Mum told me that was wrong. She said people shouldn't say one thing and do another. It made me angry."

"Where did you go when you got out of the car?"

"I was dirty, so I went to the gym."

"Did you take anything from the car?"

"I had to take the photos. I couldn't let anyone else see them."

"How did you get into the gym?"

"Five, one, nine, four, five. I took off my clothes and had a shower. There weren't any towels, but people always left clothes hanging on pegs and forgot to collect them. I dried myself and looked into the open lockers. I found tracksuit bottoms and a top that fit me. There was a box of matches in one locker. I sat and ate my lunch while I watched the photos burn."

"Did you take your lunch with you when you left the estate on the quad bike?" asked Gus.

"No, it was in the car. I had to take it. Mum said we mustn't waste food."

"What did you do after you ate your lunch?"

"I went back to the bike, put on my fleece, and rode back to work."

"What did you do with your dirty clothes?"

"I hid them in the bushes on the edge of the estate."

"What did you do with your knife?"

"I washed it in the shower. It was dirty. I took the belt off my trousers and used it to hold the tracksuit bottoms up. They were too big for me. The knife's still in the sheath, next to the rubber duck. My trousers are in the wardrobe at home. Mr Jackson told me to wear something smart today."

"After you left the gym, what did you see when you walked past your mother's car?" asked Gus.

"I didn't look," said Martyn. "She lied to me. Every day when I was growing up, Mum said I must tell the truth and not do anything wrong."

"When did you see Martyn that morning, Mr Jackson?" asked Gus.

"I didn't see him after he arrived in the office to ask what he should do. I told him to mow the grass between the trees, and I'd remind him to stop work at one to get to the café for his lunch. Martyn said he wasn't hungry when I called at a quarter to one. He carried on working until the police rang. I went to collect him and couldn't understand why he'd done so little work. It wasn't like him."

"And you didn't think to mention that until now?"

"I had no idea Martyn had left the estate."

"Did you know he could ride the quad bike?"

"I'd seen him. The other lads told me how much he enjoyed not having to walk everywhere."

"We're ready to pass Martyn on to our colleagues, Mr Jackson. They will determine the charges they believe are appropriate."

"WILL a jury ever convict Martyn of murder, guv?" asked Alex as they left Bourne Hill police station to return to their cars.

"Ralph Tucker and Serena Campbell both told me people misjudged Martyn. If he's slow-witted, how did he work out how to react after the violent outburst that ended with his mother's murder? Martyn can't claim he did that while the balance of his mind was disturbed, can he? He removed the photos, burned them, showered, changed clothes, and then cleaned the murder weapon. Martyn was clever enough to use the fleece to cover the missing shirt and stash the bloodied clothes. No, he's got a lot to answer for."

Monday, 27 August 2018

GUS HAD JUST SAT at his desk when the phone rang.

"Freeman? It's Kenneth Truelove here. DS Mercer notified me of the extraordinary matters you uncovered while solving the Reeves murder. You never cease to amaze me. I've set the wheels in motion to investigate the historical exploitation of underage girls by Street, Francis, and others. The enquiry will also look into the possible murder of Maureen Glendenning. I'm holding the first session of Operation Oakleaf at noon."

"A catchy title, sir," said Gus.

"Did you have a better idea?"

"I toyed with Figleaf, considering most of those photos, sir, but you're much better at these things than I am."

"You can't rest on your laurels, Freeman. Don't be late for our meeting."

vinci-books.com/deadreckoning

A cold case. A relentless detective. A killer's perfect alibi.

Kendal Guthrie, a man with a knack for stirring up trouble, is
found dead. But how did the killer manage to arrive at Guthrie's
farm before him on that fateful night? With time, distance, and
locations holding the key, Gus Freeman and his team must
navigate the treacherous terrain of Salisbury Plain to unravel the
truth.

Turn the page for a free preview…

Dead Reckoning: Chapter One

Saturday, 25 August 2018

Alex and Lydia had to make an early start. The train journey to Edinburgh Waverley involved two changes and took over seven hours, whichever way they approached it. Alex offered to drive overnight because Lydia wanted as much time with her mother as possible, but Lydia judged the extra hour they might gain with Eleanor wasn't worth the effort.

"I like my bed too much," she had said as they drove back to Chippenham from the Old Police Station on Friday afternoon.

"I enjoy sharing it with you," said Alex.

Somehow, they dragged themselves out of bed to make it to Bath Spa station to catch the train.

"I called Eleanor last night to say we would arrive in Edinburgh by a quarter past three this afternoon. Providing there were no delays," said Lydia.

"How long does it take to reach her place from the station?" asked Alex.

"Twenty minutes on the bus," said Lydia. "Eleanor's happy for us to stay with her, thank goodness."

"You stayed with her in Craigmillar the last time you visited," said Alex. "Her house is big enough, isn't it?"

"I didn't have you with me last time," said Lydia. "I didn't know how she felt about us sleeping together."

"I get it. Eleanor is your mother after all's said and done, even though you're twenty-five. We didn't have this problem with Chidozie. It made more sense for us to book our accommodation that weekend."

"With the eye-watering price of our train fares today, saving the extra cost of a hotel bed for the night was more than welcome," said Lydia. "We're not made of money."

"It means we can risk treating Eleanor to another fine dining experience tonight," said Alex. "Do they serve haggis in August?"

"Ugh," said Lydia, "haggis is an acquired taste. Despite the number of Burns Night suppers, my Dundee parents forced me to attend, one I never acquired. We'll avoid the restaurant where Chidozie and Rosa took Eleanor. It sounded fantastic, but variety is the spice of life."

"It was *that* expensive?" grinned Alex.

"Eleanor didn't elaborate on the phone, but I reminded her that Chidozie and Rosa were used to the costs of restaurant meals being far higher in the Netherlands. Edinburgh prices wouldn't have seemed excessive to them."

"Your father is a wealthy man, Lydia. You couldn't have missed that while we were in his company. He bought his place in Dubai at a great time. Heaven knows what it's worth on the open market today. I can't wait to visit."

"That's something I need to discuss with Eleanor this weekend. If possible, I'd like us to arrange our trip to stay with my father to coincide with hers."

"Even though Eleanor told you she and Rosa got on well, you still have reservations about them spending too much time together."

"Two's company," said Lydia.

"Five provides safety in numbers," said Alex. "Less chance of awkward moments."

"My thoughts exactly," said Lydia.

No sooner than they got comfortable in their seats, they had to grab their things and get off at Bristol Temple Meads, the first of their scheduled changes.

As they boarded the train to Birmingham New Street, Lydia's thoughts returned to yesterday afternoon.

"What did you make of Martyn Street?" asked Lydia. "I'd ruled him out as a suspect."

"Gus took Luke to the Wilton café for their first meeting with Jackson and Street. Their reports in the files didn't point towards Martyn being the killer. He lost his rag at something Gus said, but neither Gus nor Luke made much of it. The witnesses who contributed to the murder file described Martyn as a hard-working giant with a quick temper. Most painted him as slow-witted or backward, but he fooled everyone. Martyn was far more capable than many people imagined. Gus led him through the sequence of events unfolding when he left the engineering factory. Gus gambled the solicitor wouldn't jump in to suggest his client didn't have to answer. Whether Martyn has genuinely erased stabbing his mother from his memory or not, I don't know. A court will decide. It will help if Salisbury police discover the remnants of the bloodied clothing and the murder weapon Martyn admitted having hidden. Gus believes we've got enough evidence for a guilty verdict."

"We don't always see the results of our labours, do we?" said Lydia. "I mean, actually going to court for the trial and helping to find the young woman Gus mentioned after you guys returned to the office."

"You mean Maureen Glendenning," said Alex. "Gus thinks Bourne Hill are the right people to take that search forward. Luke and Neil did most of the leg work yesterday, trying to find her in the UK or Spain. I only heard what they told Gus late yesterday. What did you and Blessing contribute?"

"Not much," admitted Lydia. "We finished updating the Freeman Files and then searched social media for signs of a Maureen Glendenning. That proved a fruitless exercise. Neil hadn't found evidence of a wedding in the reasonable period he researched in the morning. Just after lunch, Blessing trawled through the recorded deaths since 1968 without luck. It's an unusual surname, so the chances of everyone missing a mention of a Glendenning are slim. By the time you and Gus returned, we had resigned ourselves to accept that the poor girl was dead."

"What about Maureen's child? Did Luke try to learn who adopted the baby? We're assuming Maureen put the child up for adoption, but the mother's name would appear on the paperwork."

"Gus told London Road what we knew," said Lydia, "after he informed them he'd wrapped up another cold case. Gus didn't discuss it with us, but perhaps he thought it better for the fifty-year-old man or woman not to find out. How would it help them?"

"You searched for your birth parents when you were old enough," said Alex. "I wonder if Maureen's child ever started the process?"

"I'd be surprised if Graham Street's name appeared on the birth certificate," said Lydia. "He was an evil man, wasn't he?"

"He wasn't the only person from the investigation who was a bad lot. That's another side of the Marion Reeves case that feels unsatisfactory," said Alex. "Everyone who deserved to stand trial died before we uncovered the truth."

"Maybe an investigation will find culprits in the sexual exploitation affair that are still alive," said Lydia.

The train pulled into Birmingham New Street just before eleven o'clock. Alex and Lydia switched trains for the final time. Another four hours, and they would arrive at Waverley Station.

Lydia looked forward to meeting with Eleanor again and introducing her to Alex. Because of the type of relationship she'd developed with her birth mother, Lydia wasn't nervous. The nerves would set in when the couple travelled forty miles further north to Dundee to meet the people she called Mum and Dad.

"A penny for them?" asked Alex.

"I was just thinking about what we might do this afternoon," said Lydia. "There won't be much time for sightseeing before we travel into Edinburgh for a meal. Eleanor isn't a night bird. She'll be tucked up by eleven o'clock, so we can't eat too late."

"While you were miles away, staring out of the window, I scrolled through a few places of interest on my phone," said Alex. "We could use the hop-on, hop-off open-top bus service to check out the hot spots. Eleanor will guide us to the best options, and we can get to as many as possible tomorrow morning. If we make an early start, we can fit in lunch somewhere with Eleanor closer to home and then get a taxi to the station to save a few minutes."

"That sounds good," said Lydia.

The train trundled into Waverley Bridge on time. Alex

put an arm across Lydia to stop her from rushing for the carriage door.

"Let the eager-beavers go first," said Alex. "Give them ninety seconds to trample over one another in a rush to get off the platform. Then, we'll follow behind them and decide the best exit to catch that bus to Craigmillar."

"You're not a fan of crowds, are you?" said Lydia, gathering her things together.

Alex grabbed his bag and, taking Lydia's hand, led her off the train. She had to admit the worst of the crowds had dispersed as they strolled along the concourse.

"I know it's a Saturday afternoon," said Alex, "but this place is busy, isn't it?"

"Waverley Bridge handles twenty-five million passengers every year," said Lydia. "There have been so many changes in recent years. The main station facilities stand in the middle of a large island platform surrounded by platforms on four sides. There are eighteen platforms, which connect to Scotland, and a range of train franchisees run trains between Edinburgh and every major city in England."

"Were you a trainspotter when you were a young girl?" asked Alex. "You seem to know the place inside out."

"My parents brought me into Edinburgh quite often when I was growing up," said Lydia. "The train was the easiest way to travel. This city was where I was born, after all. When I left school, I wanted to be an actress, and it was a toss-up whether to find a drama school here or in Glasgow."

"What made you choose Glasgow?" asked Alex.

"It was further from Dundee," said Lydia. "I knew I was adopted, and the need to find my birth parents was growing. So I felt I should get far enough away to find my path if that makes sense?"

"You realised the time had come when you needed to stand on your own two feet," said Alex. "No matter how well-meaning your parents were, they stifled your true character."

"Gus might have preferred it if I'd remained a home bird," laughed Lydia. "I'd turn up to the office in a sensible twin-set over a knee-length tartan skirt."

"You wouldn't look out of place in this building," said Alex. "How long has it been here?"

"Since the late 1860s," said Lydia. "The booking hall floor featured beautiful mosaic tiling when it opened, but there have had to be too many changes in recent years for the original features to be so prominent. It's such a shame. The station no longer allows access to cars because of the heightened threat of a terror attack. The taxis used to drive right onto the concourse. Now they have to queue outside."

"Cars parked next to steam trains right where we're standing must have created a terrific atmosphere," said Alex. "The pollution must have been deadly, but nobody knew it back then."

"The covered escalators over there will take us to Princes Street on the north side," said Lydia. "We can catch the bus outside."

Twenty minutes later, they reached Eleanor's home in Craigmillar. Lydia rang the bell.

Alex didn't have a particular picture of what Lydia's mother might look like. But, when he had met Chidozie Barre, the family likeness was striking. Chidozie was tall, muscular, handsome, and confident. There was no doubt Lydia was his daughter.

Eleanor had a slighter build, and her ginger hair faded with age. It was more rosy-blonde than copper these days.

In a decade, the grey and silvery-white highlights would become more dominant.

"Come in, you two," said Eleanor. "You've had a tiring journey. Sit yourselves down and relax with afternoon tea. Lydia knows where your bedroom is. You can get settled in later."

Alex and Lydia dropped their bags at the foot of the stairs, sank into the comfortable sofa, and did as instructed. Eleanor left them and returned from the kitchen several minutes later with a trolley. The top shelf held three plates laden with food, plus a pot of tea and a small sugar bowl. Eleanor pointed to side plates, cutlery, cups, and saucers on the bottom shelf.

"There are the makings, you two. Get stuck in."

Alex looked at the sandwiches, cakes, and scones on offer. He'd need to walk the three miles into the city to make room for an evening meal. Lydia had already dived in. She was always hungry.

"So, you're the famous Alex Hardy I keep hearing about?" said Eleanor.

"Famous rather than infamous," said Alex. "I'll settle for that. It's good to meet you too, Eleanor, finally."

Lydia had demolished two sandwiches and was deciding which cake to go for next when she spotted something in a vase on the mantlepiece.

"A red rose," she said.

"A single red rose, Lydia," said Eleanor. "Chidozie brought it when he and Rosa visited. It's on its last legs now. I ought to have thrown it out, but I kept talking to it and saying you would be here this weekend."

"He didn't forget what he'd given you when he arrived for your first date," said Alex. "How romantic."

"Mmm," said Lydia. "I hope you weren't encouraging him, Eleanor?"

"Don't be foolish, girl. It wasn't to be twenty-six years ago, and we've both moved on. I'm so glad you and Chidozie found one another. Rosa told me about your time with them at the Lady Eleanor. Despite the name, it sounds like an interesting place. Rosa said that Chidozie was disappointed they were losing their chef."

"A five-star restaurant has snapped up Lucas Romeijn, I imagine," said Alex. "His food was spectacular. Chidozie knew they were lucky to have held onto him for as long as they had."

"Lucas, yes, that was his name," said Eleanor. "He leaves at the end of this month. Chidozie and Rosa were interviewing people to replace him after they flew home. I haven't spoken to them since."

"Where did you take them while they were here, Eleanor?" asked Lydia.

"They took me to The Table in the evening," said Eleanor, "to see how the other half lives. We spent a lot of time here chatting. If it had been just the two of us, I think Rosa would have enjoyed a few hours of retail therapy on Princes Street or George Street. I liked her. We got on well together."

"They invited you to Dubai in the autumn, didn't they?" asked Lydia.

"You know they did. I told you on the phone. Why, what's the matter?"

"Nothing," said Alex. "We got an invitation too. How would you feel if the three of us flew out there together?"

"That sounds a marvellous idea," said Eleanor. "I'd get to spend a whole week with my daughter. And her partner, of course. Are you sure Chidozie and Rosa wouldn't mind?"

"I can't see why," said Lydia. "If you were there alone, they would feel duty-bound to keep you entertained every minute. When they close the Lady Eleanor and escape to Dubai, they deserve a rest after a busy summer. We can let them do their own thing while we three explore Dubai, then get together in the evenings. Us girls can go shopping one day while Chidozie and Alex can chill out by the pool."

"We'll need to stay for two weeks to fit everything in," laughed Eleanor. "You've got it worked out, haven't you?"

"I try," said Lydia.

The afternoon tea took its toll. Alex glanced at his watch as Eleanor wheeled the empty trolley towards the kitchen.

"We can forget the open-top bus ride," he said. "I'd better ring around to book a table. Then, when we get our gear upstairs, shower, and get ready, it will be time to leave."

"How far away is the Castle, Eleanor?" Lydia called out.

"Half a mile, dear. It's worth a visit if you want to take a walk later."

"I've found a restaurant a mile from the Castle," said Alex. "I'll ring and check if we can get a table."

Lydia joined Eleanor in the kitchen.

"It's a beautiful evening," said Eleanor. "People think we don't get warm sunshine here in Scotland. We do, not as often as we would like, but you learn to enjoy it while it lasts."

"Once we learn what time we're eating, we'll plan our night," said Lydia. "Alex was hoping you could point us towards the best places to visit. He's never been this far north before and wants to see the sights."

"You don't need me to tell you it will take more than a couple of hours tomorrow morning to do that, dear," said Eleanor. "I'll come with you if you wish. We can whet his appetite. Maybe you'll both come back again soon."

Alex was standing in the doorway.

"We'd love to, Eleanor. I've booked a table for eight o'clock at the Condita. It's less than a mile from the Castle. I hope that's okay?"

"That's fine," said Eleanor, "it's one of the top ten restaurants in the city. I'd better hunt for something to wear now."

Alex and Lydia carried their bags upstairs to the bedroom.

"Eleanor only has one bathroom," said Lydia. "Perhaps it would be best to catch the bus into the city and get off as close to the restaurant as possible."

"She said the Castle was only half a mile from here," said Alex. "The restaurant claims to be a mile from the Castle. Surely, we can walk it?"

"This is Scotland, Alex," said Lydia. "They have castles everywhere. Craigmillar Castle is half a mile south of this house. Edinburgh Castle is probably two-and-a-half miles away to the west. So either we walk to Craigmillar Castle, look around, and then get a taxi, or we skip that trip for this evening and take a stroll towards Edinburgh."

Ninety minutes later, everyone was washed, dressed, and ready to leave. Eleanor laughed when Lydia explained Alex's confusion.

"I know a shortcut through Prestonfield that will get us to the restaurant inside in forty minutes. As long as you promise we'll get a taxi home, I'm game."

"If we leave now, we'll make it in time," said Alex.

It was almost half-past eleven when Alex paid the taxi fare and tottered up the path behind Eleanor and Lydia. The restaurant meal had been excellent, and Eleanor surprised them by knowing a great bar just around the corner. So much for her being early to bed every night.

Perhaps she was on her best behaviour when Lydia came here before.

Any thoughts of a long lie-in disappeared when Eleanor knocked on their bedroom door at seven o'clock.

"Two cups of tea on a tray outside the door," she trilled. "Breakfast will be on the table in twenty minutes."

Alex groaned. Lydia fetched the tray, and the two coffee-lovers started the day with a strong cuppa.

"We need to shower and get dressed," said Lydia. "We're not at home now."

The smells of a fried breakfast wafted from the kitchen and drew them downstairs well within the twenty minutes allowed by their host. Sausage, fried egg, streaky bacon, baked beans, tattie scones, fried tomatoes, and toast adorned their plates.

"That looks terrific," said Lydia.

"How can you face a cooked breakfast after the glasses of single malt we drank last night?" asked Alex.

"This is the best cure I've come across," said Eleanor. "If you want to see the sights of the city and endure a seven-hour train journey later today, you'll need to line your stomach, Alex. Get stuck in. There's more tea in the pot when you're ready."

"I'd prefer a black coffee," said Alex, "if there's one going."

"There might be a small jar in the cupboard," said Eleanor. "I bought it for Lydia, in case she'd lost her taste for tea since she moved south."

"I'll get us a cup in a minute, Alex," said Lydia. "This breakfast tastes as terrific as it looks. It takes me back to Sunday mornings in Dundee with my parents. We drank tea there too. Coffee became my drink of choice when I left home and moved to Glasgow to study."

"That explains it, heathens," said Eleanor with a grin.

Alex swallowed hard and forked pieces of bacon, sausage, and tomato into his mouth.

"You're feeling human already, aren't you?" asked Eleanor.

Lydia came back to the table with two black coffees.

"The kettle was just off the boil," she said. "You should be able to drink it straight away."

Alex took a healthy swig.

"I am now, Eleanor," he said. "My appetite has just woken up."

After breakfast, Alex and Lydia packed their bags and prepared to leave Craigmillar. Eleanor joined them as they took the bus into the city. She showed them Edinburgh Castle, the Royal Mile and Holyrood Palace Park.

"It's a few minutes before one," she said as they sat in the Palace garden. "They don't fire the cannon at the Castle on Sunday, so you won't wonder what's going on. Many tourists on Princes Street have almost had a heart attack on their first visit. What time's your train?"

"There's one leaving at half-past two that shaves an hour off the journey home," said Alex. "We planned to take you to lunch, but after that scrumptious breakfast, I don't think either of us could manage more than a sandwich."

"Don't worry, dear," said Eleanor. "I can get myself a bite to eat later. Catch the two-thirty train. You'll get back to Chippenham at a reasonable time then. You both need to be wide awake in the morning."

"Gus Freeman will bring back another cold case from London Road," said Lydia.

"I won't come with you to Waverley," said Eleanor. "I can get the bus back to Craigmillar. You can walk it from here in fifteen minutes. Go down Canongate and turn right into Market Street. Ring me when you get home, and promise me you'll come again."

"We will," said Alex.

"Don't forget Dubai," said Lydia.

Eleanor hugged Lydia and Alex before striding towards the nearest bus stop.

"We've got an hour to kill before the train leaves," said Lydia as she and Alex turned towards Canongate.

Alex was scrolling through his phone.

"Caffe Nero and Pret A Manger have outlets on the station," he said. "I could murder a coffee."

"Would you share a toasted sandwich with me?" asked Lydia. Alex nodded.

They reflected on a grand weekend as they boarded the train at twenty-five past two.

"We didn't get to spend that long with Eleanor," said Alex, "but it was fun."

"Tomorrow is another day," said Lydia as she nestled her head on Alex's shoulder. "I wonder whose death we'll investigate this time?"

Dead Reckoning: Chapter Two

Friday, 13 February 2015

"It promises to be a quiet night tonight, Alf," said Rosie as she peered through the curtained window at the stormy night outside.

"My Joan often asks me why I thought it a good idea to take on a pub on Salisbury Plain," muttered Alf Collett. "There's been a pub here for over three hundred years, I told her. Where else will people go for a drink?"

"Has this place always been called the Traveller's Rest?" asked Rosie.

"As far as I can make out, lass," said Alf. "In the old days, they had stables where the car park is today. Most of the passing trade was on horseback or in coaches dragged by a team of four. The land surrounding this inn was full of farms and smallholdings, with farmers and labourers who welcomed a few pints at the end of the day. Even if it took them a while to get here on foot."

"I take twenty minutes to drive here from home," said

Rosie. "I wondered whether I'd even find the place the first evening I worked here. It's so remote."

"Every class of road, bridle-path and byway has always crisscrossed the Plain, Rosie. If you knew the quickest route to where you wanted to go, it was no problem, but it's harder since the wide-open spaces attracted the interest of the Ministry of Defence."

"When was that, do you remember?" asked the twenty-year-old barmaid.

Alf Collett heard the outside door creak. Joan constantly moaned at him to get a drop of oil on its hinges, but Alf preferred the advanced warning when a customer arrived. Alf checked the large clock behind the bar. Twenty past eight. The first of their regulars had arrived, despite the wind, rain, and occasional sleet that would keep most people indoors.

"Ask Jim," said Alf. He took a pint glass from the shelf and drew a pint of bitter.

Rosie recognised the elderly figure that shuffled through the door from the small square hallway. Jim Thornton was a retired sheep farm labourer and someone who the Traveller's Rest could rely on to turn out in all winds and weathers. The brewery wouldn't get rich on the two pints that Jim allowed himself every night, but he wouldn't give up his nightly visit until they closed the lid on his coffin.

"Not many on the roads tonight," said Jim Thornton as he came further into the warm and inviting room. "It's a darn sight warmer in here than outside. A pint of my usual, please, Rosie."

"On its way, Mr Thornton," said Rosie. "Do you remember when the army started using the Plain?"

"How old do you think I am?" scoffed Jim. "I've lived two miles up the road all my life, and I was born during the

Second World War, but Queen Victoria was still on the throne the first time they used the Plain for exercises."

"Sorry, Mr Thornton," said Rosie. "Alf just thought you might remember reading about when it started. I didn't mean to suggest you were there."

Alf Collett placed the foaming pint on a beer mat on the bar next to their only customer. Jim Thornton handed over a crumpled five-pound note and took a healthy sip of his drink.

"I passed Dave Vickers on his bicycle half a mile back," said Jim. "He's got a better memory than me for facts and figures, young Rosie. I'll tell you what I know, and maybe Dave can fill in the gaps. He'll be here directly."

Alf listened out for the creaking door. Sure enough, Dave Vickers strode through the inner door, cycle helmet under his arm one minute later. A manager of a building society branch in Amesbury, Vickers was in his early fifties, single, overweight, and rosy-cheeked after his cycle ride.

"Golly, it's perishing out there tonight. Evening all," said Dave. "A pint of the usual, please, Rosie."

"I don't understand how you drink cold beer on nights like this," said Rosie with a shiver. "That will be three pounds, please, Mr Vickers."

Dave Vickers moved away from the roaring fire to use the contactless payment machine next to the old-fashioned till on the bar. Jim Thornton tutted and nodded at the two one-pound coins next to his pint glass.

"I can remember when decimalisation came in," Jim moaned. "Forty-odd years ago, a pint of bitter became eight new pence overnight instead of one shilling and sixpence. That's when prices started climbing. It should have been seven pence ha'penny by rights, but the brewery screwed us with a crafty price rise."

"Just over six-and-a-half percent," said Dave.

"If you say so," said Jim. "I know I've got a one-pound coin in my jacket pocket to place alongside these two on the bar when I want my second pint."

Alf Collett could tell where this conversation was heading. Jim Thornton needed to watch every penny as a pensioner. Sheep farming was an honest living, but it didn't give its labourers an inflation-proof company pension when they retired. Jim's state pension and a few savings were everything he had. Jim's wife had worked at a local nursery throughout her married life and wasn't in the best of health these days, which didn't help matters.

"You're a different generation to me, Dave," said Jim. "I thought you had more sense. How will anyone in the future learn the value of money if they tap their way through life without counting the pennies to check they can afford what they're buying?"

Dave Vickers had heard Jim on his high-horse about contactless payments before. Jim was old-school, and Dave hoped cash didn't disappear while people of Jim's generation were still around. Change was painful at any age, but to change the habits of a lifetime was nigh on impossible.

"We'll agree to differ, Jim," said Dave. "I know what I can spend while enjoying a beer on a Friday evening. It's as easy for me to control my expenditure with my phone app as for you to ask your wife for six quid before you leave the house."

Rosie laughed.

"Cheeky young beggar," said Jim. "I don't have to ask permission to pop out for a couple of beers."

Dave took his pint and sat closer to the fire. Alf eyed Jim's glass and prepared to pour his second and final pint for the evening. As Jim took a long swig, almost draining the glass, the outside door heralded another customer.

"Oscar," said Alf. "We haven't seen you in here for a few weeks. Everything alright up at the house?"

Oscar Wallington was the estate manager at the nearby manor house. Alf wasn't sure which regiment Oscar served in, but Oscar left his quarters at Bulford Camp and settled in the area with his family when he'd done his duty. The job at the manor house suited a man well-versed in a disciplined life.

The locals who used the Traveller's Rest reckoned the estate was on the verge of bankruptcy when Oscar took over from the previous manager four years ago. Today, it was in a far healthier financial position, and it wasn't only Oscar's highly polished shoes where the sun shone.

"Best laid plans, Alf," said Oscar. "You know how it is. My wife kept telling me she sticks religiously to this dry January caper. I thought I'd enjoy the extra Scotch we got in for Christmas and New Year and then take a break from the booze in February. After the day I've had up at the manor house, I thought, blow it, I'm dropping by the Traveller's Rest tonight for a wee dram."

"A double?" asked Alf.

"I wasn't aware there was another measure, old chap," said Oscar. "A splash of soda, if you please."

Alf prepared Oscar's drink, and Rosie escaped from behind the bar to warm herself by the fire.

"It could do with another log," said Dave.

"I'm not made of money," said Alf. "It'll be quiet tonight. You can get off home when that fire dies, and I'll close early. Rosie has a tricky drive ahead of her if this weather closes in any further. You appreciate what the Plain can be like this time of year."

"Give that fire a stir with the poker, Rosie," said Dave. "There might be enough life to keep us warm until eleven o'clock."

Jim Thornton finished his first pint and handed his glass to Alf.

"Did you ever wonder what those copper and brass items were hanging in the fireplace, Dave?" he asked, winking at the landlord.

"They look old," said Dave, "but they're for decorative purposes these days, aren't they?"

"Rosie asked why we suffer cold beer in the winter months," said Jim. "One of those Victorian utensils was for warming your beer. Sticking a red-hot poker into a glass of dark, malty beer is an English winter tradition stretching back a thousand years. My grandfather used to drink in this bar and enjoyed sitting where you are now, supping his mulled beer every winter. He told my father he was often troubled with headaches, stomach ache, toothache, coughs, colds, and other rheumatic diseases when he drank cold beer. However, as soon as he started drinking his beer as hot as blood, he stayed in good health throughout the winter."

"It doesn't sound very hygienic," said Rosie, making a face.

"I imagine that was what they used the conical warming vessel on the right-hand side for," said Oscar, sitting on a stool at the bar nursing his double whisky. "Alf's predecessors would fill the vessel, stick it deep in the fire and watch for the foam to form. Then use a tool from the fireside set to help lift it out and pour the warmed beer into a customer's glass. I can't see it making a comeback. Health and Safety would have a field day."

"You still haven't got your answer yet, Rosie," said Jim.

"Ask Mr Wallington when the MoD became so interested in the Plain."

"I was going to ask Mr Vickers," said Rosie.

"I don't know much about those days, Rosie," Dave said. "I learned at school that Salisbury was a prosperous place several centuries ago. Why build a cathedral there if it wasn't? The wealth came from the wool and cloth trade. Those industries declined in the mid-nineteenth century, and Wiltshire had become one of the poorest counties in England by the turn of the century. There were extensive areas of Salisbury Plain where few profitable businesses had survived, so the Ministry of Defence thought they could put the area to better use."

"The training area covers roughly half of the Plain," said Oscar. "The army conducted its first exercises in 1898. From then on, the MoD bought large areas of land until WWII. The one hundred and fifty square miles of land they own makes it the UK's largest military training area. Much of that land is rented to farmers or licenced for grazing. The army keeps fifty square miles for live firing. Public access is greatly restricted or permanently closed in those areas, as you know, Rosie. I'm sure the route you took to drive here tonight was anything but as the crow flies."

"In the dark, it's hard to see crows," said Rosie. "I nearly always get lost, but somehow every lane or track ends up at this pub."

"Our ancestors got a few things right," said Dave Vickers. "They knew the priorities."

"Where do you live, Rosie, if you don't mind me asking?" asked Oscar Wallington.

"Stratford-sub-Castle," Rosie replied. "It used to be a separate village to the north of the city, but it's part of Salisbury these days."

"You live in a cottage next to your old farm, don't you, Jim?" asked Oscar. "Is that far from here?"

"Between here and Chitterne," said Jim. "I passed Dave in Tilshead cycling from Shrewton on my way here."

"I can't imagine you cycling here, Mr Wallington," said Rosie, moving back behind the bar to stand beside Alf Collett.

"No, I've got my trusty old Land Rover Defender outside," said Oscar. "It won't be long before I can take her on the London to Brighton Rally, but she gets the job done. My journey here is around the same as yours, Rosie. Twenty minutes, give or take. My employer's Lodge House lies on the other side of the village of Chitterne."

"It's a sign of the times," said Alf Collett. "The only way a country pub can survive is for people like yourselves to drive from the nearest town or village. Jim here always has two pints and drives home, praying the police aren't waiting for him up at the crossroads. Dave doesn't drive, but you can still be drunk in charge of a bicycle. Many's the night I've locked up as Dave cycles along the road, hitting the grass verge on either side."

"I fell into the hedge one night," said Dave. "A Christmas Eve, I think it was. I was laughing so much I couldn't get up for several minutes."

"Just as well you were wearing a helmet," said Rosie.

"What about you, Oscar?" asked Alf. "Will you want another double scotch?"

Oscar Wallington tapped his nose.

"When you've spent a lifetime learning how to evade the enemy, you work out how to get back to base with no one seeing you."

Jim Thornton rapped his hand on the bar top.

"You crafty beggar," he said. "The Defender comes in handy for that purpose, no doubt."

"She's a four-wheel drive," said Oscar, "and there are a dozen fields between the Traveller's Rest and the Lodge owned by the estate. So I can manoeuvre my way back to my billet, avoiding any places the police might patrol if I've over-indulged."

"I don't think I've ever seen a patrol car out this way," said Rosie, "not since I've worked here."

"My predecessor was fond of a lock-in," said Alf. "Before you ask, Joan would have my hide if I started that game. It has to be ten years since a patrol car idled past the Traveller's Rest looking for someone to nick. As for my licences, they send a young PC during daylight hours to check them."

"Just the one?" asked Dave. "I thought they went nowhere without a colleague."

"The Plain will be unfamiliar territory to many of the youngsters they have working for the police nowadays," said Jim. "I dare them to visit certain parts in the dark, alone, without wondering if ghosts and ghouls hide behind every tree and shrub. I know the area well, and long ago, people rarely strayed more than a few miles from the house where they were born. Sixty years ago, as a young man, I can remember villages within a few miles of this pub populated by only five families."

"Inbreeding going on," muttered Oscar.

"Maybe there was," said Jim. "Perhaps they knew no different. If I developed a thirst after searching for a lost ewe, I might wet my whistle in one of the dozens of nearby pubs that have long since disappeared. When I walked into a bar, everyone's eyes turned towards me. The temperature dropped a few degrees, and conversation died until I had drunk my beer and left. There were rumours of pagan worship in those remote villages and hamlets. I can't swear to any truth behind those rumours, but forget what you believe about the world being a small place. Put yourself in the middle of the Plain, with civilisation miles away. What if a combination of the weather, geography, or circumstances cut you off from the nearest big town? Even the plague if you went back far enough. Who knows what demons might have survived in such a wilderness, real or imaginary?"

"You're a bundle of laughs tonight, Jim," said Alf. "Is it because it's Friday the thirteenth? Do you think something wicked lies in wait outside that front door?"

"I wish I had someone to come home with me later tonight," said Rose. "I'll lock my car doors and turn the stereo up full blast on the way home."

Jim Thornton turned his attention to his pint of bitter. Most of what he just said was a myth, but people underestimated the dangers of the Plain at their peril.

Dave Vickers stared into the fire's glowing embers and wondered if he could afford driving lessons in the spring. He decided it required a fresh pint while he considered. The large clock behind the bar ticked on as the handful of staff and customers sat quietly with their thoughts.

Oscar Wallington ordered another double whisky as the clock ticked to half-past nine. "The last one for me for tonight," he said.

"I don't think Dave and Jim will be far behind you, Oscar," said Alf. "Jim's hung onto that empty glass for long enough."

As Alf slipped a twenty-pound note into the till and sorted Oscar's change, he heard the creaking door. With a sigh, he placed the change on the bar and looked to see his new customer.

"That's all we need," he groaned as he recognised Kendal Guthrie.

The Guthrie family claimed to have farmed on the Plain for centuries. Nobody was too sure when they first moved south from Angus in Scotland, but they lost any trace of an accent several generations back.

Kendal Guthrie was a larger-than-life character and was universally disliked.

At sixty-seven, he was a widower; his wife, Poppy, died eighteen months earlier from a heart attack. The couple had two children. Wesley, married with two sons, lived and worked on one of the five farms currently owned by his wealthy father.

Wesley, at thirty-eight, was two years older than his sister, Helen. She married young at eighteen to Guy Stilwell, a structural engineer, and they emigrated to Melbourne, Australia, four years later. Helen and Guy had no children. Wesley had only seen his sister in the past fourteen years when she flew back alone for their mother's funeral.

Alf Collett patiently waited while Guthrie removed his camelhair coat and looked for an appropriate place to hang it.

"I suppose it's too much to ask that a pub in the back of beyond might possess a coat hanger. This coat cost me twelve hundred quid."

"The wind and rain outside can't tell the difference between it and an old parka," said Alf. "There are several spare pegs on the rack by the door. Take your pick. What can I get you to drink?"

"A gin and tonic. Slimline, no ice, with a twist of lemon. Get the girl to put it together if it's too complicated for you."

Kendal Guthrie strolled to the bar and made a great

show of removing his wallet from his inside jacket pocket. Dave Vickers admired the cut of the dark blue suit Guthrie wore. The building society manager reckoned it would cost him at least a month's wages.

Guthrie watched Alf cutting the evening's first and only slice of lemon. Then he turned to study the person sitting near him at the bar.

"Who do we have here?" he sneered. "A squaddie masquerading as a gentleman farmer. You're a long way from home, Wallington. That Defender of yours outside looks to be on its last legs. Go easy on the whisky. You can't afford to scratch my Bentley Continental GT if you leave here before me tonight."

"My Defender will get me home whatever the weather, Guthrie," said Oscar. "I served my Queen and country for over thirty years, and I was a Warrant Officer Class One for the last thirteen of those years. That's as far as you can get from a raw recruit without a commission. As far as I can tell, the only person you've ever served is yourself."

"Ooh, touched a nerve there, did I? If you fancied a better motor, General, why not do what the estate manager before you did? No wonder the place was losing money. He embezzled over a quarter of a million, or so I heard. A mere twenty grand would be enough for a car that suited a man of your calibre."

Guthrie laughed out loud. Nobody else in the room joined him. Alf knew it wouldn't phase the farmer. It was water off a duck's back. Guthrie relished the fact people hated him. He thought it was because they were jealous of his wealth.

Alf placed the gin and tonic on the bar counter in front of Guthrie and turned away.

"How much do I owe you?" asked Guthrie shifting a wad of banknotes partly from the wallet.

"Four pounds, fifty, Mr Guthrie," said Rosie.

"Ah, the vision of loveliness speaks as well," said Guthrie. "I can see you've not been busy tonight, sweetheart. Can you change a fifty-pound note?"

Guthrie laughed once more when he saw Rosie's head snap around to seek help from Alf.

"Don't worry, sweetheart," said Guthrie. "I've got several of each denomination—even a measly fiver. Put the change in the charity box for Guide Dogs for the Blind. Keep an eye on this one, Alf. She might have sticky fingers like the last girl you had behind the bar. Or was that just a vicious rumour about you and Imogen?"

That set Kendal Guthrie off again. He thought he was highly amusing.

"Well, you can't stop people talking," said Guthrie. "They tell me Joan hasn't come downstairs to work alongside you since Imogen left. You know what they say. No smoke without fire."

"Alf's not like that," said Rosie. "He's been the perfect gentleman ever since I started."

"Imogen did short-change customers," said Dave Vickers. "She couldn't get away with it with us regulars because we're too familiar with the prices. Alf reckoned Imogen was lucky if she got two pounds a night. It was hardly the Great Train Robbery."

"You'd know all about that, wouldn't you, Vickers? Our jovial building society manager offers half of one per cent interest rates. Who does that help? It means people who don't have the first idea about money can borrow it far too easily, while those of us who have worked hard for it get next to nothing for investing several million in your branch."

"I don't set the rates, Guthrie," said Dave. "Blame the Bank of England."

"Funny that, isn't it, General? Dave quickly passes the responsibility on to someone further up the chain. You must have encountered that when you were a serving soldier. Same story, but the other way around. The grunts in the trenches carry the can when something goes wrong in the heat of battle."

Jim Thornton released his grip on his pint glass, stepped away from the bar stool, and lifted his coat from the back of a nearby chair.

"I'll be on my way," he said.

"If the Devil were to cast his net in here tonight, he'd be disappointed," said Guthrie. "All shrimps and no Atlantic bluefin tuna. Jim Thornton, as I live and breathe. What a life, eh Jim? You toiled away for fifty years for Bob Ellison's father, and did you get a gold watch on the day you retired? Did you heck. Now you're spending your last days praying that your poor wife goes first. Does she realise the truth, Jim? Bob told me his old man promised he wouldn't turn you out of your tied cottage until you died. Now Bob has had enough of scraping a living as a sheep farmer and wants to sell the lot, lock, stock, and tied cottages. Fred Ellison was an honourable man; he gave you his word. Nothing in writing though, Jim, was there?"

"Bob won't go back on his father's promise," said Jim. "Not everyone is as devious as you, Guthrie."

"You might have a problem, though, Jim. What do you know of Lower Everleigh? Or farms out at Enford, Ablington, Durrington, and Collingbourne Ducis? Of course, you wouldn't have your finger on the pulse. They're on the latest list from the MoD. Five farms were released for sale to tenant farmers. Little by little, as the General here will confirm, our army is decreasing in size. They don't need the land they amassed before the Second World War. You've got to be quick when you hear a whisper of a release such as that. There's money to be made. I've got my name down for the ones that are the best fit with my portfolio. I won't secure every one of them, but that doesn't matter. Anyway, now I've heard that Bob Ellison's farm is up for grabs, that's one I want, and you know why."

"You own the farms on either side," said Oscar Wallington.

"Give the General a cigar," said Guthrie.

"You wouldn't turn an old couple out of the home they've lived in for half a century," said Dave Vickers.

"That's cruel and vindictive," said Rosie.

"No. That's business, sweetheart," said Guthrie.

"I'm not your sweetheart," yelled Rosie.

"Don't fret, petal. You're too skinny for my taste. That Imogen was a fine-looking woman, but Alf would know better than me whether her performance compensated for the couple hundred pounds she stole from him."

"That's enough, Guthrie," said Alf Collett. "I'm calling time. Ten minutes, and everyone needs to get out. Don't come back, Guthrie. You're barred."

"Hah, they have barred me from better pubs than this dump. If I want a place to drink, perhaps I'll turn Jim's cottage into a roadside tavern for a couple of years. It will take time to get planning permission for residential development for the rest of the land."

"Nigh on impossible," said Oscar.

"You've been out of the army for a while, General," said Guthrie. "Surely, when troops and their families return from the defunct German bases, they will need somewhere to live? Larkhill, Bulford, and Tilshead are right on my doorstep."

Kendal Guthrie waved his wallet as he strolled to collect his coat.

"Money talks."

He was still laughing as Alf heard the front door creak shut behind him.

"He's serious, isn't he, Mr Thornton?" said Rosie.

"I haven't heard a thing from Bob Ellison," said Jim. "I know plenty of farmers, not just on the Plain, have struggled these past few years. Several have got out altogether; the others diversified to survive. Bob's heart was never in it, anyway. Fred struggled to convince him to take over after he retired. While Fred was alive, there was no chance Bob would sell up, but it's been several years since Fred passed. Who knows? Guthrie has had his eyes on that farm for years."

"When did you retire, Jim?" asked Dave Vickers.

"Five years ago, when I reached sixty-five. I was happy to work on, but Bob reckoned I'd done enough to deserve a rest."

"Fred Ellison was older than you, wasn't he?" asked Alf.

"Ten years, maybe," said Jim. "He died two years before I stopped work. So that's seven years ago."

"When did Fred talk with you about the tenancy?" asked Dave.

"He called into the cottage and discussed it with the wife and me shortly after he handed the farm over to his son. He said we deserved to have a roof over our heads for as long as we needed it after staying with him throughout my working life. Fred carried on working until he was seventy. That would have suited me, but Bob put a stop to that. Why, what does it matter?"

"The laws have changed relating to agricultural tenancies over the years," said Dave. "I would contact a solicitor to find out where you stand."

"I can't afford a solicitor," said Jim. "Fred gave me his word. That's good enough for me, and it should also be good enough for Bob. Guthrie likes to stir the pot every chance he gets. One day, he'll go too far, and someone will put an end to it."

Jim wrapped his scarf around his neck and waited until the others were ready to leave. He didn't want to be outside alone with Kendal Guthrie. He'd heard enough from him for one night.

Dave Vickers brought his empty glass to the bar and handed it to Rosie.

"I don't think you're too skinny, Rosie," he said. "Kendal Guthrie's an ignorant pig."

Rosie giggled and collected the handful of empty glasses.

"Take care cycling home, Mr Vickers," she said. "I don't want to see you in the hedge when I drive past. I'll sing at the top of my voice to scare away the bogeyman."

Oscar Wallington was ready to leave, and he went to join Jim by the door.

"We both copped flak from Guthrie tonight," he said. "You're right. It's high time Guthrie got his just deserts."

Dave Vickers didn't pass a comment. He knew he needed to pay a visit before tackling the bike ride home to Shrewton. As Dave headed for the Gents, he noticed Rosie slipping into the Ladies next door. Two minutes later, Dave made his way outside and groaned when he saw the weather had worsened.

Alf Collett waited until the bar was clear of customers and then locked the front door. They hadn't taken enough money to make it worth opening, and Kendal Guthrie had soured what little joy the evening had brought. Alf joined Rosie behind the bar and picked up a cloth to dry the glasses she had finished washing.

"I'll finish these if you want to get off home, Rosie," said Alf.

"We're nearly done. Why do you think Mr Guthrie is so horrible to everyone? Did you see that wallet of his? He had hundreds of pounds, and his watch was a Rolex. Who needs three gold rings on each hand, anyway? It's asking for trouble."

"He'll get what's coming to him," said Alf. "If what Guthrie said to Jim is right, this place could have competition just up the road, which will finish me. Now I've barred him; he's the sort of bloke who would open a pub out of spite, whether or not it made him money. He's a swine, through and through."

Rosie shivered.

"I didn't like how he looked at me," she said. "He gave me the creeps."

Rosie fetched her woolly hat, coat, and gloves from behind the bar, and Alf let her out of the side door.

"Mind how you go, lass," he said. "I'll see you tomorrow."

Alf stood by the door and waited until Rosie reached her car. The barmaid waved a hand as she drove slowly towards the road. Alf waved back. The weather hadn't improved. It was still blowing a gale, and the chilly rain was almost horizontal.

"Friday the thirteenth," tutted Alf as he closed the door.

"Weather like this makes you wonder whether Jim's monsters are on the prowl."

Dead Reckoning: Chapter Three

Saturday, 14 February 2015

"Wesley?"

Wes Guthrie tried to clear his head. He'd stayed out late, got soaking wet as he walked home, and fell up the stairs at around two o'clock. Millie, his wife, was already awake and downstairs in the kitchen.

Millie cursed him when he finally made it to bed, and when she got up twenty minutes ago, you could have cut the atmosphere with a knife. Wes knew he had a good deal of making-up to do if he could be bothered.

"Wesley? Are you there?"

"Who is that?" he asked.

"Helen, your sister. I know we don't often see one another, but surely you haven't forgotten the sound of my voice."

"Sorry, I had a few drinks last night and am not awake yet. What time is it over there, anyway?"

"Seven in the evening. Guy and I were going out for a

meal. We've found an awesome Italian place on Southbank Riverside."

"Bully for you," said Wes. "What's up?"

"Trust you," said Helen. "It would have been Mum and Dad's fortieth wedding anniversary today. I thought I would call. Dad's bound to be thinking of her."

Wes couldn't think why. His father never gave much thought to anyone or anything except money.

"So, why don't you call him, sis? It will save me the bother."

"No, you don't understand, Wesley. I started ringing him an hour ago with no reply. Do you know if he's away for the weekend?"

"When did he ever go away for the weekend, Helen? Perhaps his phone's on the blink. I'll drive over later. It's too risky for me to drive anywhere yet. Enjoy your meal."

Wes ended the call and staggered to the bathroom.

"Serves you right!" shouted Millie.

Noon had come and gone before Wes felt human enough to drive over to see his father. It wasn't how he would have chosen to spend a Saturday afternoon. He hadn't had a day off since New Year, and after he'd finished work on the farm yesterday, he'd left Tom Dix in charge with instructions not to call before Monday.

"Who is it you're going to see today?" asked Millie as he made ready to leave the house. "The same tart as last night?"

"Don't talk rubbish," said Wes. "I was drinking with my mates. Helen called earlier and said she couldn't get hold of Dad. No idea where the old beggar went in that storm. Let's hope he hasn't wrapped his new car around a tree. I'll be back in an hour."

Wes eased the car into early afternoon traffic on the

A303. Wes, Millie, and the boys lived in Winterbourne Stoke, three miles from Stonehenge, and he was soon turning off the main road towards Durrington. Wes drove past the Stonehenge Inn and took Netheravon Road to Glenhead Farm.

It hadn't always been called Glenhead. Wes couldn't remember whether his grandfather or great-grandfather changed it from New Farm to bring a touch of Angus to Salisbury Plain. Anyway, what idiot decided it was a good idea to call something New whatever? Wes had gone to school in Salisbury, and he knew the New Inn had stood on New Street since the end of the fourteenth century, which made it one of the oldest inns in the country.

Wes continued to consider the irrationality of the study of place names as he negotiated the potholes on the lane leading to his father's farmhouse. He spotted the Bentley parked in front of the double garage. Kendal Guthrie was in residence. His father hadn't yet had a flag designed to fly from the gabled rooftop, but give him time, thought Wes as he pulled up by the main house.

Wes rooted through the pockets of his jeans, hunting for the spare set of keys he'd picked up at home. As he stood outside the large wooden door, his mobile phone rang.

"Did you have a good time last night?"

"Tamsin," said Wes. "Hello, babe. I think you know the answer to that. Look, I can't talk now. I'm standing on my Dad's doorstep. Are you at home? Can I call round in an hour? Less if I can get away from here sooner."

"I'll be here, waiting," replied Tamsin. "Perhaps you can stay longer this time?"

Wes had been seeing Tamsin Meredith for three months. The girl was insatiable. Not that he was complaining. Beautiful, too, with legs that went on forever.

"I told Millie I'd be back in an hour," said Wes. "I'll have to tell her Dad kept me talking. See you soon."

Wes rang the doorbell and listened for his father. Nothing. He could be somewhere on the farm, thought Wes. He rang his father's mobile and realised he could hear its ringtone nearby. Wes frowned. His father went nowhere without his phone. He fumbled with the set of keys and unlocked the door.

"Dad, are you okay? It's Wes. Did you have too much to drink too?"

Wes stood in the hallway and looked upstairs. All was quiet. He took the stairs two at a time and checked the main bedroom, the en suite, and the other rooms on the first floor. There was no sign of Kendal Guthrie. Wes returned downstairs and walked into the spacious lounge/dining room.

"This is like the flaming Marie Celeste," said Wes. "Nothing out of place, but no signs of life."

Wes called out to his father once more as he walked through to the large farmhouse kitchen. He glanced through the windows, trying to spot him in the garden. Wes stood by the butler sink and studied the apple trees overhanging the lawn. Where would his father have gone? Who would know? It was a lousy night, but he'd never sit at home watching TV.

Wes imagined his father had visited someone to discuss business and then drank in a pub that still let him inside the premises. He'd insult everyone in sight, drive home, and because of the weather, use the side door because it was closest to the garage.

Wes turned away from the window and crossed the kitchen to the door leading to the old mudroom. His late mother insisted that anyone, farm worker or local priest, got rid of their shoes before entering the house when there was any risk of mud getting onto her pristine carpets or recently washed flagstone floor.

Wes reached the door and opened it.

Kendal Guthrie lay face down in a pool of blood. He still wore his blue suit, the brand new camelhair coat, and a sturdy pair of muddy shoes.

Wes bent over his father's head and searched for a pulse on the side of his neck. Although he had waited until attempting to drive here, last night's alcohol left him light-headed. Wes knew at once his father was dead. His head swam, and he lurched away from the body and hurried back to the butler sink, where he vomited.

Grab your copy…
vinci-books.com/deadreckoning